# FIFTEEN
# BY CANDLELIGHT

Shonagh Koea is a fulltime writer who lives and works in Auckland. Her short story collection, *The Woman Who Never Went Home,* was published in 1987 and her first novel, *The Grandiflora Tree,* in 1989. Her second novel, *Staying Home and Being Rotten,* was published in 1992 and received outstanding acclaim. Her short stories have appeared in magazines, mainly the *Listener,* since 1981 when she won the Air New Zealand Short Story Award. The Queen Elizabeth II Literature Committee awarded her the Additional Writing Bursary in 1989.

Shonagh Koea

# FIFTEEN RUBIES BY CANDLELIGHT

VINTAGE

Vintage New Zealand
Random House New Zealand Ltd
(An imprint of the Random House Group)

18 Poland Road
Glenfield
Auckland 10
NEW ZEALAND

Associated companies, branches and representatives
throughout the world.

First published © Shonagh Koea 1993
ISBN 1 86941 183 8

Printed in Australia

# CONTENTS

# THE ANTIQUE DEALER

'DID YOU SELL your picture?' she asked amid impenetrable silence. He was reading the menu and before that he had read the newspaper thoroughly, twice. The little restaurant was chilly with silence and lack of use. It was a place where the brightness of custom no longer shone, she thought.

'I wonder if they've given up,' she said. 'I wonder if they don't bother any more.' A large, red, Chinese fan dangled over the main door. It should have been held firmly by two hooks but one had fallen out of the wall.

He did not answer.

'I definitely think they've given up,' she said. 'If they hadn't given up they'd put that hook back in the wall. They'd tidy the place up a bit.'

The clutter on the reception desk threw up a vegetable catalogue, a seed merchant's guide and a large book about growing fruit and nuts. There was nothing about cooked food, no updated menu and yesterday's newspaper ensured there was also nothing about today or for today.

'What was that, my dear?' He placed the menu on the table and she sat back then, bloomed a little like a brave china rose in last year's auction catalogue, later Capodimonte though. Definitely not Nymphenburg.

'I said, did you sell your picture? That oil?' she said. 'Did you sell it after all?'

He was an antique dealer and they had met, predictably, in an antique shop the year before the big stockmarket crash when the market was flooded with over-priced pictures that no one wanted any more, and florid Dresden of the worst sort assaulted every cranny. They met before all that.

'That's a very pleasant little figurine,' she had said to him then, thinking he looked an impeccable man, fine even, loitering behind a Georgian escritoire with ormolu mounts, a bisque-glazed ballerina in his left hand.

The owner of the shop, a mountainous woman in magenta silk that blazed with nine-carat watch-chains in confusion on a massive bosom, waited with the key to the cabinet in her hand. He was a connoisseur, knew what he wanted and exactly what he was doing or that woman would not have opened the cache of treasures for him. She knew that then, immediately.

'Very pleasant. Very fine,' he had said, as if he always talked to women in antique shops and perhaps he did, she thought now with a rising sense of melancholy. He had regarded her with very great care from behind horn-rimmed glasses. He always wore those on his buying trips, she knew that now. Mainly he dealt in pictures and porcelain but he acquired — and she knew that from experience — anything worth turning over.

'Is it of some age?' She noted he continued to look at her even though the little figure still lay in his hand.

'The age is immaterial,' he had said, and they stood in that glossy over-priced shop on a sunny afternoon in August while the owner jangled the bunch of keys to the cabinets.

'I'll leave you to make up your minds,' that big bold woman said. Then she changed her own mind. 'I'll leave you to make up your mind, John, while I go out the back. I've got a couple of calls to make. Here's the key to the other cabinet if you want to go in there. Just give me a yell if you want anything.' She whisked away through velvet curtains that matched her dress and they both listened to her dialling numbers on her old telephone.

'She seems to be busy,' he said. 'You and I are in charge of the shop.'

'In charge of the emporium,' she had said and detected an immediate glimmer in his pale blue eyes at this redecoration of his remark, the gilding of her lavish little echo. It was a generosity of words emboldened by the deduction, absolutely true she was certain, that he must be well-known in that shop, perhaps had a long history of buying there. There must have been no trouble over paying, no cheques that bounced, no problem with funds if he had

2

been made so welcome and given the keys.

'Is it marked?' she asked, thinking of the figurine.

He continued to regard her through the horn-rimmed glasses he perched on the end of his nose.

'There isn't a mark on it.'

'I meant the figurine.'

'Oh, the figurine.' He turned it upside down, looked at the underside with care. 'There's no mark.'

'I think it's early Naples.' She hazarded a guess. 'It has that look about it — something about the hands and the flowers. Early Naples I'd say.'

He continued to stare at the underside of the figure.

'I prefer them unmarked,' he said, 'then you can invent your own. And now' — and he took her arm then — 'why don't you come with me and have afternoon tea. There's a very good little stamping-ground just down the road.'

Now when she said, 'Oh, Hawky, this seems so sad and you don't even love me,' he would say, 'But I do. I love your beautiful pristine unmarked flesh,' as he bit her knees. So she wept then, amid tumbled sheets, like a little statue with a worn signature, a nearly obliterated mark of excellence upon the bronze.

'That little oil painting,' she said again now, in the restaurant. 'That one of the river and the paddock.'

'Field. It's English. Meadow if you like. Not paddock.'

'Field then. Does it really matter? Did you sell it, Hawky? Hawkington?' She avoided his Christian name, always had. Too shy to enunciate clearly the roundness and clarity of John, even after all this time, she embraced him in nicknames. To call him Mr Hawkesley would be absurd, under the circumstances.

When he still did not answer, just stared out of the little triangular window into the square, she said, 'The square looks pretty when it's nearly dark and starred with lights.' She watched him watching those streets that glimmered with greasy rain. 'And those flowers are quite nice. I haven't seen orange marigolds like that for years.' Again she waited. 'My grandmother used to grow marigolds like that up her front path when I was a little girl.' She gave him the gift of one

3

of her minuscule but telling secrets with this confidence. The little conversational gem lay upon the silent distress of the evening like tears with the sudden watery glitter of old rose-cut diamonds at a big auction. That she never spoke of her childhood was a thing she supposed he might have noticed. It was excruciating to recall. He never spoke of his ex-wife and the continuing profundity of his silence gave an acute veracity to the general belief among the other dealers that she had been extremely beautiful but wayward and had broken his heart, if he had one.

'My mother used to say they stank, marigolds.' Again she waited. 'Like polecats.' The capacity of suffering she noted in herself seemed endless. He ignored her.

'I've lost a piece of paper,' he said. Those square determined fingers were splayed on the breast pocket of his jacket. 'That piece of paper I was writing on this morning when I was talking on the phone, before you got up.'

'When you were talking to the squadron leader.' She remembered that, propped up against the arched velvet headboard of the bed. The opulent plush of the carpet, the glimmer of gilded mirrors made her think business must be improving. He had taken her to a better hotel than usual.

'I'll just give you this,' he had said, handed her the tea which she did not want, 'and this' — that was the morning paper — 'to keep you out of my way while I make my calls.' So she sat there with her hair tumbling down in baroque splendour, holding the paper and the cup like a sad child given toys too young or too old.

'I don't need the paper or tea or anything.' She had drawn herself up from the confusion of lace-edged sheets, blankets that were satin-bound. 'I don't need to be kept out of the way.'

'Brigadier,' he said now in the restaurant. 'He's a brigadier.'

'He must be quite old, mustn't he?' She was conscious of her error. 'To be a brigadier?'

'About 80.' He was turning out his wallet now. 'He's going to autograph one of his books for me.'

She waited to be invited.

'Are you going by yourself, Hawky?'

'Yes.' He was very crisp about that.

4

'Oh.' The wait was over.

For the first time that evening he smiled and she sensed that the collection of this trophy autograph was a triumph, a coup. He liked books about the war, cited the wisdom of Sir Winston Churchill, referred to Sir Anthony Eden as Eden.

'He married Clarissa Churchill,' she told him once, a long time ago. 'Anthony Eden married Clarissa Churchill.'

'Was she one of the old boy's daughters?'

'A niece, I think.' What doom that utterance held. 'They had a son.' But it was already too late.

'I might take him a bottle of champagne,' he said, 'in exchange for the autograph.'

'Champagne's very nice. I like champagne.'

He seemed to reflect on this, eyes slightly narrowed.

'I wonder if he likes champagne,' he said.

The square was in complete darkness now, the restaurant still empty as she turned away.

'This doesn't seem to be a very popular place,' she said.

'It's private. Nobody sees you here.' He was turning out his pockets again. 'I'm sure I've got his address somewhere.'

'It is unpopular,' she said, diction as sharp as rage, 'because it is not nice. I deserve,' she said, 'something better.'

A waitress approached, a thin Chinese girl with a grey pleated skirt fanning knees so fat they were a shock.

'You order now? Please?'

'Not yet, my dear.' He was very crisp with the waitress too. 'Not till I find what I'm looking for.' She padded away again, nearly afloat on stout black shoes like rafts.

'Hawky? Listen to me.' He looked up. 'Hawkington, this morning I saw you writing on a little piece of paper, when you gave me the newspaper.'

'I gave you the newspaper to read.' She noted how he paused then. 'My dear.'

'I didn't want to read it. I wanted to watch you fluffing about. I saw you fold a piece of paper in four and put it in your wallet.'

'I see.' He looked guarded.

'I don't eavesdrop. I wasn't listening. I don't care what you do, John.' So there was his name, out at last. She snatched the wallet. 'Just let me find this piece of paper for you and we can have dinner and go. I want to go. After dinner I'm going.'

The waitress padded up again.

'You like to order now? Please?'

'No. When I've found what I'm looking for I'll tell you and you can come back,' she said.

'Yes, madam.'

'You seem to have got her organised,' he said.

She did not answer, rifled through the wallet past the pile of $50 notes, the only denomination he ever seemed to have, past the credit cards and the cheques signed with flourishes by strangers. 'Here you are.' She slapped the piece of paper down on the table. 'Now perhaps we can order.'

They did not speak again till the coffee came.

'I saw your friend today,' she said then, conscious that the silence seemed enduring and discomforting. 'That man you call Sling. He always sits at the back at auctions.'

'I know that.' Snappy, she thought, oh, snappy, snappy. 'He's a long way from home. What's he doing here?'

'I didn't ask him. We were talking about flowers.'

'Where were you talking to him? And Slingsby's not any friend of mine.'

'I thought he was. I just met him in the park and he bought me an ice-cream.'

'What were you doing in the park?'

'I was keeping myself amused. You always tell me to keep myself amused so I do. I went to see the rhododendrons and I met that man you always call Sling.'

'Is he down for the Fleetwood sale?'

'No.' The power of this small piece of knowledge was as surprising as the waitress's fat knees but possibly, she thought, more valuable. 'He's come down to see his sister. She's dying. But he's left some bids.'

'What on?' Again she was conscious of that sudden abounding interest.

'Some of the porcelain.'

'He's having you on. He only buys big stuff. Dressers, chiffoniers, wardrobes as big as a house. They're into big stuff, him and that cowboy son of his.'

'No, they're not. His son's taking over the big shop and he's opening his own little extra shop round the corner, with the smalls. Figurines, teasets, that's what he's going to have.'

'Damn,' he said. 'He'll be after the Minton. So there's going to be a bit of competition, is there, from old Sling for the smalls. He's the one who bought that nice D-end dining table from right underneath my nose and sold it the next day for three and a half thousand.'

'I don't know anything about that, Hawky.'

'What sort of ice-cream did he get you in the park? Some stupid lump of vanilla on a stick, I suppose.'

'It was chocolate,' she said, 'in a French cone. It was very nice.'

'His wife's fat. I can see why.'

'His wife's dead. She died last year. He told me.'

'So,' — he leant back in his chair then — 'old Sling's splashing out, is he? Would you like something with your coffee? Would you like a chocolate. Would you have liked dessert?'

'No thank you, Hawky.'

'Fancy old Sling telling you all his business. I didn't know you knew him.'

'I've known him for a long time. I always see him at the auctions you take me to.'

'Does he know your name?'

'I've never told him what it is.' He had put his glasses on and looked at her more closely as if her name might be written across her forehead. 'He seems to know I'm always with you. Usually,' she said, 'he calls me Sparkles because he says I've got sparkling eyes and I call him Bumpy because the first time I ever met him I bumped into him beside a serpentine chest.'

'Nauseating. You've made that up.'

'No I haven't.'

'Where's he staying?'

'Same place as you,' she said, 'and me. Same place as u—' It seemed wise not to complete that sentence.

'Where are you staying?' Slingsby had asked as they

approached the hybrid block at the park. 'These are a very early one,' he said. 'They're a bigger rhododendron, more specialised. You'll enjoy this.'

'I didn't know you knew anything about gardening.' She felt oddly self-conscious, like a high-school girl out for the first time.

'I've got a very big garden at home. But you still haven't told me where you're staying.'

'At the White House.'

'Business must be good,' he said, and she dropped a little farther behind at that, reluctant as a plain debutante to go into the ballroom. 'The dining-room's good there.' They tramped a few paces and were greeted by a blaze of pink blooms, luscious and almost triumphant. 'Perhaps I might see you at dinner?'

'No.' She was very quick about that — 'Hawky never dines in the dining-room. He likes to go out, to little restaurants, to little places round the corner.'

'To little places round the corner called what, for instance?'

'I never remember their names.' It was perfectly true. They were not worth remembering.

'Well,' — and they were approaching a burgeoning bush now with a ravishing load of flowers — 'perhaps business isn't that good.'

'Oh, look, look.' Embarrassment made her turn quite wildly, nearly horrified, and she pointed to another rhododendron. 'But I know the name of that one.' She nearly shouted, as generous with the noise as the dinners were undistinguished. 'Even I know that one. It's "Pink Pearl". ' The triumph of that jewelled name nearly made up for the paucity of the cafés.

'What did you say to him in the park, my dear?' The little restaurant's quiet possessed a sudden menace.

'Nothing. I just said, "Hello, Bumpy," and he said, "Good afternoon, Sparkles".'

'I think you're being deliberately obtuse.'

'I didn't tell him any of your business, Hawky. We didn't talk about you at all. You weren't mentioned.'

'Oh.' Now it was his turn to put his elbows on the table,

his turn to clasp his hands. 'You didn't mention me at all?'

'Not even once.'

'I see.' He beckoned to the waitress. 'We might have another cup of coffee,' he said, 'and have you got a little chocolate or two, something nice for the lady to have with it? Please?' The late use of that word held a curious pathos, she thought. 'What time were you at the park, my little sweetheart?'

'About two o'clock. Bumpy said it was a pity I hadn't gone earlier or we could have had lunch.'

'So he's asking you out, is he?'

'I don't think so, Hawky. I think he just made the remark idly, how people do.'

'He's not an idle fellow. He's a very busy fellow. If I'd come to the park earlier I could have asked him myself what he's doing here.'

'Were you at the park, Hawky? I never knew you went to parks.'

'I was there about four. I went to see the rhododendrons too.'

'You mean if I'd been there a bit later I could have met you and we could have looked at the gardens together. I'd have loved to go to the park with you. I wouldn't have minded waiting. I spend my whole life waiting for you.' But he did not ask what she meant and, in her own mind, she chalked up this omission. 'I went to the art gallery this morning.' Better to babble on about anything, fill up the silence. 'I saw a lovely little watercolour — just daffodils in a vase with a string of lapis lazuli beads trailing along a table. It was a lovely little still-life. Weeks,' she said, 'at his very best.'

'I saw that. When were you there?'

'About half past ten,' she said.

'I must have just missed you. I was there at half past nine.'

She wanted to say, 'Oh, Hawky, why didn't you take me with you? I'd have loved to go.' But silence held her very firmly, nearly strangled her as she turned to pretend a continuing interest in the little window and the square, hoping that extreme stillness might mask the error of grief.

'I didn't sell it,' he said when five cars had gone by and

9

the traffic lights had changed from red to green three times. Her count was meticulous.

'I beg your pardon?' Possibly it might be safe to turn and face him.

'That little oil painting,' he said. 'I didn't sell it. It was a good offer.' It was unlike him to volunteer any information. 'But if they were willing to offer that much it must be worth miles more. I've had it cleaned, and I've rehung it. I've hung it in a place where it really looks something. I've displayed it to better advantage.'

'How much did they offer you?' The temerity shocked her.

'Sixty-five thousand,' he said, 'so I thought it must be worth ninety. I thought it was worth keeping.' He offered her the little dish of chocolates. 'Are you sure you won't have one of these, my treasure? I'll ask our little Chinese friend if I can buy the box. You might want one later.'

'Hawky, I never eat chocolates.'

'You might change your mind. And now' — he raised one of her hands as though suddenly it might be as precious as Chelsea, glorious as Sèvres, kissed it gently — 'why don't you tell me that nice story again, that one about Eden marrying Clarissa Churchill, that story you told me once and I didn't listen properly.'

# THE MAGIC WAY

THE BEST WAY to go to Mac's place is the back way, past the old dairy on the corner where the dog lies on the pavement on sunny days. That dog always sleeps outside the shop except when it's raining and you won't be going over to Mac's place on a rainy day. Mac likes to have the french doors open to get the breeze from the garden. He always used to say that his place looked its best on a fine day with the doors all open and that he was also at his best then. So it's best to go over to Mac's place on a good day and when you see the black Alsatian asleep outside the shop, turn right and go up the hill past those pink apartments. One of the people who used to live there was that man strangled in the park last summer, but it was an odd sort of crime, nothing actually to worry you at all. Someone caught him peeping on them at night — a crime of passion, if you like. It wasn't a personal matter, not a robbery or a real crime of violence so you can go up the hill past the pink apartment block and it's all quite safe on a sunny day, though I'd be careful at night.

You go past some old cottages and an Art Deco bungalow that's extremely architecturally significant and at the top of the road, where you breast the hill, turn right again at a big tee intersection. You can't take a wrong turn there, on your way to Mac's. It's either straight left or right, and you must go right. Then you can doodle along past an old school and through the remnants of an avenue of plane trees and at the next big intersection, beside a fish shop, turn right again. Mac's place isn't far down that road. You go past the bakery, past the Hare Krishna restaurant, past those big stone villas in their gardens gaunt with aged lawsonianas and pine trees grown past their prime, and there's Mac's place.

Mac likes visitors and he's easy enough to find if you take the back way, the magic way I used to call it because you never see a policeman or a traffic officer or a patrol car or anything that way. You can wear a coat that fell off a truck or carry a microwave you've just bought from a stranger and you can drink a bottle of wine and no one will ask you a single question, let alone say hello. So go the magic way to see Mac.

Mac likes people to stop down at the gate for a moment to check his mailbox. If there's anything there take it up to the house, even junk stuff. Mac likes to do his own sorting. It's a long walk down to the gate and he doesn't like to go unless he has to. I always used to stop there and clear out the letterbox. There was usually just a bill or two, just the electricity and gas and telephone, nothing special. He isn't a great man to book things up. Deals in cash, does Mac, and last summer, when things were different, he sometimes used to like to walk up to the shops on the main road to make a cash withdrawal from the bank and buy dental floss and bean sprouts and tomatoes. If I'd been thinking properly at the beginning of this last winter I might have wondered why he started saying, 'I've already been to the bank. I've cashed a cheque. We got the groceries.' I should have thought about that *we*. But Mac's a popular man and a lot of people used to make a point of going to see him and I'd just think that someone else — even Roberto — might have nipped in to do the chores. It never registered in my consciousness, as my naturopath would say.

I used to go to these classes in the management of the inner self to induce calmness and a sense of beauty, getting myself ready for Mac. So I just went happily along, calling in at Mac's place on sunny days with the french doors open and the breeze coming in nicely, just to his taste. I thought Roberto might have looked after the shopping and he thought I'd done it and we all thought Mac's sister had done his banking and none of us realised till the week before last what Mac had been up to since he stopped asking us to help with the shopping. You mark my words — study a man's shopping and you can deduce every nuance of his life. What goes in the shopping basket is the emotional barometer of each person's psyche and the hand that places it there is that of the current favourite.

None of us realised, till last week, exactly what Mac had been up to all this time, since early last summer. I mean, he often used to mention the name and say, 'What a wonderful worker. What a talent,' and Roberto might say, 'Oh yes, dear — really marvellous. Quite makes the toes curl. Does the heart good to see it, dear heart.' We were there with the french doors open and all the shopping mysteriously done and if we'd only asked where those bean sprouts had come from, and the totally unbroached bottle of gin, we'd be in better order today.

Roberto's gone away for a fortnight to see his old mother. Eighty-seven if she's a day and lively as a cricket, he says. As for me, I'm here and I'm thinking of the problem as a challenge to be overcome.

I had it all planned and it doesn't matter how many rehearsals you've had in life for plans going wrong, it's always so drear when they do. I've been thinking of Roberto, though, and how he always sits so supine after his yoga classes and he'll say, 'Did anything strike a chord today, dear heart? Was there a chord struck in that tasty chest? We've got someone lucky here then, haven't we, dear hearts.' Droll is what you'd call Roberto. 'Divulge all to your nearest and dearest,' he used to say after we met Mac. 'We are, my dear, *agog*.'

Roberto used to bring a beautiful boy with him then. He has, as Roberto would say, gone into the wide blue. Roberto's got this habit of missing the last word off sentences and phrases. 'Oh, heart,' he'd say, '*heart*, tell all to Uncle Rob.'

Roberto's boy had a wide and pouting mouth like an open rose. 'And where is your sulky little bloom?' I'd say to him sometimes till I realised the boy had gone so then there was just Roberto and me and Mac and we were happy.

'You wouldn't credit it, would you, heart,' Roberto said to me on the telephone yesterday. 'Yes, Mother, I'll say hello to my friend. Mother says *hello*.' At the airport, when I drove him out to catch his flight, he said, 'Life's a hole, heart, just a *hole*.' We'd been out to dinner together at that Indian restaurant over on the main road the night before. A sort of goodbye, I told him, and hello, heart, and I feel he got my meaning.

We cried into our birianis and drank a bottle of a not undistinguished Sauvignon Blanc.

'A rich and aromatic libation,' said Roberto when I filled his glass and we linked arms and took a draught. 'Floral tones are what I'd prescribe, dear heart,' he said and pinched a little carnation from the vase on the table and put it in my lapel. My naturopath says that if you look to the east and do not find what you desire then all that is necessary is to look at another point on the compass. I thought of it that night and it suddenly came to me then that I might never go over to Mac's place again, not after what's happened.

When we first used to go over to Mac's place we took the main road. We'd drive right across town, through all the traffic lights and we got stopped by the breathalyser patrol twice, but only on the way there. Not on the way home again. We used to hack through all that in my car and Roberto would sit in the passenger seat and say, 'My dear — what luxury — I do love your carseat covers, heart, I do really. White curly sheepskin, dear heart. Aren't you a tiger for luxury. Ooo look, heart, look. There's a wonderful shirt shop. I must trot in there one day, on my wee hooves, and see what they've got.' He was sad, though, about that rosy boy. You could tell. It was just a swanky flourish, going on about the shirts.

'You haven't brought that boy, then?' I said to him one day early on, before I knew him so well, and he said, 'Oh, you do go on, heart, don't you, and would you mind pulling those Austrian shades down a bit? The light's just killing me today, it's just killing my eyes.' So I never asked idly about the boy again. The boy was actually of no interest to us at all, Mac and me. I don't recall that he ever said a word but you had to make sure you didn't talk to Roberto for too long or that boy would sulk. He could sulk silently and ostentatiously, that boy. The hush of his sulking could fill a room.

He went off one day with someone in a band, so after that Roberto and I used to go over to see Mac by ourselves, and we all used to talk on the telephone about each other to each other. I'd ring Mac and say, 'I'm really worried about Roberto. Friend Rob may lapse into a torpor,' and Mac used to say, 'Why don't you two dear ones skip merrily over this way. Come five pm, the witching hour *chez moi* and we can have a glass or two of wine and cheer the old selves up.' They were happy times.

I read a lot of gardening books at that stage. It was deep winter when The Rose, as Mac and I called the boy, went off with the drummer. We got through till spring and this idea came to me then, this idea for a special path designed for Mac. I began to plan it and I began to plan other things like Mac spending more time here. There's an oak tree down the bottom of my garden and before it came into leaf in the spring I pruned the lower branches like I saw in one of the garden books. I made an oak *allée*, a kind of oaken archway over my new path. Everything was very wet then. The weather experts said it was our wettest winter for eighty years but I managed to get the pruning done and I made an area under the tree of beaten earth, soundly packed. There was an old fence post in the shed and I'd go out on a Saturday, if the weather cleared up, and I'd beat the ground to consolidate the earth so that, under my oak tree, at the centre of my oak *allée*, I had a living garden house ruffled with fine leaves like the trimmings for a king.

The garden roller was propped up in the shed behind some old rakes and a shovel so I dusted the cobwebs off it and on long afternoons, still with promise, I used to drag it slowly back and forth over my sylvan area beneath the tree. It was a kind of stroking of the earth, a preliminary caress in lieu of those to come. Thus I prepared the hardened earth in a solitary ritual prior to bringing Mac to see my domain. I also went to the supermarket several times and began to lay in supplies of things I knew Mac liked. Tinned peaches in genuine fruit juice, boysenberry jam in jars not tins, olives with pimento stuffing, tinned salmon in the large size.

Succeeding in life is often only a matter of adjustment. I have now altered the area, changed my shopping list and await the arrival of Roberto. Mac was to have had adzed teak

15

deck chairs. I favoured the idea of azure blue canvas on the seats with matching cushions and a small Italian table with a blue tiled top. Fortunately I had not done any of this shopping. Roberto will now lie, supine, on my new swing lounger, on chains. I bought it today and the upholstery is olive green to match his hazel eyes. On my languorous and luxuriant patio, rich with the flowers of red geraniums and a proliferation of roses pink as nipples, Roberto will recline. The beaten area under the tree may become mossed over. Who would know? Prepared as if for a mating dance, it will be forgotten. Much in life is a mystery, including the sybaritic rites of old civilisations and our own quaint ideas.

I sometimes wonder about the retail trade that might be affected by people's battered hearts and forgotten ideals. Dresses not bought because he never rang, tickets to shows that lie unclaimed in box offices, cars left unsold in car yards because the girl went off with someone else and, in my own case, the teak deck chairs that were never purchased because Mac suddenly said one day, 'I'd like you two to meet Violet,' and this big buxom thing swam out from the kitchen that Roberto and I had slaved our hearts out painting the most delicious shade of antique reseda we could mix. Roberto's a wonder with colour. You've only got to look at the way he dresses. Pure magic. Pure *Vogue*.

'Hello,' said this Violet and she put one hand on Mac's shoulder in that proprietorial way that's so offensive. 'Would you like a cup of tea?' she said. We nearly died. Luckily we hadn't sat down. Roberto's the most wonderful liar under duress so he suddenly launched forth into this great taradiddle that we'd just called in to tell Mac the track was hard and fast at Ellerslie for the spring handicap and The Chef was worth a bet as a rank outsider, ten dollars each way. Then we took off down the drive again and the only thing Roberto said was 'Victor more likely!' He's got such style.

My oak *allée* still seems to be coming along fine, but the plans are somewhat changed. I've also been back to the supermarket and bought different things. The salmon and the peaches and the jam can stay in the cupboard to be

16

emergency supplies, but I've bought different things now. I've bought cognac and cashew nut pâté, wheaten crackers, Camembert, vintage Cheddar, a pot of English Stilton, Chinese dates and chocolate peppermint creme biscuits. Roberto's favourites.

My naturopath says there are no such things as difficulties in life. No indeed. There are challenges. 'And you must meet them, my dear,' she says. 'Head on, if necessary. Go forward. Turn the page. Evolve, my child. *Evolve.*' So I have evolved and so has my plan for the garden. 'You've really got to rally, heart,' Roberto said at the time. '*Rally.*' So I've also rallied and I've put myself on to supplementary vitamins for a week or two. It takes it out of you, evolving and rallying. But I've replanned my *allée* and it should all be ready by the time Roberto returns at the end of this week.

In one of my garden books the *allée* was a much more comprehensive affair than was possible in my garden, but I've used the germ of the idea. In the book there's this border of red roses flowering with geometrical precision to form an avenue leading into the *allée*, a kind of horticultural preliminary. An anteroom, if you like. Between the roses and the gravel path they've planted a slender hedge of box, neatly clipped, and beyond all that lie the mysteries of this pictured oak *allée*. Mine is less grand and this is not France. The picture I saw was of a garden near Paris. I do have one red rose which flings itself over the steps that lead to the garden. The profusion is tasteful in its own way. The effect I have aimed for is one of ease and abundance, a joy in living among flowers. I hope this will have an effect on Roberto.

In my old plans for the *allée*, involving Mac, I had the *allée* as the end of proceedings. I imagined us making our way out there, wandering along the cobbled path I've been making and reaching our final destination beneath the oak on that firmly packed dirt floor of my sylvan garden house. That is what I thought and planned and I have given it up now. I have also given up the idea of having a narrow hedge of clipped box either side of my path and I have given up Mac.

I have given up all those ideas, not necessarily in the order

I have listed them. Instead I have been to the nursery and purchased two dozen plants of impatiens 'Futura', a good augury of the times ahead, and I shall line my path with those. Roberto returns on Friday and I will meet him at the airport. I have had my car repainted in his absence and the new sheepskin carseat covers are tailored to the latest ideas in back comfort as well as pandering to the idea of elegance. I had them especially dyed to match the car. After placing Roberto upon their robust curls I shall bear him triumphantly northwards to my oak *allée* where much awaits us, including the new garden path. Under my old plans for the garden I had the path ending at the *allée* and the effect was to be tailored, hence the neatly clipped box hedge. Roberto is a more languorous personality. Roberto is more your terrace man. I therefore replanned my path and placed it on more of an angle and curved it over the wide buttock of my back lawn as far as the *allée*. There my beaten earth area takes over the space in a curiously primeval manner like the dancing ground of an ancient and ritualistic tribe.

I never did buy the teak deck chairs. Roberto definitely is not a deck chair man. I've taken up the path again as a thread in the garden on the other side of the oak tree and it snakes round in a half-circle to the house now. I did buy a sculptural garden seat to put in my sylvan area as a statement of delicacy amidst my cave of greenery. Roberto, of terrace fame, has a great eye for quality and I want him to pick up all the nuances of my care and thought so the garden seat, upon which we will probably never sit, is French and has an antiqued paint effect in sage green. I bought it at an antique shop miles from here and when I use the word *scour*, I do so advisedly: I scoured the city for exactly the right statement, in iron and wood, of my intent while Roberto was away in Sydney nursing his bruised heart at his old mother's place by the Toukley Bridge, only an hour by freeway to the middle of the city.

He's sent me a postcard every day with all the news. Very fond of his mother, Roberto is. He goes over every year to see her and does a bit of swimming in Tuggerah Lake. Depending on his mood, he either has a dip at Pipe Clay

Point where the water's shallow right out and lovely white sand all the way — so sensual, he says — otherwise he goes to the top end where the real swimmers congregate. At night he goes home to his mother for a vodka and tonic on her terrace and then a spot of dinner. She won't have gin at any price. 'My healing time,' he says. I see him, in my mind's eye, tanned and relaxed and wandering across the rump of my lawn, into the oak *allée*, out again and thence over the curved path to the terrace where my swing lounger, on chains, awaits.

There has not been a word from Mac all this time but, as Roberto has so wisely said, 'Let us not utter the merest syllable on the matter, heart.' The day we escaped after the introduction to Violet, we noticed she had brought her car right up the drive from the street and made a swirl on the new sealing. A proprietorial gesture, indeed. *Mine*. We fled from her flagellation of Mac's bosky turf.

'One or two tiny decisions in the night, heart,' Roberto said on the telephone the next morning. 'Just ignore me, heart — it's my sinuses again.' I was on the verge of saying he sounded ill. 'I might pop across the ditch and see the old mater for a day or so' — actually he's staying a fortnight but it gives me time to get this path laid — 'and heal, heart. I must heal.'

'Of course,' I said. I felt a bit in need of healing myself, but my garden's my therapy. I've begun to feel quite happy getting my garden ready for Roberto and it's logical when you think about it. It never occurred to me before but we were both preoccupied. *We were blinded*, he wrote in yesterday's card. *Enjoying the swimming. Not many people about.* Call me selfish if you like but I was glad. *Mother says next time I come over I'm to bring you. Lovely eyes, she said, and a generous mouth. I showed her your picky. She never liked You-Know-Who!*

*Love, Roberto*, he wrote at the end. I cling to that. *Love, Roberto.* I wrote back straight away. *Looking forward to seeing you on the fourteenth*, I said. *Garden looking a picture in honour of your arrival. Have bought swing lounger, on chains* — he loves chains — *for the patio and have polished ice bucket etcetera ready*

19

*for triumphal homecoming*. You don't like to be too obvious, do you, but I thought that might make it plain. *Give my love to your mother and tell her if I come to stay I'll potter around in the garden. Tell her to get the hedge clippers sharpened*. I always think it's nice to pull your weight.

She's a great old girl, Roberto's mum. Had some sort of a hostel in King's Cross for years. A real old martinet in her own way. She ran it like a military academy, Roberto says, and even now she comes over all funny when she sees a uniform and he can't take her to the beach or anything like that. Show her a snorkel, show her a diving suit and you've got a funny turn on your hands, so Roberto says. Nearly ninety and still likes to go dancing on a Friday night.

My old feelings about Mac are no longer extant. I saw him a couple of days ago, just from a distance, at the supermarket and there were various signifiers, to quote my naturopath, that kept me behind the chocolate chip biscuits on their big stand. His hair, for instance, was imperceptibly different. His fringe was heavier and looked lank. His shirt was a sharp cerulean blue. The old leitmotifs are no longer present. The subtlety has gone. His watch was new and had a red face and a striped red strap. All these new messages coalesced to give signals of a Mac I no longer know. I went from the chocolate chip biscuits to the tonic water — I thought immediately of gin when I saw him — and nary a word passed my lips. Some day when Roberto and I are out on the patio I might tell him about Mac and the new red watch when the moss has grown over my parade ground under the oak. I had planned to have a row of zinnias in terracotta pots, swanking and strutting in their stiff way at the entry, but my impatiens 'Futura' will be better, I think. More Roberto. Less Mac. 'Turn the page,' my naturopath says. 'Cease looking to the west and glance to the east. March on.'

There were various signals, apart from the hair and the watch, that indicated Violet was still in Mac's life when I saw him at the supermarket two days ago. He had a large white loaf (toast sliced) in his basket. Also smooth peanut butter, iced Madeira cake and pikelet mix. He may have left Violet at home dusting the aspidistra on the verandah and gone forth, Mac the hunter, to find nourishment for the loved one. I, too, have gone forth. Roberto sometimes likes a Campari, on ice, at sundown and he's fond of a gin and tonic with two thin slices of lemon and ice-blocks shaped like hearts. I've got my supplies in. The heart-shaped ice-block container was a problem but I ran one to earth in a little novelty shop down in the city. *Pink.* And such a helpful man in the shop. I've got pâté, baby peas, broccoli and French beans in the freezer beside the pink ice-block tray. Very Laura Ashley — pink and green. Roberto's extremely sensitive to colour.

The house, the garden and the freezer await Roberto and as the evening breeze ruffles through the impatiens the swing lounger moves on its chains, the faint creaking a promise of happiness.

The sky is brilliant and boundless above my head. It would hardly, as Roberto would say, be beneath my feet. The leaves on the oak tree, above my abandoned prancing ground, are in constant motion in the tides of the air. Everything, even on the stillest day, seems to be faintly stirring, beyond our comprehension. The moss has begun to grow on the flagellated earth and an abundance of roses sway on my trellis, voluptuous as the undulations of a body.

I saw Mac at the supermarket again this morning, *sans* red watch, and in his basket he had spray-on starch, gherkins, some alfalfa sprouts, an old-fashioned mousetrap and a small square of soapy cheese. I've sometimes seen people sitting alone in restaurants and cafés in islands of silence and I am saddened to think of Mac in such a state. As for Violet — I cannot speak with any authority about Violet and where she might be. Perhaps the red watch had just been taken in for an overhaul.

As for me, I'm very busy here. My new neighbours climbed up a ladder to shout to me over the hedge just now. I like to keep my hedges high. 'Mr Merrill? It is Mr Merrill, isn't it?' I couldn't make out where the voices were coming from for a moment and then I saw the faces above my clipped camellias. 'Mr Merrill, there's a huge crop of tomatoes left here and *fraises de bois* gone wild under the runner beans — just hold out your arms, Mr Merrill, and we'll pass you

21

some, and more when you say the word.' I told them to call me Anthony. They seemed obliging people. Roberto loves tomatoes and strawberries. He'll be tickled pink.

I feel all the vibrations are very positive, as my naturopath would say, very magical like the way over to Mac's place used to be. I threw his telephone number in the bin last week but do feel free to give him a ring and pop over to see him. Go past the pink apartments and the Art Deco house with that amazing bay window and take the right turning at the tee intersection. You'll find him easily enough. The magic way, I always call it. The magic way.

# DEATH AND TRANSFIGURATION

THE STORMS ARE late this year. Usually by this time the rain and sleet, hail and snow are long gone. Winter stayed late this year and the farmers, mistakenly, left shearing the sheep till now. It is very late spring, too late for severe storms but such a storm did come this week and buried miles of countryside in snow. What did not die then, frozen, did so later of starvation or drowned in the floods that followed. I am not a farmer, nor was I ever married to one. I read about all this in the newspaper because I love the hills and valleys of all land. I love the breadth and depth of it so I read about the farmers and their land because I do not own any, not any more.

I remember when I was a little girl, when I lived down on the old farm, I used to go out into the middle of paddocks and I would listen for the song of the skylark which rose sharp and haunting, in air so clear that it seemed as clean as my own heart.

My own storm was late this year also, to match the weather. I thought in August that I might have escaped my storm. Most years my storm comes in July. August arrived, then September with its false warmth towards the end of the month so I had my winter coat drycleaned and packed it away. I have got it out again now, taken it from its big plastic bag, and I am wrapped in my coat because I am frozen. My cold does not come from the outside. The day is a warm one. The sun is pleasant. People in shirtsleeves have walked up and down the street. The man who mows my rented lawn arrived at midday, sent by the landlord, and he complained bitterly of the heat as he trimmed the hedge. I am frozen, though. My storm has frozen me from a line of ice inside my backbone right through the chest to solid lungs full of glacial tears and a heart blanched white with treason that is not my own. I call it treason. Other people may call it nothing or the ringing of a bell, for my storm is an annual telephone call that may take five minutes, certainly not often much longer and, if I have my way, much less.

My own storm, my telephone call, came last night at the end of a week during which farmers lost ten thousand newly shorn sheep and losses among cattle and other animals have not yet been assessed. My telephone call came as darkness fell on a grim evening of wind with a constant promise of rain, when the moon did not rise. My garden was dark in every corner and even the middle of the lawn, yards from any trees or hedges, was unlit by star or sky or the bloom from a stray light anywhere.

'Hello? Is that you, my dear?' I had picked up the telephone and my storm, thus, began. The voice still has its old *timbre* but it is a little frailer now for a year has passed since I heard it last and the exigencies of bronchitis, age and infirmity have taken some juiciness from it. Perhaps next year I may not have to endure my storm.

I said nothing. Farmers receive some warning about the weather, about storms. There are weather forecasts. My storm is always a surprise.

'Hello? Dear? Are you there?' So I said I was and I sat down on a small chair beside my telephone. My house is small. Most things in it are small but once, a long time ago when these people knew me differently, I lived a larger life on a larger scale. I had large chairs and a large house. I sat at the head of a huge dining table, polished oak, nearly twenty feet long, and I used to laugh idly as evening fell, a gratuitous mirth which I would think now was a luxury.

'I just popped out from the bridge table — we've got such a lovely four going — to give you a little call. We tried to get you last night but you didn't seem to be there. And the night before that we had a dinner to go to. You know what Hughie's like. He does love going out.' It is their annual holiday and they are quite a long way from home. They are doing shopping, seeing people, dining out, looking up old friends and making telephone calls in the evening to acquaintances. It is the same every year. 'We went out to dinner last night with our darling son — he's got such a wonderful practice now, doing so well, we *are* so proud — and of course our darling Helen's up here with us this time. We thought she needed a little break, our poor darling girl. Did you ever meet our son? And Helen?'

'Yes,' I said. 'I met Alexander and Helen, just the once.' It was enough. I began to freeze then, at this thought of Alexander and Helen. I remember Helen particularly. She had a round complaisant face, and her red dress was pulled tight over expanding hips. Helen had begun to run to fat.

'Our poor darling Helen's still putting on weight,' the voice pipes, 'but we've heard that Jenny Craig's an absolute saviour so Hughie's enrolled her. You knew about her divorce, of course? We said to her before the wedding, "Helen," we said, "is this really what you want, darling? Are you sure?" we said, but she went ahead with it. It was so embarrassing, of course, with the dresses all bought and the cathedral booked. The engagement was off and on so many times we lost count. Hugh adores the boys, though. My darling Hughie just loves the boys — she had three beautiful, beautiful boys — so that's a bonus from the whole sorry business and she's picking up the threads now.'

I sat there, thinking of Helen, the bright, bold child of the fortunate. I met her only once, after my husband died. I went to a party they gave because he had promised to go — was it their fortieth wedding anniversary? something like that — and he died suddenly so I went instead, the very last time I ever honoured old obligations, loyalties that were not my own. I went to their party and I, too, wore red. I wore a red silk dress he once bought me in Jaipur. It had been brought down from the hills by the hill people. Who else would come from the hills but the hill people? My storm addles my brains. Helen was there, at the party, and she came up to me and said, 'Are you an Indian?' I don't think anyone else spoke to me all evening. The following day I caught my flight home, having checked out of the small hotel where I had spent the night. It had been a simple excursion and one I never repeated.

'Are you still there, dear? You sound so far away. Are you

there?'

'No.' My voice sounds bleak.

'Oh, you always were such a joker. I do hear a hint of laughter there now. You did know, of course, that Hughie always calls you our laughing Amaryllis?' Because that is my name, you see, but people seldom use it now. 'I was telling you about Helen's darling boys, wasn't I. They're so artistic. They're the great joy of Hughie's life. Hugh has hopes of a musical career for the youngest one. He bought him a violin and his hands on the bow are breathtaking. He and Hugh are inseparable but he adores them all, of course, every last one of them. The middle boy's a wonderful sportsman. Hughie sees him as a famous cricketer. You must remember how Hughie's always loved his cricket.'

I do remember that. I do recall how Hugh loved cricket. When they used to come to stay, hot summer afternoons would pass with the sound of the television, faint, from the back of the house, from the old morning room downstairs which was, ironically, always at its most pleasant in the afternoon. Hughie used to sit there in a big wing chair watching the cricket on a huge television set with remote controls that Gerald hired every year because our own television set was small and unreliable.

'Now that's what I call a television set,' Hugh would say at the beginning of their week's visit.

He would sit there watching test matches from the Oval, or anywhere, and his wife who telephones me annually now would say, 'Hughie does so love his cup of tea at four o'clock but don't worry about anything too elaborate to eat. Just something simple, if you wouldn't mind.' I would know it was time to stop hiding upstairs in my bedroom, to stop trying to snatch a fleeting siesta in an armchair, when the big clock in the hall struck four. Beyond my chair were the bedroom windows and outside our land stretched out for more than an acre in the middle of town, and beyond that was the wide blue sea. I owned land then.

'Oh, we were always such friends.' The voice is mellifluous in my ears and my little house has grown colder.

'We were.' She has used the past tense and so have I, but

the certainty and confidence in her voice have blossomed. She will not notice my own diffidence.

"Hughie always speaks so well of you. He's never forgotten those lovely — well, they were really house parties you used to put on, weren't they. We never quite knew how you managed it. Dinner would appear as if' — the confident little laugh is deprecating now — 'by magic. Of course, as you know, we're great churchgoers. We don't believe in magic. No, no. Hughie always puts you in his prayers and my dear father, bless his soul, was a minister and so was my dear brother. He's still alive, by the way. He's marvellous for his age, just marvellous. It's having faith that does it. Faith is the answer, my dear. *Faith.*' The voice is full of faith and certainty, it possesses the buoyancy of insulated ignorance. 'No, no — it wasn't magic at all. It was probably just plain hard work. You were,' she says, 'a wonderful girl. Wonderful.'

'I was.' The past tense again.

When they came to stay I used to keep the hedge clippers under the sink in the kitchen. He liked his breakfast, on a starched cloth, in the kitchen at seven thirty. She liked hers on a tray, upstairs, in her bedroom at eight fifteen. He liked freshly percolated coffee and rolls after something cooked. She liked tea and two slices of whole wheat toast. He liked marmalade. She liked raspberry jam. In between these two breakfasts I would run up the drive with the hedge clippers clasped in my hands and I would clip the edges of the lawn.

'Such a sight,' Hughie would say. He might have wandered out on to the front verandah, coffee cup in hand, to finish the last of his breakfast. 'A manicured lawn, edges all done. That's a fine sight on a sunny morning.' Then, cup still in hand, he might go on an inspection of the trees and shrubs. The rhododendrons had thrips, he said, which left a silvery bloom on the upper side of the leaves and brown castings underneath. Thrip dung, he claimed. 'Just a light spraying would cure it,' he said. 'It wouldn't take a moment. Haven't got a sprayer? I might pop in somewhere when I'm in town, if I've got time, and see if I can hire one for you. They're so easy to use even a child could manage it.'

'Darling Hughie's often wondered, before you left the big

27

house did you ever get rid of those thrips on the rhododendrons?' she says now.

I honestly cannot remember. I remember the last day I spent at that house. The dust had, long ago, settled on everything. The man I hired to mow the lawns every fortnight had done his best. No one can ask for more than that. I did my best, but the place was, more or less, overgrown. I cannot recall actively regarding a rhododendron at that time. The ivy grew wildly after the funeral — perhaps death prompts the rampant advance of ivy, do you think? I recall a vision of ivy all over the western boundary. I remember the violets had spread under the magnolias and when you bent right down you could see a great swathe of their faint flowers among the weeds and debris. People used to throw things over the front fence. When Gerald was alive nobody threw things over the fence but after he died I often found rubbish on the lawns. I think it was a gesture of contempt for a house occupied solely by a woman, and a woman who suddenly, due to mischance, lived alone in what became a most unsuitable property. I cannot recall the rhododendrons and perhaps this is fortunate.

I remember on my last day in the house I tried to go over all the carpets with the vacuum cleaner, and the vacuum cleaner fused. I left it lying in the middle of the floor on the top landing and I just walked away. Perhaps the new people found it. I do not know. I walked away downstairs and I picked up my purse and I walked down the drive to the street and I never looked back at my house, not once. I have so many recollections of things I wish to forget that, perhaps, to have forgotten the rhododendrons and their thrips is a blessing.

After they had their separate breakfasts, and inspected the thrips, they used slowly to get dressed for the day. He preferred showers. She bathed. It took time and while they were, thus, busy I did the dishes.

'Isn't it wonderful how you manage, my dear,' she would say. 'Isn't she wonderful, Hugh?' And old Hugh, fastening his gold watch round his wrist, would say I was indeed wonderful and she would say, 'Just give me a tiny hand with these, dear, if you wouldn't mind,' and she would hand me her pearls to fasten round her throat and her sapphire brooch for her lapel. The day would have begun.

'Hughie's begun to think of schools for the boys, for our darling Helen's boys. Are you there, dear? You're so quiet, aren't you, these days — but, of course, it's so very understandable. I always say to Hughie, "Hughie," I say, "don't ever lose your sense of humour. Hughie darling," I say, "when we cannot laugh at God's little jokes in this wonderful universe of ours we can consider ourselves dust, Hughie, dust." You must never lose the gift of laughter, dear, and I think I can hear a tiny hint of it now, if I listen hard. Just excuse me a moment.' There seem to be murmurings and I wonder if bridge is to begin again. Have they had their break and is she called back to the bridge table again? But no, it is not to be so easy.

'Yes, Hughie, yes darling — I'll ask her.' So it is Hughie who has prompted the mutterings, I think. Hughie who has formulated the scheme of conversation during this lull in their game of bridge. 'Helen — yes, darling, I'm asking her now, I am, I am — Helen has told us the most extraordinary story, dear, quite extraordinary. We're all absolutely convinced it can't be true. Helen says that a friend of hers says she saw you one day striding along a not very nice street and you went into a vegetable warehouse, dear. Yes, Hughie, I'm just asking her now. She said you were wearing black — what do they call them? *stovepipe* trousers and a funny little coat thing and such a great mop of hair not even styled any more but piled up on top of your head and tied with string. And emaciated, she said, absolutely emaciated. "Well," I said, "it simply could not have been our Amaryllis, not the Amaryllis we know." I said, "Amaryllis has always been" — well, you remember what you were like, dear. Always so elegant.'

'Yes,' I say. 'I remember what I was like.'

'I knew it couldn't be you.' Her breathing changes slightly then, it seems to suggest physical activity.

Is she making hand signals, I wonder, sending an urgent semaphore to Hughie. No-it-was-not-her-she-is-not-emaciated. They have not seen me, you see, not for years.

'But it would have been me,' I say and there is power in my precision with words. 'Yes, indeed. I know that vegetable warehouse. I go there quite often to get things. I always walk. I live nearby.'

I know the girl behind the counter at the warehouse by sight. She has a sharp voice but she is quite a kind girl.

'Dad?' she called that day I went over in my black trousers and Gerald's old leather jacket. 'Dad? It's that lady that buys the spotted pumpkins. Are there any out the back? Dad?' Her father came out then from the storeroom, a big blocky man like a giant onion and so pale, and he showed me where the spotted pumpkins were.

'Free to take away,' he said and walked away. I think he was embarrassed.

'Helen's friend said you had such a big bag. She said it looked extremely heavy. They were most concerned.' The old voice sounds embarrassed as well.

The humble pumpkin is a forgiving and splendid vegetable. I remember I cut out all the rotten spots as soon as I got home — I carried three pumpkins — and I chopped the good parts up into serving pieces and froze them all on trays. Later I might make pumpkin soup and I have a recipe for baked pumpkin which is a complete meal. Nothing more is required except a piece of black bread. I had no idea, when I walked home with my three spotted pumpkins, that eyes had observed my passage through the streets, that people had assessed my burden. I had taken a blue bag I bought once in London and I wrapped each pumpkin in a sheet of newspaper so the interior of the bag was not soiled. I will not get another bag as splendid as my blue one so I must look after it. On the way home I became aware that three big pumpkins might pull the handles of the bag from their moorings so then I walked along hugging the bag as if it were an unwieldy child.

'If you could see our very lovely Helen now you'd weep,' she says, this proud mother of a fat and middle-aged child. 'Our poor darling.' There is almost a sob. 'Every advantage. Hughie even sent her to France, you know, to ensure her accent was accurate. She was a debutante, so nice —

30

debutante of the year.' A sigh now. 'Hughie has such hopes of Jenny Craig. We've pinned ourselves to Jenny Craig. Her friend, Helen's friend, said you were very, very thin. Emaciated, she said. And such a bag to carry, my dear, such a burden for you and she said the wind was appalling. The wind would cut you in half like a knife, she said. You mustn't do too much.' The reproaches now. 'You must look after yourself.'

'I only make pumpkin soup.' Deliberately now I misunderstand. I make this inane remark.

'You always were such a cook. Yes, Hughie — I've given her your regards.' Perhaps there is more semaphore from the bridge table. 'We've never forgotten those wonderful dinners you used to cook — absolutely no effort to you, was it. As I said, dinner used to appear as if by magic, just magic,' and she lengthens the word so it sounds almost like a bray. *M-a-a-g-i-c.*

There was nothing magic about it. I used to cook beef in red wine, chicken in sherry, Hungarian goulash and I would pack it all into the freezer, in boxes neatly labelled the previous week. In the evening, while they had a brief late siesta, I would get out a big square of something large enough to poleaxe a regiment. Thus was dinner manufactured. I used to be able to toss a salad quickly while they walked round the garden again. 'So manicured. I do like a manicured lawn,' and there would be that endowment of words again, that braying. *So-o-o ma-a-a-nicured.* By the time they came inside again, clattering over the quarry tiles, the main course would be unfreezing and I'd have potatoes baking. It was organisation, not magic. Once they stayed a day longer than I expected on their yearly migration through the houses of friends. There was nothing to give them for dinner. My frozen squares had all gone. Gerald found me sitting on the edge of the bath, crying into a bath towel. After seven days — seven breakfasts in separate locations, seven lunches, seven dinners — I could not think what to cook.

We went out to dinner that night. Gerald took us all out to dinner.

'Gerald is so-o-o kind,' they said. 'So-o-o kind.' He was

31

dead less than a year later. They saw the report of it in the newspaper and the telephone pealed in that house in which his ties and laundry still remained as if needed tomorrow while his body had been carried down to the funeral director's chambers.

'Amaryllis? Is that you, dear?' she said that night. 'We've read about it in the paper. We must come at once. Hughie says to tell you he'll answer the door for you. We'll help with letters. You'll need someone, won't you, because you haven't got anyone. Gerald always said you had no family, just no one. Tragic for you. Tragic. You'll have people knocking at the door and people ringing up and driving you mad, dear. What you need is rest and quiet. We'll come and help you. We'll insulate you, dear. You've always been so kind. Ring us tomorrow. Ring us at six. We're always home at six in the evening. We'll have worked out by then exactly what we're doing and when we're leaving and everything. The moment Hughie read it in the paper he said, "She won't have anyone. We must go immediately." That's what my darling Hughie said, didn't you, darling?' Perhaps there was the sound of nodding in the distance then too, a vague semaphore. I had not yet learned to listen for such things. 'Well — till tomorrow then. Just get through till tomorrow and we'll be on our way to help you.'

I believed them. It is the irrevocable loss of that belief that I grieve for now.

My garden is sodden today. There was rain overnight and my pink roses are full-blown and dying. I recall hearing the rain drumming on the roof sometime during the night. I remember I hung up the telephone receiver. They were starting another rubber of bridge. I heard Hughie say so, from a distance. Perhaps he was becoming impatient. I have never actually spoken to Hugh since it all happened. She is always the one who telephones now. I imagine, perhaps wrongly, that they might discuss the call. 'We must ring her,' they might say.

'Will you speak to her or will I, Hughie? It might be easier if I did it, darling.' Easier for what? Or for whom?

'And don't forget, my dear' — her laughter has a slight edge

32

to the tinkle now — 'you still haven't sent us that photograph. Yes, Hughie — I'm reminding her, dear, I am. Hughie so loves his gallery, as he calls it. All his poor dear departed friends — my poor darling Hughie. Yes, darling — I *am* coming. I won't be a moment.' Perhaps my storm may be over soon, I think. 'If you could just remember, dear, to send darling Hughie a picture of Gerald, the tiniest snap would be sufficient. He could get it enlarged and put it in a frame with all the others. "All my friends," he always says. "So sad. All my friends gone." He says a prayer for them all, you know, but you've never sent us Gerald's picture and Hughie would love one.' There are mumblings in the background now, bear-like grumblings that could emanate from a large and hairy animal being poked with a stick. 'Yes, Hughie, I've just asked her again and I'm sure she'll really try to remember this time, dear.'

I say I will with an insincerity that makes my head ache.

'Hughie's devoted a whole wall in his bedroom — we have separate rooms, dear, at our age —'

'Yes,' I say. 'I remember that.'

'— to his gallery, as he calls it, of friends. He's got them all up there, all his dearest friends now so sadly departed, and a lovely photograph, taken from the air of our very lovely home and pictures of the garden and Hughie's favourite tree. Yes, darling.' There are more whisperings. 'Yes, I'll tell her it's your Memory Lane. He says to tell you, dear, that it's his —'

'Memory Lane,' I say.

'Oh, you are so sharp. So you were listening, dear. I felt, just for a moment or two, that your attention was wandering. Our darling Helen suffers from exactly the same lack of concentration. I was reminded so vividly of her a moment ago — you have the same abstracted little voice, forgetfulness, an inability to retain a thought. So like our own darling Helen.

'It's stress, of course. The divorce has been a great strain for us all. He buried all his assets this way and that, hither and yon as Hughie always says, most of it hidden so she's got very little out of it. Our poor Helen now has a very diminished lifestyle. She has to make do with a much smaller house. Hugh goes round every week to mow the tennis court and the grass is so poor he could weep, couldn't you, dear.' There are more murmurings in the background. Hughie is, perhaps, nodding and agreeing. 'What Hugh would like to see is complete returfing of the whole area but we can't even contemplate it at present. The boys must have their tennis. We have hopes that the oldest one might make the grade as a professional. Meanwhile' — and there is that tinkle of laughter again — 'darling Hughie's on lawn-mowing drill. Anyway, do try to remember Gerald's picture for Hugh's little gallery. It would give him such pleasure.'

Gerald seldom had his photograph taken. I have only one picture of the two of us together and we are smiling on a summer's day as if summer will never end and we will always be in our own garden, together. I do not feel inclined to give them one of my few pictures so that Gerald might appear in Hugh's gallery of sham, his cavalcade of fraud.

Their offers of help were, of course, a fraud. I remember when I telephoned them at six o'clock on that evening after the funeral. They were a long time coming to the telephone and I was passed, like a parcel, from one to the other.

'I'll just get Hughie, dear, to talk to you.'

'I'll just pass you back to my darling wife.'

'I'll just let Hughie have a tiny word with you, dear.'

'Perhaps it might be best if it came from another woman.'

I forget who said it first. I think if was Hughie.

'You must realise, my dear,' he said, 'that we have our own daughter to think of. You must have some relatives somewhere? Perhaps if you really put your thinking cap on you might be able to think of a cousin? Or an aunt? You must be able to think of someone, surely? I'll just hand you back to the lady of the house.'

'Hello, dear. Hughie's just handed me the phone. Has he told you? He has. Oh good. Well, we've been thinking overnight and it really isn't a possibility to come and help you after all. We have our own family to consider. Our very lovely Helen, as we've already told you, is in real strife with her marriage. We never thought he was good enough, never.

Anyway, what we've been thinking is that you must advertise for someone to come in every day and keep you company, someone who could answer the door for you and cope with callers and help you with answering letters. You've had a hundred letters already?' The voice was triumphant. 'Well, there you are — an admirable solution to the problem. So glad to have helped you solve it. Yes, I know we did promise but one says these things in the heat of the moment. The news of poor Gerald's death absolutely shocked us. However, my dear, get on to the advertisement first thing in the morning and we'll look forward to hearing from you. Cheery bye.'

I was beautiful then with all my years of comfortable living. Betrayal was familiar to me when I was a child, but I had forgotten its sting. I remember once, down on the old farm, waking up one night to hear someone say, 'Just another mouth to feed.' It was a frightening thing to lie in my little bed in a sunroom that opened off the living room and to know I was just a mouth in the face of a poor relation's child when I had believed, until then, that I was a listener to skylarks. Until I spoke to Hughie and his wife that night much later I had believed for a long time that I was loved and wanted and would not, thus, have to pay someone to keep me company. I did not believe, until that night, that I was so unlovely people would have to be paid to speak to me. Religious Hughie told me so, his name like a gust of hot air, the news relayed via his wife.

In the afternoons, when they came to stay all those years ago, I would drop off to sleep in my big chair up in the master bedroom. Gerald would be at the office. Sometimes I might hear stirrings in the bedroom next door. Cynthia had also sneaked up the stairs for a rest. Have I told you her name? *Cynthia*. The name, for me, matches a hiss.

Hughie, far away in the garden, would blunder about plotting war on thrips, a battle with the thistles in the lawn, the making of a curved path in front of the sitting room, all of this to be done by other people. From far away it was sometimes possible to hear odd drifts of his garden soliloquy. 'A good strong man once a week for an afternoon . . . perhaps

35

a retired farmer. . .landscape architects. . .a lawn expert. . .a work gang of the unemployed. . .perhaps two strong girls. . .' When he was tired of his own company he would come back to the house and he would play the piano with a light and relentless touch so the sound penetrated every corner. *Girls and boys come out to play.* That was his tune. *Girls and boys come out to play, the moon is shining as bright as day. Leave your supper and leave your sleep and come with your playfellows down the street.* It was time to get up. Time to make his cup of tea with something simple to eat, nothing elaborate. Time to go out. I would get the car out of the shed and Hughie would direct me.

'Turn the wheel a little bit more to the left, and a little bit more, my dear. Now straighten up. Straighten up. We'll make a driver of you yet. I must speak to Gerald about this area.' His eyes would narrow then and the look would be empirical. 'The whole space needs redesigning. Landscape architects could give you a huge paved circle with a turn-around for the car and even a nice little fountain and a statue.' Gerald would have been at the office since seven in the morning. We would have crept downstairs in the very early morning like naughty children in our own house and while Gerald ate his muesli I held his hand because I wouldn't see him again till dinnertime.

'Good luck,' he might say at the front door and he used to wave to me from the gate. By that time I would have run upstairs again to have a last look at him from the big bay window on the upstairs landing. Then I went downstairs again to put Hugh's starched cloth on the table ready for his breakfast at seven thirty. I have never been able to inflict a regimen on anyone, even myself. It is a mystery to me now how they managed to impose their routine on us, but they did. We knew they always had separate bedrooms, their exact meal times, how Cynthia did not let Hughie have a brandy after dinner.

It was perfectly understood that no disparaging remarks were to be passed about either Methodists or Anglicans because Cynthia's father had been a Methodist minister and Hughie was a devout Anglican. To be a cricketer was a marvellous thing and, failing that, to watch it was miraculous, dinner had to be served promptly and without a fuss and swearing was outlawed. They were really Gerald's friends. He knew them a long time ago, long before he met me and we were married. Gerald married late and I was very young and I disappeared from Hughie and Cynthia's ken early because he died young. Their voices — Hughie's and Cynthia's — come to me now like an echo, the recollection of them like a pang *douloureux*, painful only because it was all such a waste of time.

At Gerald's funeral an old lady fought her way through the crowd to clutch my lapels and say, 'He'll never see you grow old and ugly,' and I thought of it that day I walked home carrying the spotted pumpkins. I felt glad that Gerald cannot see me as I am now, a thin woman who wanders about carrying pumpkins. I could sell my jewellery, of course. I could sell all the things Gerald bought me. I could sell the sapphires and the diamond earrings, my gold bracelets, everything he bought me. They are never worn now but I keep them like a recollection of good times not forgotten. Sometimes in the evenings I get out my jewel case and I go through everything again. The amethyst brooch he gave me when I was twenty-one, the diamond watch he gave me one Christmas, the pearl and turquoise hoop ring when we had been married for ten years, the turquoise and gold bar brooch he put on my pillow the year Cynthia and Hughie stayed an extra day.

They were his old friends, you see. He knew them a long time ago when he was very young and things were different. They were part of his perception of a brief golden youth in a distant spot, now long gone. It is my opinion now that it never existed but Gerald never came to that realisation and it is my opinion, again, that he was lucky never to know it.

'Hughie's waving to me again. Yes, darling, I have told her she's far too thin. And yes, darling, I've told her she must look after herself.' There are more muffled noises. Perhaps she is waving back to Hugh now. The voice is reedy but determined. 'Mind you, my dear, you're so lucky to be a thin breed. Such a tiny frame! You must take great care. Our poor darling Helen — I won't bore you with that again, dear, but we do have very sincere hopes of Jenny Craig, not that it's cheap. The enrolment fee at the diet school is just the beginning but we're offering as much support as we can to our own darling. Hughie goes every week and collects her food. You have a counsellor, you know, or perhaps you didn't, and they give you an allocation of food. It's far from cheap, dear, far from cheap, but if we can get Helen back as she used to be — such a lovely, lovely girl. You'd weep to see her now.' I have a definite feeling the sight of Helen would simply make me flee, not weep, but I say nothing. 'If we can get our darling back on the rails again who knows what the future may hold for her? Perhaps she may marry again.'

Cynthia's voice expands and warms then as if it springs from a bright and gracious smile, the charming grin of the bride's mother clad in beige lace of the best sort, attending Helen's second nuptials. The bridegroom will be a well-padded but discreet stockbroker greying at the temples and with a large car at the door of the registry office. The boys could be pages. Perhaps the oldest one, if he were too old to wear a little velvet suit with a bow tie, could trim the beginnings of his downy moustache and carry the ring for his new stepfather. 'Are you still there, dear? You sound so very far away.' I am indeed a long way away. I live in a world they do not comprehend and have feelings they could not imagine. 'Helen's friend said it was a freezing day they saw you out and such a heavy bag, too. I said, "Oh, she is a naughty girl, isn't she!" Their car was heated — they have this wonderful French heating system because he's something big in electronics and he knows all about that kind of thing. Such a kind man — Helen's friend has nothing but the best, just what we would have wanted for our own darling girl but it was not to be. They all thought you were very naughty to be out on a day like that, carrying such a load. Whatever would Gerald say, dear?'

I often wonder what Gerald would say. I sometimes dream of him and I see him only in profile, then he turns slowly and looks at me. His eyes are full of anguish and I wake up screaming.

'Helen's friend said absolutely not a soul was out that day. The streets were empty. You were the only person out walking, such a naughty girl to be out on a day like that when everyone else with a grain of sense stayed at home all warm and dry.' Cynthia's voice is playful now. 'Yes, Hughie — I have told her, I *have*.' She seems to be waving again. I hear faint movements. I do not say that was the only day the special on pumpkins was advertised. I do not say I no longer have a car. I just let her run on.

'We do have just one free evening the day after tomorrow, dear, and we could come to dinner if you had time? You haven't? That is sad. Perhaps another time. Yes, Hughie — I really am coming this time. I'll have to go, dear. They're wanting to start again and I've got three very impatient faces looking at me. It's been so nice talking to you and hearing all your news. We're so glad everything's fine. Now, do look after yourself. It must be years since we've seen you properly. It would have been so nice to see you and see where you live. Hughie's waving to me again. He says to tell you he always puts you in his prayers. As you know he has deeply held religious convictions that have greatly illuminated his life. Yes, darling — I'll ask her. Hughie wants to know, did you take our advice about paying someone to stay with you, dear? We were really quite worried about your being alone but I think Hughie saw the sense in paying someone.' There it is again, my horror in treachery, my terror in duplicity, my realisation of lies and deceit, the loss of friendship that never actually existed. 'You could even pay someone to help you now, dear. You could have paid someone to pop out and do your shopping that very cold day. You really must look after yourself and think of getting help. Our own darling daughter, the very apple of Hughie's eye, simply would not be able to manage without our help.'

I have already begun to sink down, slowly, to the floor as she rings off. Finally she has gone and as I fall I am certain that my own lack of words will never be noticed. I have not said goodbye. I have said nothing.

After the funeral, when they had finished speaking to me

on the telephone about how I must hire someone to help me, I went halfway up the big staircase. It was a beautiful staircase. I have a photograph of it here somewhere. The panelling glows golden in the light of a lost sunny afternoon. The stairs lead ever upwards, round three bends punctuated by a carved and turned newel post. The rug is a red Persian runner with a border of dark blue. The men who carried the coffin down the stairs had to hoist it shoulder-high because the balustrading blocked the way on the bends. Life could not make Gerald stay but his own architecture had sought, vainly, to do so. Like a wooden and staying hand, the staircase had tried to keep him in his own house. On that vile evening after the funeral I went halfway up the staircase and I lay down upon the snake of carpet that wound up to the top landing and I heard my own voice echoing in my ears like that of a wildcat or a panther stricken. I lay on those stairs and as evening fell I screamed from loneliness and despair, desolation and betrayal. I screamed in savage terror amidst the kithless emptiness of the house, knowing then, irrevocably, that I was so unloved, so unrequired by the world, that I would have to pay someone to keep me company. Down on the old farm, the night I heard them say I was just another mouth to feed, I knew I was a child who was, thus, a nuisance. I was not a listener to skylarks ever again. The night Hughie and Cynthia told me I would have to pay someone to stay with me I knew, again, that I was horrible.

Every year when they telephone again, just once, I hear the echo of those old screams, but I do not scream now. My house is small and close to the road. All the properties jostle each other for space. Children walk up and down the street and play there. If I screamed now I might frighten the innocent.

I remember I cried myself to sleep the night I realised I was just a nuisance, just another mouth to feed, but that was a long time ago. I was a child then. Now it takes longer. It could be an arithmetical equation — how many tears do you have to shed per sector of body weight so an adult, at last, sleeps exhausted on the floor beside her telephone?

After they have finished with me, Cynthia and Hughie, I find it difficult to move so my storm these days is one of falling and stillness.

The floor of my house held me kindly all through the night and my cat must have found me because she was beside me when I awakened this morning. We are all loved by something or somebody, even if it is just a cat and the dead.

I have sometimes wondered if a living person's spirit can haunt a property. Do I now haunt those old stairs on fine summer evenings? Has the phantom of my desolation stained the floors of that place? You would have to ask the people who live there, the people who bought it. I live differently now.

# PLEASURES OF THE PAST

ON SUNNY DAYS, when the wind came from the north, the terraces that comprised the lower garden lay like warm and inviting earth smiles curving round the mild brow of their hill.

Arthur and Nancy did not know that, though, on their first visit to the property with the land-agent when all the For Sale notices decked the front wall. On the first visit they saw only tangled vines, skeletal trees, a jungle of rampant weeds cascading in disarray. The terraces were beneath all that, like secrets known only by spiders, hedgehogs and inquisitive neighbouring dogs who knew the arcane byways below the enveloping canopy of growth.

It was only much later, too, that they remembered the odd little breeze that kindly fanned their first inspection of the property, soft as a breath on their cheeks. They recalled that warmth when the actual physical exhaustion of the move faded and the idea that the garden was tenanted had taken root.

'I think this is where the old chap grew his onions,' the agent told them on that first day, and he kicked idly at the pernicious weeds. 'And there's his grape.' He nodded towards dry tendrils clamped round a tree trunk. 'They say he had wonderful circulation right to the end,' he said, 'and she was as fit as a flea, so they say. If you ask me, it was all the exercise. They wouldn't leave,' he said. 'They wouldn't go till they were carried out.'

He shrugged as he waved one arm at that wild hillside.

'People take one look at it,' he said, 'and they go away again. Everyone's been here — the Mackintoshes, Dr Lovegrove and his lady-friend, Trudl and Frank (you'd know them), the Marriotts. They've all been here and they've just gone away again. People these days don't want the work.

42

Now the old people were different,' he said. 'It was their whole life. They loved it.'

A giant reticulata camellia loomed over their heads, two dead branches clawing the remainder.

'It's sprung variegated leaves,' said Arthur, 'on the left, see?' and he pulled carefully at the high golden branch. 'You could breed a camellia with yellow foliage from that.'

'Ah,' said the agent, triumphant now, 'so you're going into horticulture.'

'That's not my line.' Arthur was looking round at the majestic herbaceous violence that surrounded them.

'If you ask me, it's dying.' The agent plucked roughly at the tree, shivering. 'It's cold up here,' he said, blew into his balled hands and stamped his feet. 'The day the Marriotts came we all nearly died. They couldn't get out of it fast enough.'

'I find it rather warm,' said Arthur. 'What about old Nance there?'

'Nancy,' she said, 'and I'm quite warm. I think it's really warm and pretty. Look at those flowers down there and feel the warm breeze.'

'Onion weed.' The agent turned up his coat collar. 'Onion weed and oxalis. You'd need to get professional eradicators in.'

'It's beautiful.' That was Arthur. 'You'd have to bring it back to what it was. You'd have to be dedicated.' Nancy, alarmed, suddenly saw a real interest in his expression. 'Look at the view,' he said. 'I can see over the tops of trees.' The warm wind fanned through the overgrown garden, clung fondly to their frozen ankles though the day was an icy one in mid-winter with the promise of snow on the ranges later.

'It's a warm place.' Arthur smiled as if summer started the following week. 'You could grow zucchinis. I could have an apricot tree. I've always wanted an apricot tree.'

'I think the old boy had one' — the agent gazed at the thicket of undergrowth — 'but it died.'

'I'll grow another one,' said Arthur and that happy warmth came again, lay like a silk scarf over their arms. Nancy took off her coat.

'I don't honestly know how you can do that,' said the agent and crossed his arms over his hollow chest, coughing.

'I've found a sort of path.' Arthur wandered down the slope and was climbing round a fallen bush. 'I think I've found some steps. Nancy? Get me my boots from the car.'

'Please,' she said.

'Please,' said Arthur. 'Anything. Just get them.'

'Arthur's a bit of a gardener, is he?' The agent regarded her curiously as she eased through the long grass in those unsuitable shoes.

'Arthur likes land.' She tossed the boots down the slope. 'Arthur likes property. Arthur likes owning things.'

'What's he doing now?'

'He seems to be digging a hole,' said Nancy, 'with a stick, I think.' Arthur, booted, had stopped far below in a clearing.

'Through those weeds? He'll be lucky.' The agent lit another cigarette.

'The soil's wonderful, just wonderful. I've found potatoes growing. I've found a lemon tree.' Arthur's glad cry rose from the depths. They watched one green branch toss wildly. 'I've picked a lemon. I'm tasting it.' There was silence now.

'He can't be eating a lemon, can he?' The agent's cigarette smouldered, forgotten, between his fingers. 'Not really?'

'Arthur often eats lemons,' she told him. 'Arthur's a stoic. Arthur has his teeth drilled down to the bone without novocaine. Arthur had an operation once without an anaesthetic because he says they aren't good for you. Arthur', she said, 'doesn't understand pain.'

'They'll need potash to sweeten them,' called Arthur at last and the remnants of a broached fruit flew into the air, bright and joyful like a small balloon.

'He needs his head read,' said the agent. 'He can't be thinking of buying the place, can he?'

'I haven't the vaguest idea,' she said. 'Arthur doesn't ask me anything.'

'Arthur's no spring chicken. I remember Arthur donkey's years ago, at high school. I remember Arthur before the war.'

'He's very fit.' It was Nancy's turn to shrug now. 'Arthur does exercises every morning at ten minutes past six exactly.'

44

The earliness of the hour seemed to make Arthur's callisthenics sound even more onerous than they were.

'But you wouldn't want a place like this?' He pushed his hat to the back of his head. 'Not at your time of life?'

'And what time of life is that?' she wanted to know, annoyed. 'When I was young all I did was work and now all I do is work. You live and you work and you die. That's what I think.'

'All that housework? All that gardening?' He was a persistent man. 'I could show you a dozen lovely little apartments — no maintenance, metal joinery, the lot. I've got three on the books right now completely paved.'

'You'd have to housekeep here in a peculiar way.' Nancy was wading through raging privet. 'You'd have to do what that batman did in the short story. He polished all the change in the general's pockets so no one noticed the uniform wasn't pressed. What a shame the names of all these things are lost. There's a name-tag on that old rose but heaven only knows a name for the rest. I do babble on,' she said, 'don't I?'

'You've lost me,' said the agent and he sat down on a tree stump. 'I'm completely flummoxed.' He gave her that curious look again. 'You weren't a local girl, were you?' She shook her head. 'I didn't think so,' he said and seemed relieved. 'I don't honestly know how you can stand there like that. I really think that you'd better drag him up yonder to see the bad news.' He nodded towards where they had last seen Arthur eating a lemon. 'There's all new shagpile for starters, and new lining and all new plumbing. There's no end to it.'

He shunted Arthur through the front door as though he were a naughty old boy and he a wise but worn nurse who tends bad children.

The old stairwell windows cast a brave and brilliant light within that shuttered house, and as they climbed slowly up through the dust motes Arthur said, 'I must live here, I must live here,' and so it seemed to be decided.

They moved on a glacial day in mid-spring, domestic squalls over the haphazard breakfast table matched only by the bitterness of stinging rain before midday. Vicious lightning late in the exhausted afternoon illuminated the livid

45

old scar along Arthur's right cheekbone, mark of Nancy's own dinnerplate, and her own wary expression which had paled over the years before the poisonous chill that surrounded them.

She slept that night in an armchair before a dead grate. It was filled with old ashes and a stained and scabrous bandage that still conformed to the shape of a thin strange limb.

'Good morning,' said Arthur after the following dawn and she thought perhaps it might be a better day. He placed a piece of bread and butter on that sinister hearth and said, 'Will you find some plates and spoons by tonight? I'm going to the office now.' He climbed back over a pile of boxes and from far within the dusty house a door slammed behind him.

The garden claimed all immediate attention. Vile fuchsias branched out anew from shattered stumps after Arthur faltered over the final axe blow. That was the first time they heard the footsteps scuffing through the dead leaves, gentle footsteps stopping just short of where they were clearing malignant brushwood from a window.

'Did you hear that?' Arthur put the axe down. 'This is ridiculous.'

Later he began to break in the old orchard, finding the earth terraces that lay beneath their burden of riotous herbage. As Nancy worked in the rose garden she could easily hear him climbing up again through the tracks he had made.

'Nancy, did you come down just now? Did you walk behind me?'

'I've been here all the time.' She worked indefatigably in the gardens round the house. 'You must have heard an echo of my steps up here.' Yet she had not walked anywhere, had remained in the same place digging tussock with the new small spade.

Arthur was not fooled.

'I just came to see how you were, Nancy.' He often hacked up through the garden to see her with an unaccustomed concern. 'Are you sure you're not frightened? Are you frightened, Nancy, when I'm away?'

'I'm fine, Arthur. I'm always fine, thank you. You know what we've agreed — I'm fine, you're fine and never the twain shall meet.'

'I thought I heard the footsteps again.'

'I've told you, Arthur, it must be an echo of mine up here.'

'It sounds like a man.'

'Perhaps it's an echo, then, of another garden.'

Of all her statements that was the most true. The firm tread of the wildwood and the soft footfalls she denied in the upper garden belonged to the time when their garden had its heyday. The old roses would have been in their prime and pride, and the dead apricot tree borne bounties of amber fruit.

As tendrils of ferocious jasmine clutched at her throat and burdens of convolvulus provided a felling weight she heard footsteps herself. She thought they would come from an old-fashioned size two, a fine little lady's shoe in glossy leather polished to the radiance of snakeskin. A navy-blue shoe. Black seemed too dark for that light elderly tread.

In the evenings they sat, embattled and exhausted, with their backs to upstairs walls, and they read seed catalogues and lists of new roses with wary eyes on the stairwell, though their own remembered unease from the spreading land about them was the only thing to haunt them indoors. The interior was pervaded only by the scent of soap and paint and the cigarette smoke of tradesmen.

Outside, under sullen sickle moons, the garden was lapped by waves of unexpected blooms from a drift of white hydrangeas and the abundant flowers of the ancient rose 'Tour de Malakoff', encircling copper beeches and magnolias like a watchful army and the lone cypress a warrior king. In the daytime white daisies shuffled uneasily in a rising wind as Nancy, seeking expertise, read question-and-answer gardening columns in newspapers. The writers confided their difficulties with dianthus or marigolds which, they said, were dying of disease or neglect. Nancy thought they had discovered this acceptable way of stating their own misery. If she had written herself to such publications she would have said that she had neither strength nor courage left, that

47

she did not know what to do. These very statements reinforced her idea that gardening was a microcosm of life and the problems found therein, blight for instance, were part of a greater malaise of the spirit.

'You'll be entertaining,' the new neighbours said, waiting expectantly for the crunch of many vehicles on the drive, but they remained on the property alone amidst the baneful woods and thickets formed in the years of neglect, the hollow barking of a distant dog the only sound to break the silence.

'If we still knew all the old gang we could have them round,' Arthur used to say, but currents of false hope or sudden wildness had borne away most of their friends. The ranks of the middle-aged had been decimated by disease, breakdown, drink and abandonment, and those remaining often took up peculiar dietary habits, younger men or women, or all three.

'But we don't, so we can't.' She sat, immured on the upstairs landing while Arthur fossicked in the drinks cupboard.

'Our medicine, my dear,' Arthur always said as he placed the glasses on the tray with an odd camaraderie, a sudden unfamiliar old-world courtesy.

Throughout their work the footsteps came, cautious but curious, the garden visitors never far behind the increasing paths of their lawnmowers. The steps followed them everywhere as order advanced upon the tangle and one season became another, the notion that the garden must be restored becoming a claiming thought like a manic political belief among extremists. On rainy days as another winter began, they even ventured forth, as though called, to weed feverishly before another squall struck the lee of the house.

Small things, like forgotten gifts, awaited them in the long grass. A copper funnel was the first piece of munificence and, polished, lay like a trophy of rewarding kindness by the hearth.

Later, when the full grip of winter almost stopped them in their tracks, they found a porcelain saucer gilded with laurel wreaths like those for a victor. In the depths of heartless chill the old gazanias flung out an abundance of black-eyed sunny flowers and they knew then that the garden sensed the coming of a better spring, had sent them this friendly message of comfort.

They kept a fire flickering in the grate throughout the darkest days, stoked it lavishly with logs found under the ivy hedge, and sat before its warmth. Their conversation, always now polite and gentle, was about extra seed potatoes, new hoes, the best rose spray, safe subjects that brought no tempests upon them.

Nancy sometimes stood at night watching the dark land but no shadow ever disturbed the passage of the moonlight over the lawns and even the old dog nearby barked glumly, without conviction, as if what disturbed him was the memory of old frights and agitations from distant seasons, irritating cats now buried beneath gaunt trees.

On the coldest days the footsteps began to draw closer, pattering along nearly at their heels like pets, and Arthur would call out, 'How's your friend?' as she pruned the roses back to the first good outward bud.

An extra strength came to them as frosts subsided into a damp and misty spring. When their axes felled the wild daturas along the last untouched boundary they found beneath them, lashed to the earth with creepers, a great arc of white camellias that looked more like roses. When the days grew longer and the sun had more heat, when the dew in the corners dried out before midday if they were lucky, they trundled out the lawnmowers again and stripped more rank tussock from lost areas. On starry nights, as Nancy watched the garden, the exposed white roots glimmered like a promise beneath pruned trees.

Summer brought a bountiful innocence of flowers that replaced the old ruin of weeds and underbrush just as, indoors, the lightness of new paint and their own determined hands upon scrubbing brushes brought a guileless order to the burdensome chaos.

They bought each other new gumboots for their second placid Christmas and the burden of work diminished so there was time to wander about the rose garden in the evenings as darkness fell. The footsteps drew a little closer then, first a small echo away, then half an echo, accompanying them on the rounds of the flowerbeds like fond and contented favourites, all allies of the omnipresent garden.

When Arthur was away Nancy often now ran gladly out through the french doors into the warm dark arms of the trees, smiling like a person who is loved, to fetch forgotten secateurs or a sunhat left by the rosemary.

'Aren't you frightened?' asked the neighbours. 'All alone?' 'But I am not alone,' she said. 'I am never alone,' and realising it was an error, added, 'There is an old dog.' The footsteps came closer again, then, to within a heartbeat.

When summer filtered into benign autumn they picked the fruit from burdened trees, hung herbs and flowers to dry beside sunny windows. Their mowers sliced through grass that ceased to look amputated and fell in deep mossy stripes, rich and green, beneath their feet. The reticulata camellia with the disparate branches had buds forming for its annual profusion of blooms that were as familiar to them now as each daisy in every manicured corner, but no ancient tread disturbed the silence, no soft footfall followed them within the confines of their hedges. The garden was empty, at last.

Until the heat of winter fires warmed them, they had a chilly and absurd sense of loss like people who have suffered a secret bereavement, the news of which had been brought to them over high mountain passes from a nostalgic country far away. They spent their days working quietly, in that decorous way they had now, among the mulched flowerbeds, brightening only when Nancy said one day, 'The name of the white hydrangea is "Madame de Mouillière".'

# EDWARD AND LALLY/
# TED AND PAM

HER TEETH — HER *new* teeth — reflected in the mirror (also new) above the chiffonier looked, Lally thought, simian. Definitely like a monkey's teeth. She sat there, at the dinner table which the latest decorator had lacquered green, and toyed with a piece of Greek cheese and a spinach cracker, running her tongue over those teeth again as if it might be sandpaper and could make them smaller. Perhaps that other specialist, the one in the Art Deco building, might have been a better man to go to than Edward's favourite little tooth man, as he called him, down in the inner city. Edward always said he was the biggest name in capping.

She smiled slowly at herself again in the mirror, without promise, and the teeth were still too big. Like a melancholy tiny marmoset — for the last five years she had been on only 800 calories a day without a break — she bared the teeth again.

'They're too big,' she said. 'I see that as the salient problem.' They had been, she and Edward, to classes in vocabulary management and tried to utilise unusual words in a natural way to create a greater atmosphere of personal productivity in the vocalisation sphere.

'Indeed, yes.' Edward had heard this, far away at the head of the table. Maida was cutting grapes off their stems with a pair of sterling silver grape scissors which the decorator had purchased to give a focal point to the dining-room. Maida popped the grapes into Edward's mouth while Grahame, her husband, poured himself another glass of port. They all said Grahame was a mass of cellulite and desperately in need of a detoxification programme, if only he'd ask for help. 'Thank you, Lally, for that very valuable contribution to the discussion,' said Edward. 'An over-

51

weighted partnership, as you have so very accurately divined, an over-balanced portfolio of investments and commitments, far too many drones on the payroll — and what have you got?'

'A disaster.' Maida put another grape in his mouth. 'Open wide, darling. No, Grahame — you don't deserve any.'

'Maida's come up with exactly the right word.' Edward's smile was rapturous. 'She's captured the leitmotif. Top marks so far to Maida.'

So, Lally thought, it was a competition, was it?

She smiled at herself again in the mirror. A monkey, she thought.

'I was talking about my teeth,' she said. 'Do you think my teeth look too big?' The mirror with its distinctive glaucous depths gave her face a mossy cast and the teeth looked almost yellow. The effect was, she thought, autumnal. The decorator had given the mirror an inlaid imitation marble backing in forest colours to give all reflections profundity. The bill for all this, plus for the new quilted chintz drapes, arrived the day before the capping and Edward's cry of horror had also been profound.

'No,' said Grahame. It was the first time he had spoken for more than an hour.

'No what?' Edward did not look away from Maida and her bright and perfect smile.

'No, Lally's teeth don't look too big.' Grahame was pouring another glass of port.

'Why do you think Grahame and Maida stay married?' people often said. 'I mean, he's like the invisible man. He never even says anything. What on earth keeps them together?' And once Lally heard herself say, her own voice echoing in her ears like that of a knowing and wilful stranger, 'Maida keeps Grahame because he's her springboard. She springs off Grahame for these affairs she's always having and when she falls back in a heap she's got old Grahame to go home to. The thing that keeps them together is precisely nothing and that's why it's so valuable and no one can wreck it.'

'What a truly dreadful thing to say.' Someone had said that.

'A truly, truly dreadful thing, indeed.' Perhaps it had been an interested and defensive Edward, she thought now as she looked down the table again. Maida had begun to cut into the Brie while Edward looked at Maida and the cheeseboard with unequal relish.

'Now if you really want to see wonderful little toothy-pegs,' he said, 'look no further than Maida.' His glance was embracing and nearly shameless.

He had wide peripheral vision caused by a lifelong astigmatism. His latest contact lenses, which also altered his eye colour to deepest azure, came from Lautour, who cost twice as much as anyone else but was such a fascinating and inventive dialogist that it was worth paying the extra money just to hear how he escaped from Estonia with the Russians on his heels. Edward claimed everyone said so, everyone indeed, so it must be true.

"I must congratulate Maida on her comprehensive grasp of the corporate state.' Edward opened his mouth very wide, to show his capped back molars, as Maida placed a green grape inside one of his cheeks and a piece of cheese inside the other.

'Maida's grasp is certainly always remarkable.' Lally heard her own lispings with unease. The teeth were definitely too big. Her mouth felt slightly uncomfortable, as if it might be too small, and she thought that her recent liposuction might have caused such pain that all her membranes had shrunk with anguish. And hope. They had shrunk with anguish and hope, then disappointment, so there was now not sufficient room to speak. 'I think we're all very much aware of Maida's grasp,' she said and grasped one of her own slim thighs under the table as she spoke. Thighs, dimpled with cellulite or not, were a real problem after forty.

'Her grasp is toothsome.' Grahame was pouring himself another glass of port. 'Her grasp is ambrosial, or so I'm told.'

'Delectable,' said Maida, as she began to nibble Edward's shoulder. He had enrolled the year before last at the best gym in town, recommended authoritatively by Crossan, who was the big man in face lifts and specialised in the removal of dewlaps above and below corporate, and other, chins. It

53

was the only fitness centre that acknowledged the actual face, the *visage* as it was called, must not be stressed under exercise while the flab below was pressed to the limit of human endurance. The regimen claimed to provide stress relief for all membranes plus the central nervous system in one to one and a half hours on the very first day.

Lally could perceive, from the faint rippling of the fabric, that Edward was flexing his enlarged biceps under his new silk shirt. It was a *nouvelle* designer label from a landlocked principality within sight of the majestic Pyrenees where the population was reputed to be of extreme beauty and slimness into advanced old age. He now took two sizes larger in shirts due, in part, to the meagreness of the cut and mostly to the actual development of his sinews. For casual, but charming, catered dinners at home like this one, he wore his shirts pulled tight across his pectorals and knotted at his (now) very slim waist. The development of his deltoid area had also been, in a word, exceptional, to quote the resident medical man's quarterly report from the gym. Lally had perused it only yesterday with a rising sense of horror. She had not enrolled there yet due to the liposuction and the teeth and the face lift and a few other things including treatment for the varicose veins that sadly marbled her right calf. Inertia of a general nature came into it too. There would be such a lot to catch up on in the exercise field. If mopping tears was not ruinous for her new eyelids she might have wept. Edward's trapezius was now beyond comparison, according to the critique, and his latisimus dorsi verging on breathtaking.

'I'm concentrating now on the gluteus maximus,' Lally heard him say. Maida was still gnawing his upper arm. Her lips had been tattooed baby pink so the sleeve remained pristine. 'To put it in layman's terms,' he said, 'the bum.'

'The bum indeed.' Grahame was eating another spinach cracker with Brie. His glass was empty again and he regarded Maida with anxious and hollowed eyes. 'The bum indeed. Laymen indeed.'

'Oh, Edward, stop biting me.' Maida's shriek almost cut the cheese. 'And Grahame — stop being such a pain. Isn't

Grahame being a pain?'

'Leave Grahame alone.' Lally thought her own voice, coming from behind the big new teeth, was almost surprising in its familiarity though the lisp was new since the capping. Her vowels were rounder these days, too, and Mrs Van Utteridge, the therapist, claimed her *timbre* was two tones lower.

'You sound as if you could have come from anywhere,' Mrs Van Utteridge said at the end of last term and Lally said, 'Well, I'm not quite sure that's what we, I mean I, I don't really know who I mean' — and she had given a nervous little titter — 'I'm not sure that's what we had in mind.' She repeated it now as she looked at the teeth again in the lacquered mirror. 'I'm not sure that was what I had in mind.' Simian, she thought. *Simian*.

'I thought,' she had said to Mrs Van Utteridge, 'I'd sound as if I came from somewhere, well, different.' Mrs Van Utteridge clapped her lightly on the shoulder. Her private creative dancing lessons taken over more than three decades had made her inexpressibly light on her feet, and elsewhere. Her hand on Lally's shoulder had tightened, the skin on her fingers matchlessly pure. All age spots had been removed by an avant-garde method which caused no scarring and resulted in the holistic completion of psyche and epidermis. Her hands always seemed to blush slightly, particularly round the palms and the tips of the fingers where they were touched by money. Her bill arrived in a scented pink envelope patterned with a botanical print, completely accurate and in exquisite taste, of the modest violet (in sepia) as a smokescreen for the immodest contents.

'But I must say,' Edward always said as he wrote out the cheque in payment with his sterling silver pen (Pierre Cardin and a new line), 'quite categorically, Lally, you do indeed sound different.' He flexed his pectorals again as he said this. They had been trained in a myriad of small exercises to use in all moments that may otherwise be wasted. For instance, Lally read book reviews instead of the actual books while the beautician built up her nails with a recognised protein derivative, a process which took exactly thirty-four minutes per nail and was of such paralysing boredom that all emotions were drained.

Maida was tickling Edward in the ribs now with one manicured hand. Her nails looked exactly like pearls, another novel process which was imperceptibly more expensive than any other.

'Let me feel, Edward. Let me *feel*.' She had transferred last term to a new clinic where they taught a vaguely foreign manner of speech. Maida's vowels, Lally noted, were suddenly almost Gallic. She mouthed soundlessly over her new big teeth. Her own vowels were now crippled, she decided. 'Let me feel, Edward.' Maida was using two hands now.

'Feel away,' said Grahame and reached for the last cracker. 'Don't mind me.'

'There's been great development, hasn't there, Edward.' Maida was ignoring Grahame, her head nearly touching Edward's so they looked like conspirators. 'I do notice a great difference.'

'So does Mother.' Lally spoke to her own reflection. 'Mother notices a great difference in everything.' No one was listening. Grahame was eating cheese. Maida continued to finger Edward's ribs. Edward was looking at Maida.

'We all notice a great difference in everything.' Maida turned her big round face towards Lally. Years ago, when they were all at school together they had called her Moon, but that was almost forgotten now. It was silted over by foreign vowels and clothing of such aggressive raw silk that it looked, to the uninitiated, like sacking. The cosmetic surgeon had been unable to alter dramatically the shape of Maida's face but had rearranged the contours so her profile was almost handhewn in the most delicate way possible. Her psychological profile was also high in the world of charities, particularly those that attracted maximum publicity for minimum effort.

'Hear, hear.' That was Edward. 'Yet again Maida's come up with exactly the right phrase.'

'Thank you.' Maida kissed him. 'We particularly notice a great difference in how you look, Lally.' The voice was suspiciously encouraging.

'Me?' Lally looked at the teeth again in the mirror. 'What about me?'

'Think how wonderfully you've come on, Lally.' The moon beamed from the head of the table, beside Edward. 'Nobody could possibly pick your age. You look at least two or three years younger than you are, doesn't she, Edward?' She nibbled his earlobe, perfect since birth so it had required no renovation. There was a long silence.

'Thank you very much indeed, Maida.' Grahame had roused himself from a crumpled position in a chair that looked too small to hold him. 'I feel sure Lally's very grateful for that, aren't you, Lally? Two years younger than you are, after all your pain and anguish.' His voice was sepulchral now. 'What a wonderful thing. I feel sure those very kind words — those kind and well-intentioned words — from our own very lovely Maida, our sociable Maida of whom everyone speaks well including the man at the service station and a few thousand others as well, I feel sure Lally's going to be effectively enlarged psychologically by such graciousness.' There was another long silence.

'I wonder' — Edward coughed slightly as he spoke — 'if we should do something about getting Grahame home. I think Grahame, dear kind soul that he is, could be just a tiny bit in need of popping home.'

'Home indeed.' Grahame stumbled slightly as he stood up. 'Sent home. Naughty Grahame. Naughty Lally.' He glanced at his reflection and that of Lally who stood beside him. 'Teeth too big,' he said. 'Only two years younger than she is.' He wandered out into the entrance hall. 'Coat,' he said. 'Coat.' He leaned against the wall while Edward put his jacket round his shoulders.

'The thing I've really got against you, Grahame,' he said, 'is your unrepentance. Your whole body's a mass of cellulite. You're more than ten kilos overweight — and what do you do about it, Grahame? Nothing, Grahame. You do nothing, and that's what really gets my goat. It's your arrogance and your pretentiousness, your inability to acknowledge that you need to improve that gets me right where it hurts most.'

'And I've already told you that you're a pain.' Maida wedged him in a corner. 'Now just stand there, and don't move an inch. He's got a very negative attitude,' she said to Edward. 'Not like you.'

'Lally?' Edward's voice was sonorous. 'Run and ring a taxi, will you? No, go upstairs, darling, not downstairs. That little catering man's still out there.'

The upstairs hall held a cool gloom that was reassuring, she thought, and the mirror up there was kinder. She looked young, the teeth smaller.

'Lally? Lally?' Edward's voice was echoing up the stairwell. 'I think he's passed out.' Muffled noises came from below. 'He's fallen in the cupboard.'

I must ring Mother tomorrow, thought Lally as she dialled the number for the taxi. Far away, in a distant suburb, the old lady would be asleep now, blissfully unaware that the area was not a highly rated one in real estate terms. She had been born there and would die there. *Is that you, Pammy?* Her mother's voice would echo over the line. The telephone in the old house had been there for years and even rattled slightly when the receiver was lifted. *You don't sound like yourself at all, dearie.* That's what she had said last week. *Been to the dentist? Have you had an injection? Capped? Had your teeth capped? What did you do that for, lovey? Pammy? Are you there?*

'Are you there, Pam?' she said to herself as she waited for the taxi company to answer. 'Where are you?'

Years ago they had been Ted and Pam. *Give my regards to Ted*, her mother always said, the old voice squeaky with the effort of goodwill. *Tell Teddy hello from Mum.* Proceeding with extreme dedication to upward mobility, almost before it had been invented, they had become Eddy and Pamela by the end of their seventh form year at the old high school, before they got A bursaries. By the time their respective degrees had been completed they were Edward and La-La, and from there it just required a tiny final step to become the trendy Lally. *Pam? Are you there, dear?* her mother always said on the telephone. *I don't know, Mum. I don't know who I am.*

She had been Dux of the school once and her mother still had the medal in the china cabinet. *Pam Driscoll, Dux* — plus the year, which she preferred now not to think about. Edward had been captain of the First Fifteen, which had seemed important at the time. Was it, she wondered now in the upstairs hall, just the first fifteen? And was it dux, not Dux? Did distance and time diminish or give a correct perspective? Their marriage and mating, not necessarily in that order, had been a cliché. Maida had been a year younger and in a junior form though, in her late teens, she had been crowned Miss Grosvenor Raincoats in a minor beauty pageant. She was thus equipped to weather storms of all kinds, including those caused by her early and necessary marriage to Grahame, the school's fat boy (another cliché) who studied engineering in the technical course. He had, predictably, grown into a fat engineer and their twin sons, who were also fat, were studying engineering (repeat cliché). They would become fat, round-faced engineers (ditto).

'Lally? What are you doing up there?' That was Edward's voice again. 'Are you inventing the taxis?' A muffled titter from Maida. 'She's quite hopeless,' Lally heard him say.

He had one hand two or three inches above Maida's bare right shoulder, like a kind of arrested digital elevation, when Lally went downstairs again.

'You'd be so much more graceful, Lally, if you'd come to my yoga classes with me, even just once.' Maida's round face seemed to beam goodwill. 'We concentrate on the common denominator of complete inner meaning. My guru could do wonders for you.' There was a long silence. 'He's a really marvellous person and he makes designer letterboxes as a sideline. He makes all the tiles for the roof of each one while under self-hypnosis.'

'Marvellous.' Edward's admiration was frightening, Lally thought. 'You must give me his number,' he said. 'No, don't tell me now.' He placed a playful hand over Maida's bright and perfect mouth. 'Give me a little tinkle at the office. Perhaps we can arrange a course of classes for Lally's birthday.'

Now Maida was staring out of the little window beside the front door.

'There's no sign of the taxi,' she said. 'Are you sure you

rang the right number, Lally? Edward says you're really silly about numbers. Edward says you're always getting them wrong.' The red leadlight panes of the casement cast a bloom over Edward's face. He might have been blushing, Lally thought, if that were possible. Kreisler, the stained glass artist, had assembled all the glass in the red/blue colour spectrum to promote healing and homeopathic goodwill, a useless piece of expense Lally thought now. They might as well have had an ordinary window, or none at all. 'Yoga could be of extreme help to you, Lally. Clumsiness of the mind and body are specialties —' Maida was interrupted by the sound of a car. The taxi had arrived at last.

Later, after they had loaded Grahame in, Lally watched as Edward stepped forward to kiss Maida on one perfect cheek.

'Ring me, I mean us,' he said, 'and let me know you're home safely.' There was a vague murmuring, something about tomorrow. 'Bye bye, dar —' He coughed. 'Bye bye, Maida.'

Standing back on the pavement — the débâcle was best viewed from a distance — Lally put one hot hand on the ivory splendour of her left cheek. The tucks taken beyond her hairline to lift the forehead, the reshaping of her eyelids, the implants in her (now) pouty lips, were all useless. She could see that now. To have reached the end of a painful search for perfection only to discover that the manufactured beauty was charmless was a piece of cosmetic horror that not even yoga could cure.

'Lally, what are you doing?' Edward's voice with those well-trained vowels seemed to come from an imaginary land of felicity in which she was a masterpiece redundant before completion. Her navel had not yet been lifted and placed slightly off-centre as a statement of life's enigmas and also, after their classes in caring about the universe, a mute protest about the destruction of the South American rain forests. The operation would now never be done. 'Lally, you can't sit in the gutter. You'll ruin your legs. Lally, we can talk this through. I'll ring the clinic in the morning.'

As the taxi drove away she could see Maida regarding its

60

ceiling with the daintily lascivious and proprietorial look of a bride rampant. 'Au revoir, Edward,' she called through the open window. 'Give me a ring.'

# THE FACE OF THE LAND

IT WAS NEARLY spring before they finally set off on the expedition. The old lady wore her rings and her hands gripped the top of her bag ferociously, so he knew she had brought her money, a great day.

'You're late,' she said, fingers snapping at the catch. 'I've been waiting.' She was sitting on a little chromium chair just inside the door, an unassailable position that gave an enveloping vista of the streets outside.

'I said nine,' he said, 'and it is nine.'

'Ten past. It's a good ten past by my clock.'

'Then your clock's wrong.' He had gathered a momentum for himself now, had drawn himself forward from the sudden anguish of being a late boy again into his present secure middle age. 'Your clock must need regulating. I'll take it in.'

'I've been waiting. They've been watching me.' Behind her, at an internal window, he saw a row of faces above knees, tartan-clad in woolly rugs. 'They said if you didn't come I could go on the outing. They said Matron would get another ticket. Ha.' She breathed on the glass, misting it over the faces. 'He's come. He said he would. He says it's just nine. He says the clock needs regulating.'

They sat, impassive, and he wondered what time Matron got them up. As he helped his mother down the steps she turned and smiled, waved.

'Let them put that in their pipes and smoke it,' she said. 'I told them you were coming. I told them you were taking me to all the places I ever lived.'

'Not all,' he said, 'surely? And besides, it's only a picnic. We might not be able to find anything. The roads might be different now.' He noticed she was wearing her best navy-blue coat and her shoes twinkled over the pavement to the car.

'I know it's only a picnic.' The hands were very firm on the rim of that bag. 'I polished my rings this morning,' she said. 'You can do it with toothpaste. I read it in a magazine.' So she had got herself ready, he thought, creeping round in the early morning with toothpaste and shoe polish and the clothesbrush before anyone stirred.

'We were up at the crack of dawn today.' Matron appeared from behind the camellias that masked the drying green from the road. 'Now be a good girl for me,' she said to his mother, 'and don't get too excited or we'll have to have a valium tonight and we know what we'll miss.' She leant forward, pink-cheeked and confidential. 'They hate going to sleep before that one about big business, the one with all the smart outfits.'

'It's the news I like.' His mother looked quite grim, he thought. 'And after that I like current affairs and the outdoors.'

'Miss Mary Quite Contrary, goodbye then,' said Matron and pushed her head further in the window of the car. 'They all have their funny little ways.'

'Her,' said his mother as they drove away, 'and her valiants. She can keep her valiants. I sleep like a top. I've still got my wits about me.'

'Nobody said you hadn't, dear,' said his wife, silky and sulky in the front seat, turning to look again at those rings.

'Just how much longer will she go on for?' she would say that night. Their days with his mother always ended in the same way. 'Eighty-seven. Isn't it long enough? Haven't we had enough?'

'There's no choice in these things.' His voice of reason, the legal training, calm and measured. The opposite example of his parents taught him that.

'She'll live to ninety-one. She'll live to a hundred. I'll die of exhaustion and she'll still be going.'

The sun came up slowly from behind the hills as they took the coast road, the brightness showing them the benign face of late winter as he drove along the crest of a ridge.

May had been a pleasant month, very suitable for a country picnic, but the old lady developed bronchitis. June was busy.

He had an audit through the firm that ran into July. Later that month a virus rolled into the home one dank day, plundering the ranks in the armchairs.

The old lady came through it with a deep and lasting cough and when they saw her on the last Sunday of that month she was sitting up in bed wearing the best pale pink bed-jacket, a triple feather and fan two-ply pattern that his wife said was total angst even if you could do it. The road maps were spread out over the counterpane, and they knew it was time.

'I know the way. I know it off by heart.' She was pointing over the back of the car seat, gesturing far beyond the bedraggled factories and the tannery to where the hills met the clouds in a purple haze and distant houses sat like fullstops punctuating the landscape. 'Up there,' she said, 'take the first turn left after the petrol pumps. Just keep going till I say. I know the way.' He could not doubt it.

'But Mother' — that was his wife again, turning to look at those rings — 'a lot changes in fifty years.'

'Fifty-two,' said the old lady, 'if it's a day,' and already he could hear the beginning of the scene.

'She's always got to be so right.' Betty would say that. 'She's always got to dot every i and cross every t. She's always got to have the last word.'

'It's fifty-two years nearly to the day that I came up here.' He felt, rather than heard his wife sigh. 'It was raining cats and dogs. Your father dropped my best teaset on the way and broke everything except two saucers.'

'I'm sorry,' he said, as if he had done it himself, and his wife stirred uneasily, coughed. She was from a devoted family and did not comprehend hatred.

The sounds of the years echoed in his ears as he took the hill road, the patches of dappled sun like the isolated pictures in his mind of dinners splashed on walls, the mark of a hand on flesh. The recollections were always brilliantly lit by bare electric bulbs swinging wildly in bleak farmhouses. Their whole lives seemed a play before rustic footlights and he the terrified audience, a stolid child hiding in grotesque shadows.

'Don't take any notice of her,' his father would say in the morning. 'We were only funning. She was just singing,' and he would smile that jackal's smile, eyes as cold as steel.

'I laughed when he died,' said his mother as they took a small gorge. 'Do you remember that?'

'I do,' he said. 'Very well indeed.'

'Turn left here, left I say.' The old arm was flung out, coat sleeve like a banner, and he took the left-hand fork in the road at too high a speed for safety, a sort of driving effervescence in gratitude for a change of subject and direction.

'Is it far?' his wife asked. There had been no word or movement from her since that sigh.

'A mile or two,' said his mother. 'Just past that bend up there, that was the first place we had. Then we moved up the road to another place and after that we went into the ranges, bigger places but not such good land.'

'You can call on us,' said the neighbours at the door, 'any time. Have you just got the one little boy? If Mummy needed someone you could run up the road and get us, couldn't you, dear,' and the lady bent right down, took his hand and looked into his face so closely that he still remembered the clear pale hazel of her eyes. They moved again later that season, their disharmony now a known thing in the neighbourhood, a piece of local knowledge that became an unsavoury myth to shame them.

'There,' said his mother from the back seat and he eased his foot off the accelerator, wondering if this might be the house of that old night. 'You can see the chimney past the trees. Stop at the blue gate.'

No gate remained and the chimney, when they waded through rough grass to reach it, reared up alone in a desolate field like a sentinel saying, 'Why did you do this to me?' A fragment of path led nowhere and below the hedge a few early spring bulbs snatched at the sun.

'It's amalgamation,' he said. 'It's the new way with farm management. It's all amalgamation these days. Lots of the old farms don't exist any more.'

'It was quite a good place,' she said. 'We made a living

65

out of it. I told him it was a mistake to go.' He heard again those shouts that roused the neighbours in the night.

'Where next?' he wanted to know.

'Up the road.'

Another chimney awaited them there, but its mantelpiece remained together with the roofless shell of a separate wash-house open to the wide sky, richness compared with the first stop.

'Ah,' said his mother, and pecked through the long grass like an old sparrow after a crumb. 'I had all my brass up there and your Aunty Vera's blue vases.' The hand rested on the old shelf for a moment. 'It had a lovely grain, this wood,' she said, 'then.'

The mists of early morning had evaporated, even from the deeper reaches of the valleys, when they reached the next place. Embarrassment, he remembered, drove them deeper into the high country.

'This was my wash-house.' Another wash-house, he thought. Did a desire for cleanliness last longer than anything else? They used its fallen door as a path to enter. 'Rats,' she said. 'Did you hear that?' The old hand darted forward and touched the wooden walls with the sharpness of a lawyer's, making a valid point.

'They haven't looked after my tubs. You had to keep the plug in those wooden tubs, and an inch of water in the bottom or they cracked. Someone hasn't bothered.' She made it sound like an accusation that had a legal basis.

'It's amalgamation,' he said again. 'The old farms aren't economic units any more.'

'They were,' said his mother.

'They aren't now.'

'Well, they were.'

'They're just run-offs now. They use the houses for sheds or storage or hay or anything.' It was like stabbing someone, he thought.

'They pull them down.' She stood, an accuser again amidst scattered masonry. 'This was a nice house. It had french doors with pretty little panes. I won prizes for jam here.' She was stepping through the weeds to the car with meticulous attention, like a lady picking her way through city rubble in fine shoes.

'Over there' — she seemed to know the ground so well — 'I had my azaleas and my magnolia.'

They were nearly at the car when she looked back, saw something. She was off again, almost skipping through the grass, and he thought of that threat of a valium.

'What is she doing?' His wife mouthed each syllable clearly through the window of the car. 'What is she up to?' She held up a vacuum flask and a biscuit tin but he shook his head. Not yet.

Beyond the rough hedges reared a giant tree, the great branches silvered with bark spreading across the curve of a hillside.

'It's my tree. It's my magnolia. It's still here.' She was almost running through the rough paddock.

'Watch out for stock,' he called. 'Don't fall. Don't trip.' A broken hip was just what they needed.

'Spoilsport.' There was a jauntiness about her now.

Beneath the branches a few early bluebells insinuated themselves through matted grass while the blooms on the tree, peachy pink in the brightening sun, lay softly like the nests of mythical birds.

'I planted this.' She had one hand curled round a flower while a fantail played round her head, coming so close it seemed to caress a cheek. 'Do you think the souls of loved cats become fantails?' Her voice, he noticed, was quite clear and strong.

'I beg your pardon?' He must have misheard.

'I said, do you think the souls of loved cats become fantails?' The little bird flew closer.

'I shouldn't think so,' he said, 'What an odd thing to ask. Why would the souls of loved cats become fantails, for heaven's sake?' His wife was mouthing something else through the window of the car. So difficult to please them both, he thought, fragmented attention swinging from one woman to the other.

'You didn't take any notice of a single thing I said all day,' his wife would say that night. 'It's called being dropped like a hot cake.'

'Don't be ridiculous.'

'So I'm ridiculous now, am I?' He must not fall into that old trap.

His mother was still holding the flower.

'I was happy here,' she said. 'I had a lovely cat. The heart went out of me when my dear old Matilda died.'

She sank down on those creaky old haunches among the weeds where the magnolia's late leaves would throw a summer shade, leaning towards the little fond bird as a child holds up a cheek to be kissed.

'They like anything that disturbs the air,' he said, 'anything that gets the insects moving. They feed on the wing.' That legal training again, inexorably arid.

'Feed on the wing, do they?' She was heading for the car. 'I sometimes think you've got as much imagination as a hen,' she said, 'and that's insulting the hen.'

'What about a nice cuppa?' His wife had the picnic-basket open. 'What about a nice bickie?'

'I couldn't eat a thing.' His mother slid into the back seat. The lid of the hamper snapped shut.

'We'll have to stop for lunch soon,' said his wife and he felt another sigh. 'We'll stop at the next nice place with a view.'

'No view for me, please.' That voice from the back seat. 'I'd like a cosy place out of the wind, where I can't see out. I don't want a place where I can see far.'

'I'd rather have a view.' His wife again.

'I'll see what I can do,' and now it was his own sigh he felt. 'It's a matter of finding a safe place.'

'Not anywhere near a bend, thank you.' He could see his wife's hand drumming on the hamper's lid. 'Not after what happened to the Cardwells, and what compensation did they ever get is what I want to know. I don't honestly see why you couldn't have got them back their no claims bonus at least.'

'I don't think we'll go through all that again,' he said. 'Not now.'

From the back seat came the sound of a small cough from

his mother, abrasive like the voice of the crow.

'Just stop anywhere, darling.' There was an unaccustomed warmth in that tone and the endearment was unfamiliar. 'Anywhere does me. Just stop anywhere, dear.' Fond again.

'I still think,' said his wife, relentless hand on the hamper, 'that you could have done something about that bonus.'

'Here,' said his mother. 'This looks a nice place,' and he slid the car thankfully into a gap between two old gates where the grass was surprisingly short, where it was easy to see no trapping drain or swamp lay hidden.

'Give him his first,' said the old lady. 'Keep the men happy is what I say. If you knew at the beginning what you know at the end things might have been better,' and she laughed that crow's cackle again, a hand creeping along the back of his seat to touch his shoulder. 'When we get back,' she said, 'I must give you my rings for Betty.' He felt his wife stir sharply like a child caught in a naughty deed. 'At my age,' she said, 'you don't need much.

'When old Mr Wilson went last month his son couldn't find his big gold watch. It was there the day before,' she said, a calculating crow now, 'but on the actual day it went into clean thin air. Betty might as well have my few bits and pieces.' His wife turned round to the back seat, flask in hand like a big red exclamation mark.

'I don't know what to say,' she said. 'It's very kind of you. I don't know how to thank you,' — there was a delay — 'Mother.'

'You enjoy them, my dear. You put your gladrags on and go and knock them in their socks. You'll be able to, now the girls have gone.'

'I think,' he said, 'that it's stop them in their socks. I don't know where you hear these sayings.'

'It's television.' There was that cackle again.

Solicitous now, his wife put a sandwich on a little tray, then another.

'Just say if that's not right,' she said to his mother. 'Just say if you'd rather have something else. I've given you ham, but there's pâté. You know who likes pâté.'

'Leave the pâté for him, then. He has to do the driving.

69

He has to do all the work.' The hand slid along to his shoulder again. 'The boy must have what he wants.' Was he seven, he wondered, or fifty-seven?

They found an avenue of flowering cherries at the next stop.

'They're early,' said his mother. 'It was always warmer here.'

'A micro-climate?' He had done part of a science degree.

'No,' she said, 'I mean early, just early and warmer. My aquilegias were a byword.' She was picking a bunch of the soft white cherry blossom, the flowers hopeless to hold on their limp little stems. They flopped over her hand like the small corpses of dead fluffy animals. 'I remember planting these,' she said. 'I remember when you came home from school I showed you what I'd done.'

'I remember that,' he said, and she smiled at him brilliantly like a lost mariner who has found a known landmark.

'I'm very pleased with what I planted,' she said. 'I'd forgotten,' and she walked back to the car with a remembered elegance that shocked him.

At the next stop there was an early flowering rhododendron.

' "John Peel," ' said his mother. 'I planted that. Always a good doer though it's inclined to sucker badly if you don't watch it.' She could go on *Garden Time*, he thought.

They came upon a whole house after that. It teetered on the edge of an incline with a jocular air like a retired actress who enjoys a little drink before lunch.

It was stacked with hay from floor to ceiling, and more hay over the verandah windows gave it the blinkered brooding air of inoperable cataracts.

'Drive on,' said his mother. 'Don't stop. They've cut down all my trees. I can see stumps.'

The remainder of the afternoon produced a sudden upland wealth of oaks, a soft fringe of birches that led up an old entrance drive, a flush of early pink leaves on copper beeches.

'I planted all these,' said the old lady, enthroned among rugs on the back seat. The chill of dusk was coming down. 'People used to drive for miles to see my gardens.'

It was after dark when they drew up where the tartan knees had farewelled them in the early morning.

'They'll be watching television,' said his mother. 'I've been out all day, from dawn till dusk. I'll tell them all I've been kept out all day.'

There was a sudden movement of the old hands and the rings were in his wife's palm.

'Safer with you, my dear, than with me.' That cackle again. 'Enjoy them,' and there was that remembered elegance in her walk again as she took the steps with aplomb.

The sudden looming bulk of Matron provided a buffer between the outer world and the internal windows, now vacant. From deep within the building, from some sort of architectural stomach, he thought, came the sound of cutlery vigorously applied to plates.

'Tea's nearly over,' said Matron. 'We've just cut into the last of the pie.' Another accuser, he thought. 'I'll have to get one of the girls to do her a nice little egg. I'll pop you into bed, Madamski, and you can have a little something on a tray.' She had turned away from the old lady. 'I'm not sure I like her colour,' she said.

'She's been out in the fresh air all day.' Betty clutched the rings, he noticed, but he was grateful for that unfamiliar warmth. 'She's had a good lunch,' she said, 'and a good afternoon tea — late, with protein.' That would be the cheese puffs, he thought. A protection seemed to come from her and he sensed a closing of ranks.

'I'm just going off to change my shoes,' said his mother and padded away.

'I don't like the look of her,' said Matron. 'That high colour. . .'

'She's excited. My husband took her to see all her old gardens. She was a wonderful gardener in her day. Her trees,' said his wife, 'were marvellous, better than the Botanical Gardens.'

'You don't say,' said Matron. 'I'd no idea.' She had taken a step back.

'I don't want a valiant.' What strength there was in that voice as his mother returned with her slippers. 'I'm not

71

having a valiant, and I don't need any tea.'

'No tea?' Matron took another half-step back.

'My son's wife's a wonderful cook. She's a better cook than my friend Mrs Jarvis ever was and she won prizes at the show. I've had enough to eat to last a week and I'm not going to bed till I've watched my programme,' she said, 'and the late news.' Push your luck, he thought.

Later, from the car, they saw the lit window of the corridor open and she leant out.

'I've changed the face of the land,' she called and the voice echoed, robust and sure, across the carpark. 'My trees, my trees,' she called. 'I've changed the face of the land.'

They saw her walking along towards the television room, the bright red cardigan round her shoulders as brilliant in the gloom as 'John Peel' had been in that last valley at dusk, the glorious trusses of flowers casting a beauty where none had been before. There was in her walk, he thought, a springing vitality like that of a gardener who, in viewing barren winter stalks, knows with certainty that by high summer roses will be rampant.

# THE TEA PARTY

HE HAD CHOSEN the best chair, the largest and most comfortable, and now crossed his legs with an easy swinging movement that belied his age. He was — and she knew this from her own private arithmetic — exactly seventy. He was tall, alarmingly well over six feet, very lithe — again alarmingly so. This languorous swing of the long legs was frightening, she thought. Frightening. And he was definitely seventy, she thought, going through the sums again in her own mind. If his younger sister was sixty-one and he was nine years older than she was, he was definitely seventy. And it checked out the other way too. His elder sister was seventy-nine when she died last year and that made him seventy as well because she was ten years older than he was. It all worked out.

Those legs, though, those lithe, slim, very long legs, those hard legs could wrap themselves around someone with a strangling grip. Even now they could do that. From his large face, pale as unripe Cheddar, his bleached blue eyes regarded her with an unmistakable warmth, also alarming, above cheeks sagging with bloodhound pouches.

'And how long iss it' — the voice was heavy with sibilance — 'since your hussband iss dying, did you say?'

'No, I didn't.' She waited for a moment. 'More tea?' In her distant chair, positioned for safety and observation and with resentment, she placed her hand on the handle of the teapot as some may clasp the hand of a friend. And it wasn't even as if she liked tea, she thought. She had served tea deliberately, knowing he preferred coffee. 'I am not liking tea,' he had said once. 'I am preferring coffee. In old Bawaria we are always preferring coffee.' Curiously at bay in her own house, oddly ill at ease because he was coming to visit, she had decided on tea. Tea. He disliked tea. And she had smiled thinking of tea and how she had not wanted to ask him there, to her house. 'Tea?'

'Aha.' His smile, seraphic in imagined contentment, was also childlike in conceit. 'Ach so — Manfred iss finding out about you.' He spoke of himself in the third person, perhaps from self-importance, perhaps from lack of facility with English. She could not tell.

'Manny iss finding out that you are liking tea.' He patted her hand in a playful way as if she might have been a kitten, as if he were a kitten. His arms could have been purchased wholesale by the metre and could reach her anywhere. The whole thing, she thought, was quietly out of control in the worst possible way. 'Your hussband, your late hussband — he iss liking tea? What iss called the English tea at four in the afternoon' — she saw him glance at the clock whose little hand pointed squarely to the figure three — 'but not to be worrying about wrong timing. Manfred will not smack. Not today.' He laughed, a peculiar sort of noise like a groan from a full oven. She began to pour his second cup of tea. The first had been tossed down the hatch in one gulp and may even now, she thought, have made its sudden way into one of those legs with the slim and marble-like shinbone exposed above an immaculate and very expensive cotton sock. He wore beige linen trousers and they fell in pleats so splendid that she could not doubt that they had been, like the socks, extremely expensive. And she could not doubt either that the hips that held them up were as slim and lithe and hard as the legs, even though he was seventy. Upon this thought she closed her eyes.

'I'm sorry,' she said. 'I wasn't listening. What was that you said? I wasn't paying attention.' It was one of her small persecutions, undetected mostly, that were exerted on guests she disliked — making them say it all again. And she listened to his answer with her eyes still shut. Surely he must go home at, say, four o'clock, she thought. He wouldn't really stay till five? Or would he. She opened one eye just a sliver. He looked very comfortable.

'Your hussband' — again it sounded like a hiss — 'he iss liking the English tea? Perhaps he iss living in England? He iss.' She had nodded in a tired way, like a dying thistle. 'Ach so!' The pouches under his eyes and the dewlaps beneath his chin trembled with delight at disclosure. 'And here iss picture of house, of other house where you live when hussband alive before coming to little house suitable for widow. Excellent.' He stood up to look at the painting again. He had had a good look at it when he arrived.

She thought again that the visit was a mistake. But what can you do, she said in her own mind, if someone nags and nags about it, and then nags more after that so you think that if you ask them, just once, you'll have peace? What can you do about that?

His perusal of the picture, second time round, was leisurely — to comprehend exactly, she thought, the size of the place, the exact sweep of the lawns, the extent of the garden, the avenue of trees that led to the front door.

'He iss very rich man — hussband.' He was sitting down again now. 'Travelling and staying in England and liking the English tea viss cakes and sandwiches and beautiful big house set in trees, just so. Yess,' he said and took a long draught of tea, 'I am getting picture.' He recrossed those fine long legs again, formidable in their presentation and preservation. 'Just excusing me, pleasse.' He stood up again to straighten a picture above her head. 'I am vishing to help. I do ziss in most caring way possible.' He sat down again. 'You are having people to advise you about sings? You vill be needing zat. You vill be needing advice. If you are asking my advice I am telling you — look after the cents and the dollars take care of zemselves. And now' — he patted her hand again — 'I vas asking you, a long time ago when I arrive, what supermarket you are shopping at and still zere iss no answer, but Manny will not smack for zat, not today.'

The tone of admonishment was as kittenish as the play of his hand on her own again but she thought, suddenly, that he could be a man who was unpleasant over the cost of butter, or flour, or sugar. Or anything. Very unpleasant. But not about his own clothes. His clothes — and she looked him up and down — were verging on majestic. The jacket hung in such soft loose folds that it must be raw silk. His cream shirt fluttered faintly. Silk again. And his shoes were of cream suede, without a mark, and held his long slim feet tightly and fondly as a — but she stopped there. As a what holds a what, she thought, and blinked and looked away. The whole thing was — and again she stopped. Revolting. Obscene.

'Did your wife have nice clothes?' Her voice was as soft as the scones on the plate in front of him, soft but sharp as the fine vintage Cheddar she had grilled on top of them to give savour and piquancy. She ignored his questions about the supermarket.

'Wife?' One of his pale hands took another offering from the plate. 'So good.' He took a bite. 'Wife hass been dead for twelve yearss.'

'But did she have nice clothes?' The questioning, she knew, was uncompassionate and nearly rancorous.

'No use buying clothes' — he shrugged — 'for person dying. My wife hass operation and comes home to die.' The silence was profound. Even the street outside, filled with traffic to the TAB and the Lotto shop at the top of the rise, was hushed. 'Iss so sad for me,' he said, biting into the scone now and she wondered where the food went. He was so tall, perhaps he was not actually fat, though thick round the middle behind the draperies of raw silk, because it was simply all spread out over a wide area. She sat there, thinking of this. 'Iss so sad to see person die.' He had finished the scone. 'But I do my best.' He brightened at this cheering thought. 'I giff her buss fare so she doesn't haff to walk home from supermarket viss shopping.'

Her own silence joined that of the street.

'Would be too heavy,' he said, taking another scone, 'to carry shopping home uphill, not vell. I am doing best to help. So sad for me,' he said with his eyes closed and a small piece of butter on his full lower lip, 'to see her die. But' — he was dusting his hands on the little dinner napkin she had placed on his plate — 'now I am enjoying zees — what is zere namings?'

'Scones,' she said, 'cheese scones,' and heard in her own voice the penetrating defeat and exhaustion of a world full

76

of women who have to carry the shopping home in all weathers, uphill, even if they are dying.

'Scoon, scoon—' He experimented with the word which lingered on that greedy mouth. 'Iss good, scoon. Manny iss liking.' And he leaned forward then to squeeze her upper arm, one stiffened finger extended (arthritis? she thought...no) to touch a chilly nipple through her dress. 'And still, my dear' — she had a notion that he had rehearsed his first use of this endearment to soften her up for later planned depredations. Looking at those long hard legs and the shinbones that were like marble she had no doubt that these might be considerable. If they occurred, which they would not. I must watch out for my angina, she thought, because her heart was beating oddly. It felt heavy and thudded in her chest and there was that pain again, so she tucked her left arm in, ready for it, and began to breathe slowly in and out to a count of ten. 'My dear, I still haff not heard where you are doing shoppings? Take care of the cents and the dollars are taking care of themselves. Already I am telling you ziss. Now, where do you do shoppings?'

'All over the place.' She sketched a wide and vague arc in the air above her head, might have been saying she did her shopping in the sky. 'I buy whatever I need just wherever I happen to be when I remember I need it.' His silence was punishing, his expression that of the archetypal, but wolfish, benevolent dictator.

'Must stop ziss, pleasse. I am pleading viss you — pleasse to be stopping ziss extravagance. As I already telling you, take care of the cents and the dollars take care of themselves. I am tellink you now, and I am speaking from za heart' — he struck himself on the chest with one fist and the sound was solid as if he were full of food and always had been — 'you must be shopping at Foodland and taking own bags. Zere you will find greatest savings. Alsso, iss good to discuss needs and wants. I get on to ziss later, some uzzer time. Iss first visit to beautiful home.' He looked around again. 'Today we are happy and laughings.'

'Yes,' she said and knew this was a remark of the unfortified. A feeling of obliteration had come over her, a

77

rubbing out of the idea of self. Even the pain diminished before this onslaught. Like a palimpsest, she was to have all her own inscriptions re-engraved, all her own ideas stamped out. Even the shopping would be severely supervised. *Are you sure you are needing ziss cocoa? Are you really vanting ziss soaps? I sink I cross zem off listings.* 'But I only asked you to afternoon tea,' she said aloud, in her own defence for this inner argument. 'Nothing more,' and he clasped her arm again with that alarming warmth.

'Next timing, perhaps dinner for Manny.'

Take care of the cents and the dollars will take care of themselves might be inscribed upon her heart, she thought, instead of Oh listen to the wind, hear the song of the bird, how beautiful is the sky.

'You are not listening to wise words.' He stood up again and walked to the other side of the room. 'Again,' he said, 'iss crooked.' He straightened another picture. 'I do ziss in most caring way possible.' But this time she followed him, right on his heels like a little beast of the free fields.

'I think you might have forgotten something about this picture,' she said. His expression of innocent conceit was well-worn, had received a thousand airings. 'I think you might have forgotten this picture is mine and' — her hand darted forward, free as a bird — 'it's always crooked. It is a tradition that it's always as crooked as this.' She tipped it to a wild angle and heard her own lie echo boldly through the house. 'You would not understand,' she said, 'and no one could expect you to.' Receipt of this fastidious little denunciation seemed to increase his appetite and he took two scones.

'So good,' he said, and swallowed them both whole. 'I am glad you are mentioning tradition because zat brings me to subject of family and family traditions. I am,' he said, and bared his teeth, 'sso looking forward to meeting family. You haff photographs of family? No?' She shook her head, unwilling to submit her children to examination of that sort. Even if they were moustached and bearded, broken-hearted after torrid affairs with insensitive girls who had each ear pierced four times and wore a different earring in each hole, even if they were in need of improvement, they could not be submitted to that scrutiny with its promise of constant revision and renovation.

'Zay are doink vat their muzzer says? No?' Once more she shook her head. 'Vell, we will be talking about ziss anuzzer time. Today iss happiness and laughings.'

She bared her teeth, like a bite. Copying from him.

'I sink truly zat it would be a good idea if shoppink habits change.' He had not dealt with that subject drastically enough yet, she thought. 'I recommend, and I say ziss in the most caring way possible, that you giff up driving car to supermarket. Catch buss instead. Also, if you are taking best advice from Manfred, you are not doing any Christmas shoppings till after Christmas. You have done Christmas shoppings? No matter. Next Christmas will be different. At Christmas,' he said and bit deeply into the last scone, 'prices escalate.' Perhaps he read the finance pages of the newspaper, she thought, to get ideas about money. He must have learned the word *escalate* from somewhere. 'Best to leave all Christmas shoppings till January sales, zen zere are bargains and having Christmas in February. Always I am telling my wife, no Christmas shoppings till January sales pleasse.'

'Ah,' she said, 'so you said please, did you? How very generous.'

He stopped chewing.

'Ach so — I am seeing.' The innocent smile again, wide as a yawn. 'More jokings. So funny.' He patted her knee. 'In old Bawaria we are fond of jokings and laughings. Iss good fun.'

'In the realm of fun,' she said, 'what did your wife think, and your children, about not having any presents at Christmas?'

'Iss difficult.' He spoke after a long pause. 'Wife understands. She iss adult. Children not so good. Problems viss children. They are wanting presents and cakes, but I am speaking to them many times and,' he said, 'zay understand, at last.'

'I see,' she said.

'But we are talking about supermarket, and buss' — there was that hiss again — 'to supermarket.' So he had not finished with that subject yet, she thought, and sighed. 'Fare iss only one dollar —'

'Ah.' Now it was her turn for triumph. 'But you said take care of the cents and the dollars take care of themselves. What about spending an extra dollar on the bus when you don't have to, when you can drive a car.'

'I am seeing.' There was more of that laughter like a groan from an oven, a full oven, she thought. He had eaten all the scones. 'Iss jokings.' His hand clutched hers again. 'So droll. I like.' It was hopeless, she thought. Hopeless. 'In old Bawaria we are liking the jokes. But I haff all worked out for you to do.' His methodology was simplistic, and time-consuming. 'First you are catching buss to Foodland with all discount tickets cut out of paper night before and comparing prices viss other supermarkets for best buy. Then climbing on buss again for Astro-Bargains and doing remainder of shoppings zere at discount prices, viss tickets if paper has any, zen home again.' He gave a shrug of infinite wisdom and artlessness. 'No use of car,' he said. 'No wear and tear on engine. All shoppings done at lowest prices.' He stared at the empty scone plate. 'Iss good. You are needing guidance, zat iss why I tell you secrets of shoppings. And, also, I am looking forward to meeting family and telling zem shopping secrets and uzzer sings. So good.' He held out his cup. 'Also I am so enjoying English tea. Just like late hussband.'

'You are not at all like my husband.' If words could cut he would have bled.

'He iss not such tall man as Manny? He cannot help ziss.' He regarded now the second plate of food — a fruit loaf cut into slices. 'Home baking,' he said. 'Iss excellent. I am liking. In old Bawaria I am haffing home baking. Mother make homemade bread. You are making homemade bread? Can learn. Iss easy. Mother makes homemade bread every day. Wife' — and she waited for him to pause but he carried on, rushing through the cooking — 'only makes bread every second day. Iss sick, though.' He was biting into the loaf now,

80

chewing with satisfaction. 'Very sad for me to see. It takes her one full year to die.'

His approach to people and food was, she thought, holistic. He simply consumed everything, consumed them all.

'You must do shoppings properly and you haff not got your hair tied up viss ribbons today. I am liking hair tied up viss ribbons. Also frilly clothes — I am liking. You haff frilly clothes? No?' She had shaken her head with daunting vigor. 'You can be getting some. Watch for sales.'

'But I don't like frilly clothes.'

'Frilly clothes iss good.'

'No they aren't. I don't want frilly clothes. I won't have frilly clothes.'

'We speak of ziss some uzzer time.' He took another piece of loaf, her most economical recipe into which she had put only a half measure of sultanas, certainly no peel or cherries or angelica. The afternoon tea must be sufficient to be called by the name but not sufficient for him to note any generosity, she had thought before he arrived. He must see that he had been invited, after months of delay, to a display of unavailability. It was nearly a year since he had corralled her in his dining-room and made her eat a pikelet. But a crust would have been too much for him, she thought now. A crumb would have been misinterpreted.

'But, my dear, you are not eating. You do not eat between meals?' She had murmured something. 'Ach so. Iss saving on housekeeping, eating less. I haff eaten all scoon and begin loaf.' He spoke with authority. It might have been an official edict, a monarch's *tour de force*. His wife, dying, must have carried home tonnes of food, she thought. Tonnes of it. 'You are not liking sweets?'

'I prefer cheese.'

'Ah — cheese. Yess, alsso I am liking cottage cheese. I am eating five hundred grams of cottage cheese per week.' She did a few rapid calculations. Twenty-six kilograms of cottage cheese to carry home every year. His smile, meanwhile, was a happy slot into which he poked loaf. 'So good and I am so happy. We haff much in common,' he said, 'now both

81

liking cheese. Alsso I am liking cheesecake. You are liking cheesecake? No?' There was his hand on her arm again.

'I don't like cake,' she said.

'Can manage without cheesecake. In old Bawaria we are always making beautiful cakes. We are liking cakes in old Bawaria.'

'I hate cake.' She was almost shouting. 'I loathe cheesecake in particular. Cheesecake,' she said, profane in the exuberance of rage, 'is shit.'

'Sheet? I am not understanding sheet.' He sat, another piece of loaf in hand, in such a state of greed and doubt that she had no heart to continue. He must, surely, go home soon?

'It doesn't matter,' she said. 'Really it doesn't. Of course you don't understand sheet. Would you like some more tea?' and she went away to the kitchen to boil the kettle again. As soon as he goes, she thought while she waited for the tea to draw, I'll have a good stiff gin.

'I must congratulate,' he said when she returned. He was wiping his mouth with the dinner napkin. 'Iss excellent.' The slices of loaf had all gone. 'And also' — he beamed — 'house very clean. You are excellent housekeeper. Iss good. I am liking.' He looked round the room, at the paintings, the china piled on the chiffonier, some Persian rugs for which there was no room on the floor so she had rolled them up, like umbrellas, for display in a large Chinese urn. 'Too many sings in house, though.' He gave a shrug of those large lithe shoulders, to show perhaps that this was of no consequence. 'But much china and paintings can be sold and monies put in savings bank to earn more monies.' He fondled her hand for a moment. 'I am telling you ziss for own good. You are needing guidance. Take care of the cents, my dear, and the dollars take care of themselves. Also — zere iss danger of robbery.' His smile became oily as he produced this strategy for fright. For terror, she thought — I'll have two good stiff gins. 'Und murder. Zere iss danger here of murder.'

'Robbery? Murder?' She was curled up in her chair now. 'How do you mean, robbery and murder?'

I wonder, she thought, if I went out to the garden shed

82

and got the axe. I wonder if I could slice his head neatly in two, but she could imagine the whole melodrama already. She would have to ring her oldest son at the hospital.

*Hello, darling, I've got some very bad news. I'm really sorry.* It would be like the night she found his father dead. But this would be murder, not like that other innocent demise. *I'm ringing you from the police station, darling. I've just killed someone. Are you still there? You know that man I know vaguely and I see him sometimes at art shows and he tells me about his sisters? And he nagged and nagged me to go to afternoon tea at his house? And then he nagged to come back here? You know that man? Well, I had him to visit today, just to get him over and done with before Christmas, and he was so arrogant I couldn't stand it any more so I put the axe through his head. Yes, dear, I'm at the police station.* How could I do that, she thought. And he had his final exams soon and mustn't be upset.

'Zere are more loafings? I am enjoying loafings. I sink you are in daydream while Manny talking.' He was eyeing the empty plate, leitmotif of the afternoon. The clock struck five.

'Five o'clock, and so soon.' She stood up. 'I'm afraid I'll have to say goodbye to you now. I have another appointment.' With peace and quiet, she thought. With silence. With security of thought. With the idea, perhaps quaint, that she was safe in her own home and would not be robbed or murdered. 'I'll go and ring you a taxi.'

He followed her into the hall, watched her look up the number in the book. A large index finger pinioned the page.

'Ziss iss cheapest taxi company,' he said. 'I tell you ziss for your own good. You are needing guidance. I am seeing zat. So extravagant, so-o-o extravagant' — he lengthened the sound so it was like a hoot — 'but a good woman at heart.' He smiled again, kind as a headmaster who is going to beat someone later and she noted that his hands, wide and pale, were like spatulas and were curiously pliant. He flicked his handkerchief over the telephone as she dialled the number. 'Just a little dust. Nossing to worry about. Rest of house iss immaculate. Do not sink about it for one moment. Manny iss already forgetting.' More flicking from the handkerchief. 'So many sings.' He had picked up a figurine.

'Burglars, even at ziss moment, could be waiting under house listening to footprints, zen sawing up through floorboards to strip house bare.' He waved one of those lengthy arms. 'Everysing gone. If you are lucky zay just tie you up. If you are not lucky zay murder you. Ziss is what will happen.' His satisfaction, she thought, was almost happy. 'You need protector.' His big yellow face shone with relish. 'When my own house iss burgled I find chair in lavatory to tie me to if I come home and disturb. You laugh. I see you laughing.' The voice was harsh now. 'Ven you are robbed and murdered, ven zay tie you to chair in lavatory you sink of my wise words. All ziss must go.' He gestured again at her pictures, her china, her furniture, the carpets. The taxi was tooting at the gate, though, so he bolted out the front door. The cost, she thought. He was probably thinking of the meter ticking over.

As he settled in the back seat she bent a little to enunciate clearly through the window, his big face only a handspan away. 'I think you have forgotten something,' she said. 'I think you've forgotten that the pictures are mine, the china's all mine, the furniture's mine. I think you might have forgotten that. And as for the chair in your lavatory' — the taxi driver turned a bewildered face towards them — 'I think they put it there to sit on themselves while they drowned you.'

'Wunderbar, wunderbar. . .more jokings. In old Bawaria we are liking jokings.' He had rallied. 'Next time I am coming to visit I am telling you ideas about doorbell. Doorbell in wrong place — must be moved.' She was already turning away. He darted one of those flat greenish hands out the window to detain her and plucked a cat hair from the front of her dress. 'You are having cat? Ach so — iss clean? Cat? Goes outside to do business?' He pondered this. 'Cat can stay, for the moment. Alsso, I haff not asked you about your face.'

'My face?' She put one hand up to cup one of her own cheeks.

'No, no. Your face. Your church. Vere do you go to church? What iss your face?'

'Oh, my faith,' she said, 'my *faith*. I haven't any. I don't go to church. I have no religion. My religion is the idea of democracy, the rights of the individual, the dignity each person deserves to have even if other people' — and she stared right into those pale blue eyes — 'do not understand his, or her, aspirations. I believe in the right to privacy, the sanctity of each person's home.' Listening to herself she thought she might never stop. 'The right we all have to do as we please, without supervision or intrusion by strangers, if we pay for ourselves and keep ourselves quiet and plain and do not break the law. I believe in self-worth, peace, privacy.'

'We talk of ziss some uzzer time.' The driver was drawing slowly, irrevocably, and deliciously, away from the kerb. 'I had hoped zat you were a Lutheran or a Calvinist.' The driver, sepulchral behind the wheel, turned to give her another ghastly look. 'But iss plenty off time for zat. I look forward to next invitation.' He flapped a hand out the window in a slapping movement — a rehearsal, she thought, for later planned admonishments. 'Such vunderful scoons and loafings. Wunderbar —' The taxi had gone round the corner.

The cat, unseen all afternoon but not unseeing, climbed out from behind a rose bush and sat on the letterbox. They regarded each other, eyeball to eyeball, for a long moment and their mutual comprehension seemed to be perfect.

'Mummy's going to have a gin,' she said, 'and then she's going to have another one, and you can have a nice drink of milk in your bowl. Then we'll hunt around and find that padlock for the gate.'

They wandered up the hall together, side by side, in a state of complete tranquillity and understanding, to restore the quiet of their house. From far away she could still hear it, 'Oh wunderbar, wunderbar. . .', echoing faintly from the main road as they welcomed peaceful evening in.

# YOUR FATHER, THE BIRD

IN THE EVENING they went down to the water. At that time there were seldom any people in the park so they walked the wide pathway to the lake with an air of command as if they owned it all. It was familiar territory and they had gone that way many times before, had gone that way for years. Years and years. More than twenty years' walking, in the evening, down to the water, so they knew the way well.

They went the same way as usual — through the little stile at the top of the hill where three roads met in a splayed junction the shape of a chicken's foot, their own road the middle toe. The path beyond the stile went on a secret curve through a rolling lawn with plantings of azaleas which in winter were bare of anything except the scent of sulphur spray to kill the lichen. But it was high summer now and the azaleas were covered with fine leaves after the abundance of the spring blooming. That brought flowers pale as a flush on a sick cheek or red as dark blood seeping away in the night. It was back in the spring when they were first told of the sickness. Illness flowered then, too.

The path took them through the spreading grove of azalea bushes, past the start of the tall trees and into deep bush that went right down to where the water of the lake waited, a dark and glossy eye in a hollow socket of land. There was no sound except for the slight noise their feet made on the gravel path and they walked with the insolence of freebooters on the public trails of the park, only stopping now and again to swap the bag from one to another. The woman had carried the paperbag to the chicken's foot intersection and the man took it from her when they climbed over the stile.

'Hold this,' she had said and went first, as she always had done. For more than twenty years, forever. Then she turned and held out her hand to him, this man who now held the bag, as she had done since he was hardly more than a baby, but like her even then. She was his mother, though now they looked just like a man and a woman walking along through the park in the evening, towards the water of the lake.

When he was very young he had liked to walk free and upright in his little brown leather shoes and had never been held back by reins or straps that tied him into a pushchair because he never sat in one. He liked to walk, free. At the stile they had always stopped while she went over first like a wild free creature and swung him up after her, to the safety of the top step so that he might be wild and free too. She was very young then and, fretting for her own loss of freedom, gave it to the child like a salutation of love. It was always custom that took her over the stile first, but when they were both over it now he kept the bag.

'I'll have a turn,' he said as they set off into the park with its hollow eye of dark water a mile away.

'I thought I'd give it to you later. Further down.' The density of the bag and the eerie weight of its contents were things she wished to keep from him.

'But it's my turn now,' he said, so they turned in silence, with no more argument, and went down the wide gravel path. During the day people went down there to get ice-creams from the kiosk or to hire boats. It was an innocent way that was taking them to the water though once a girl had been strangled not far from where they were and died in her running clothes at exactly eleven o'clock on a sunny summer's morning. And a boy who jumped in the lake drowned there by accident while he was skylarking with some friends. But mostly it was an innocent way, and they took it now with stealth, smooth-faced forgers of an artless outing to a public place.

The water of the lake was shallow enough to wade in at the edges and only the depth of a tall man at the centre, under the bridge — a silly ornamental tracery of adzed logs and branches that took people from one side of the lake to the other, a futile exercise as each side was similar and the view was much the same. In this deepest part of the lake the reflected eye of the rising moon met that eye of black water as the two of them walked down through the trees, with the bag.

The path took a ridge and wound slowly down to the water. The trees were very thick and high, blotting out any light from the rising moon, but they knew the way well and never altered their speed or tripped or faltered. Sometimes the man with the bag took a short cut across the line of a curve and the woman, his mother, knew he had gone only when he stepped from the bush on the other side of the bend. They were so stealthy, the pair of them. The ground was damp underfoot because the soil was rich here and held the moisture. On the other side of the park, nearer the sea, the loam was inclined to be sandy. Trees did not grow there very well so no leaves fell to give richness season after season. They had, she thought, chosen the richest and greenest part of the park — or he had, the man who had become ill back in the spring. He had told them what to do, and they were doing it. So they walked on through the trees to the water. They walked nearly in step, not from domination or obedience, because they were not like that, but because they were curiously similar, oddly identical in their own separate ways, though he had become someone she no longer knew very well.

He came home at breakfast-time one day and she had said 'Oh, darling, I thought you were dead. I thought you must have been killed in the night. I thought you'd been in an accident.' He had looked at her with bland and secret eyes. 'If it itches,' he said, 'you have to scratch it.' She knew then that she did not know him any more, so when he came home in the holidays she did his washing and ironing and put his dinner in front of him in the evenings, if he was there, and that was all. That was how it was.

Their legs were the same length though. Their hips measured the same on the old tape measure in the sewing box, and tonight, for the last walk down to the ring of water, they wore an assembly of each other's clothes, all black because they did not wish to be seen. She had taken a pair of black cords from his wardrobe, had often worn them before but did not tell him that. They each had their secrets, though hers, she thought, were more innocent. He wore one of his father's dark suede cheese-cutters. She had a black beret pulled down over her left eye, raffish and rakish and Frenchified, and gave him her black jersey.

They had waited, like brigands, for the coming of darkness and until the moon began to rise, an inspection from the sky. Sometimes she went upstairs during the afternoon to see if he was all right, and he was always just sitting indolently in the same position in the green armchair beside his bedroom window. There was a book on his knees but he was not reading. Its pages remained the same, exactly distributed from one side to the other, so she thought he had opened it in the middle and left it there. Afternoon and twilight passed and they did not eat. They had not eaten anything since yesterday, and empty of everything, including thought, they awaited the coming of darkness while the bag rested in the shadows under the hall table. A stranger coming into the house would not have noticed it and would not have thought it strange that the pair of them sat so still for so many hours in the heat of the day. The summer had been very hot and people did that.

At midday, when the heat was fierce, they had walked down the hill, down through the centre of town to collect the bag, and they walked back home again while the tar melted on the roads.

'I think we should walk,' he had said when she took the car keys in her hand as twelve o'clock struck.

'Yes.' So she put them back in the drawer, knowing that he had, inexorably and inevitably, divined what she had tried to hide from him — that the journey to collect the bag was a terrible one and it must be seen to be so by their traverse of that parched little town on foot in the heat. They must be burned and baked and seared. She had known that, his mother. And now he knew it. They must all be scorched and branded by the heat, must all burn. It had been a fair household and they had, all three of them, always had the same. It was always fair.

The parcel, the bag, was bigger than they expected. She thought it would be light and small, holding a handful of sand. But when the man in the office — and they did not think who he was or where they were because they did not wish to acknowledge these things — when the man in the office brought out the paperbag it was as big as the largest size sugar at the supermarket. She heard her son give a slight intake of breath, not quite a gasp. And it was so heavy. It was so heavy, and dense.

Yet he had been a smallish, neatly made man with no hint that the crushed bones from his frame would make so much. They remembered him — she remembered him, she thought now — standing in that slim and languid way beside the drinks tray and saying, 'Do you want a martini?' to the boy when he was how old? Fourteen. Thirteen. It was difficult to remember because the years had passed pleasantly and each one had seemed much the same. Perhaps it was fifteen, she thought. 'And if you wanted a bottle of rum, you could've taken the one from here, you silly bugger.' He had kicked the door of the liquor cupboard, just lightly with his neat foot. 'There wasn't any need to go down town and try to buy one. You can have,' he had said, 'anything you like, without asking. Olive? Or a twist of lemon?' So, she had thought, that telephone call had been from a publican, that one when she heard him laughing upstairs a moment before. The boy had been trying to buy a bottle of rum at some liquor store. The slimness and the glimmer of amusement behind the dark eyes were now in the bag that they had carried in the fire of the sun at midday and took down to the water in the evening.

At midday they had walked back home through the town, past the bakery where once a man called Lindsay Hartfeld made wholemeal bread, before big-company takeovers bought him out. They went past the best dress shop in town where a green suit with matching hat and gloves was displayed in the window together with an Edwardian Japanese bronze vase, waist-high, which contained a branch of magnolia in full bloom. The fallen petals made cupped hands for alms of some kind, but they had nothing to give, she had thought, from their currency of malaise. At Joe's the fruiterers old Joe himself had been out on the pavement putting more spotted peaches and apricots in the bargain boxes and the new manager of the furniture store in the upper part of the main street had had flannels packed in threes in cellophane bags to attract the holiday trade. Pink, yellow and blue, they had been folded in diminishing squares, a lovely gift, $4.99 each or only $8 for two.

Canny, she thought. That furniture store was always canny. In a small town everyone knew everything. The manageress of the dress shop was known to be artistic and the owners had a beautiful garden with fine trees. It was all a known and explored mythology.

'Are you all right?' he had said to her then, and she just said, 'Yes,' and so they walked on, past the sports shop that sold luminous ski gear in winter and now had a special on green tennis balls, also luminous. Past the Chinese takeaway where there had once been a cake shop, and outside there, at dawn, the man who was now in the bag used to park his bike and eat a bag of yesterday's cakes while he sat on the pavement with his feet in the gutter. Perhaps forty years ago he had done that, before doing his paper-run. He had been a paperboy and never knew that he might be carried past the old cake shop in a paperbag on a sunny, searing day in high summer.

'You ought to get something for that cough,' her son said as they walked by, and she said, 'I will,' when they turned into the street that took them out of the business area and towards their own house. It was then she saw the bird, the tui. The song came first, long before the sight of it, and the clear notes conquered the noise of traffic as the chant of a sage may silence a multitude.

'Look,' she said. 'Look.' And there was the bird, dark as midnight, glossy as hope, at the exact apex of Mrs Donovan's cherry tree till they drew abreast, then it flew along beside them through the baked streets, over tar melting in the sun that had already left a great welt of red across her shoulders.

The Donovans had always lived in that house. He had told her that because he had always lived in that town from when

91

he was born and knew all about it, forever. He knew whose house was painted yellow till 1956 when it was painted green by the son who took it over, and he knew which shop had a blue front door till someone married a second wife, younger and ambitious, and she had it stripped back to the natural wood.

'And the Donovans aren't really called the Donovans,' he used to say. 'They came here, way back, and had some other name no one could say, so they made it Donovan — to make it easier. That's what they did.' He had known all those small things, the man in the paperbag, and he used to tell her about it, just idly, just conversing idly, when they walked places because he liked walking.

'I think it's my turn now,' said her son, and he took the bag as they turned another corner where the tar was dissolving and the welt on her shoulders became deeper where the sun burnt it. Everything was melting or burning.

'Look.' She pointed to the bird which had begun to fly along beside them. 'Look at the bird.' It went in great loops and trails, tucks and frills, from one tree to another, one garden to another right up the road to their corner. To their house. It was not beguiled by the house on the corner whose garden had been laid out in the last year or two by landscape architects. People stood in the street to watch full-grown trees lowered into place by cranes for that garden. The house itself was two-storeyed with a verandah running round two sides of both floors. A huge old villa, that's what it was, built a long time ago by someone who had made money out of bricks or mud or anything. Groceries. Cartwheels. Paint. It was a town like that. Once the house had been painted Reckitts blue all over — a bargain buy perhaps — and this shame had stained and powdered it for years till a new owner broke himself painting it white. He went bankrupt and his wife had an affair with the land-agent while he tried to sell it for the marital settlement. 'No brains, but a lot else,' the man in the bag had said, walking by. The wife had hair frizzed out in a horizontal bob and had her bust hitched up (professionally) in a hospital that specialised in cosmetic surgery. The bird was not beguiled by all that and flew with them into their own plain garden, sitting at the top of the apple tree to sing a fine song in the sunlight.

'Your father is a bird,' she said when they went into the cool dim house. 'Would that be possible?' but he just put the bag down in the entrance hall, an odd glimmer at the back of his eyes, and she thought that perhaps the boy was becoming his father because the glimmer was suddenly identical, the man in the bag was becoming a bird and the bag was becoming lighter.

For the rest of the day they lay around the house. They listened to the singing of the bird which stayed in the apple tree on the highest branch, and they waited for darkness. The man in the bag had been their security, and now that he was not there they felt, in their own minds, that they had none. They sat lightly, like those whose tenure is brief. Already someone they did not know had come, claiming to be a best friend, and wanted the gold watch. Someone else had offered to take the piano away, out of kindness. It was a town like that.

She sat downstairs and listened for the sound of a creak from floorboards above, anything, but there was always silence except for the singing of the bird. The bag in the shadows of the hall was a little core around which the house gathered, revolved and shrank. By evening, when the sulky moon began to rise, the idea of the bag, in her mind, had taken over the whole place so the house had become the bag and the bag, again, was lighter.

He came downstairs as she watched the last of the twilight settle on the garden, the bird silent now, and when it was truly dark they went like burglars dressed in black through the chicken's toe to the apex of roads beside the park. Marauders, they went through their own garden, across their own lawns and climbed over their own gate under trees still ruffled by the flight of the bird. They took the lower way to the park where the land sloped gently to face the sun or the light of a sickle moon, a toenail in the sky.

They went past a house where once a couple had driven their daughter mad, they loved her so much, and past the place where a young mother died leaving twins and then her husband took up with the babysitter, but never married her. They went past all that.

Past the big white house on the western corner where once a harsh woman who smoked and thus dyed the front of her hair khaki boasted that she had two nests of tables — a good one in walnut with a pie-crust frill round the edges for her own friends when they came to play bridge and an old stained one, kept in a wardrobe, for when her husband brought people home from the RSA. Past an apartment where another widower lived, but old and more knowing than the father of twins, and he kept a woman round the corner. 'Well, I'm off for my cocoa,' he used to say if anyone saw him walking towards her little house in the evenings, and everyone just said, 'Yes.' They went past that place. Past the big place on the bend and a boy from there got a girl into trouble once. His father sent him off to Australia but the girl had to stay to grow old and bitter and the child died. He had told her all that — the man in the bag — all those myths and rumours, exaggerations and mysteries of the town and, as she walked along, black-clad, like a peon or a lost janissary, the town seemed to become these curious truths and miscastings just as the man in the bag had become the bird, the house became the bag and the bag grew lighter again. They had lived moonshine and now walked in it.

The park had once been full of pines, thinned now to make way for native trees, but some still ranged along hilltops, sharp and craggy as old bones and always whispering in the smallest breeze, just a tiny sound like a cruel remark between clenched teeth. She was carrying the bag as they went round the last bend in the path to the lake and they swapped it as they approached the bridge.

'It's my turn now,' he said and took it away from her. The little bridge was also part of the mythology of the place, part of the story of cunning moonshine and small deceit. A man who once won a fortune at the races had it built as a gift for the town, but whether this was a gesture of contempt to show the people they were nowhere and could still go nowhere, or whether he wished sincerely to take them somewhere, even on the shortest of walks, she did not know.

It meant that people could walk over the water of the lake in one minute, or less, or right round it in twenty. He had, perhaps, given them a choice, she thought on that dark and dreamless night. There were no sleeping tablets left so their dreams would be waking ones. The sleeping pills had all been munched up as the man in the bag died day by day, cell by cell.

'You won't cry, will you?' he had said.

'Yes.'

'You won't let them see you cry, will you?'

'No.' There was a difference to the questions, she thought, and it satisfied him because he turned slightly and seemed to fall asleep for a while.

'It's my turn now,' she said, wanting to take the bag, but he kept it tucked under his arm.

'No. It's still my turn.' So they approached the bridge illuminated by a moon swinging above the pines, thin as a mean smile. Their footsteps nearly frightened them as they began to walk over the bridge, over the tendrils of wood and creeper that hung over the deepest hole. The park was very quiet, the only sound that of night birds far away beyond a hilltop. The dark bird, the one that had followed them home, would be roosting somewhere, she thought, and would return tomorrow.

'At night the park's a sea of waving arses,' he had said once, the man in the bag, when they were out walking. He liked walks. His voice had been so quiet, the tone so scholarly, that it was a moment or two before she understood what he had said. 'Old Kennedy's always brought his house-keepers here — with a tartan rug. Didn't you know that?' She was not, originally, from that place. 'Didn't you know everyone was conceived in the park? Or a lot of them anyway.'

But the park was very quiet as they walked to the middle of the bridge and opened the bag. They had spent the morning opening things. Opening up the filing cabinet. Opening locked drawers. They had opened his big wardrobe upstairs.

'This might fit you,' she had said and handed over the

95

Harris tweed jacket. 'It's a fashion classic.' Once she had been a fashion writer.

'It looks —' She stopped there. How did it look? It looked very good. A trifle large across the shoulders. But good.

'I like it,' he had said, and she saw that the jacket, swinging a little loosely, was just waiting.

'And what about this. You've always like this.' The silver-mounted umbrella. 'And this?' A cheese-cutter hat. 'These?' More of them.

'I might wear these,' he said, and she saw his right hand slowly take a handful of paisley ties. They had sorted everything out. Who was to have what. 'I think you should have this,' he said and put a little gold pen in her hand.

'I wonder where he got it from,' she had said. 'It's stamped nine carat.'

'And also *Love from Barbara*,' he said and they stood there laughing, a peculiar sound that the house had not heard for a long time, dry and ruffling as the brush of feathers.

'I wonder who she was,' she said and opened the drawer on the jerseys.

'He probably knew her a long time ago — before he knew you. It's never been used.' There was the glimmer in his eyes again like that in the eyes, dusty, inside the bag.

When they opened the bag the bone-meal was compacted hard so they had to work it this way and that to loosen it.

'And don't ever let the bastards in this town see you cry.' The hand had come out of the bedclothes then just as it came out of the ashy bag and fell down, like dust, to the lake.

'Say it.'

'I won't ever let the bastards see me cry.'

'Say it again.'

'Hush,' she had said. 'Hush. I'll cough instead.'

Where the moon and the dark water exchanged a look, they tipped the contents of the bag straight down in a silver line, swift and true as eyes might meet across a room and the people know, irrevocably, that one day they will love each other.

*In the evening they all went down to the water.*

# NAUGHTY MAUREEN

'WHAT THE HELL do you think you're playing at?' His hand,
as harsh as his voice, grasped her arm without affection as
she stepped from the taxi.

The hotel's commissionaire stepped forward a second too
late to open the foyer doors.

'Nobody does as they're told.' The delivery had such an
edge to it that she hunched her shoulders. 'I told you quite
distinctly not to say where I was. I told you not to tell
Naughty Maureen anything. I've had her on the phone just
now. How did she find out what hotel we're staying at?'

They went across the vestibule in silence after that, across
the soft green carpet that was like sweet grass and past grand
uncomfortable sofas which, she noticed now, held people
who looked happy. She regarded them with usurious
interest, envied their minimal mastery of cheer and gladness.

Outside, darkness was falling. A chill wind had begun to
tear at the palms and fret the evening. The cloud had cleared
from Table Mountain and above the hotel an enormous rock
like a lion's head glowered.

'I don't want to get Betje into trouble,' an American woman
was saying at the reception desk, 'but the kids want a change.
They'd like to have someone different mind them nights.'

The loss of these small views of ordinariness was almost
a grief as the lift doors closed behind her.

'And you're not even mechanically minded,' he said as he
punched buttons. 'You don't even know how to work the lift.'

'That's because —'

'Shut up. Just shut up.'

Before the lift doors had finally closed there was a sudden
startling view of Robben Island far out in the bay. It
glimmered in a steely sea, grim as a reproach, ephemeral
as forgotten virtue under a rising moon.

'Do you see that out there?' Naughty Maureen, lunching vigorously earlier in the day, gestured with a creamy spoon halfway through her second helping of lemon tart. 'We kept Nelson Mandela out there and a lot of the other troublemakers.' She dug into the pie again. 'I'd have left them there to rot, hey?' There it was again, the guttural Afrikaans plaint calling for agreement or emphasis. She was not sure which.

'Naughty Maureen was an artist,' he had said early in the morning. 'I don't remember any sort of accent. Cultivated woman. I'm sure you'd like her. She could teach you a lot. Her ex was something up in Pretoria, I forget what. She was a very, very naughty lady. Naughty Maureen never wore pants.'

'That island's Robben Island,' she told him now. They were passing the seventh floor. 'Nelson Mandela was kept out there.' There was no answer. 'You can't escape because the sea's full of sharks.'

'Let's not worry about Mandela.' The lift doors opened on the ninth floor and he strode away, shadow gigantic against the lanterns. 'What I want to know is how did Naughty Maureen know where to find me?' By now he had gone round a bend in the passage and she heard the door of the suite slam. It opened immediately. 'And where are you?' She hunched her shoulders again. 'I thought you were behind me.'

'I am behind you,' she said. 'Quite a distance behind you — because I don't walk as fast as you do.' She stood carefully just inside the door as if she had never seen that room before, was a stranger. 'And I think your friend found out where we're staying because she probably looked in my handbag and saw the key.'

Oddly, she saw this pleased him. He stroked his moustache and a smile flickered.

'She always was a goer,' he said. 'Anyway, darling, you should have been more careful.' The idea of Naughty Maureen had mollified him, she saw that clearly. 'I wonder if that bloody silly room boy's put the champagne in the refrigerator. Oh, good.' He took the bottle out. 'That tonguing up I gave everyone seems to have done the trick.'

She winced slightly, remembering the shouting.

'Stop loitering in the shadows, darling. What are you looking so frightened about? Come and sit down.' The cork popped, a sound that seemed to satisfy him because he smiled again.

'I think you must have done that a million times,' she said.

'Make it two million, darling.' His reputation as a man of taste always pleased him. That was another thing she knew and noted.

'Could it possibly be three?' She was heading now for the circle of light the lamp made, flattery the ticket.

'Why don't you sit down, darling? I want to have a good look at you.' So she perched on the arm of a chair while he gave her a cursory glance. 'I don't think you look so bad,' he said, 'except for that dress. Naughty Maureen said you were a plain little thing. Did I tell you she never wore pants, darling?' The smile was a satyr's grin now, reminiscent and gleaming. 'I suppose I'd better give you a dose of falling-down water, hadn't I.' He handed her a glass of wine. 'Just help yourself if you want anything. I think I've left some peanuts for you. You know where everything is, anyway.' The wave was a vague signal of preoccupation. 'Well,' he said, 'and what did you think of her?'

'She was,' she said, 'an arsehole.' But the telephone was already ringing again, a saving clamour.

'You've made yet another mistake.' He shouted into the receiver as the glass of frosty wine suddenly bit into her hand with its chill. 'Can't you get anything right? This is Suite 937.' He enunciated with punishing clarity. 'Not 973. Do better next time.' He returned to the bottle of champagne, filled up his glass. 'Just help yourself, darling. Now, what was I saying before all that?'

'You asked what Naughty Maureen was like.'

'And what was she like?'

'I haven't met anyone like that before.'

'Ah.' The smile glimmered again. 'So she was unique, was she?'

'You could say that.'

99

'She had a wonderful mind — didn't ever suffer fools gladly.'

'I got that idea.' The second sip of champagne nearly knifed her throat.

'Isn't that nice, darling? You pulled a face.'

'Did I?'

'She used to have the most marvellous ideas.' He was staring into the middle distance. 'She had very definite opinions. Very informed sort of woman. Knew all about everything.'

'Yes,' she said. 'I got that idea too.'

He poured himself another glass of wine.

'She didn't seem to think much of you.' The voice was suddenly bleak again. 'Said you were as boring as hell.'

'Oh, I probably am.' And she sat there, grinning too now, pleased with her own innocent failure.

'What are you thinking about? Sitting there grinning like a Cheshire cat?' It was lucky, she thought, that he did not wait for an answer. 'I told you to keep her amused.'

She shrugged.

'And is that all you've got to say?'

She shrugged again.

'You're not his usual sort of girl, are you, hey?' Maureen had tucked into ostrich pâté as an entrée as one o'clock struck. Her hands were square and swollen but oddly capable, like those of a shopkeeper anxious about stock.

The waiter poured more wine into her glass.

'Getting through it, aren't I, doll?' Her rollicking laugh split the restaurant. 'This is bladdy good, hey. They serve bladdy good food.' She spread pâté on another piece of Melba toast. 'Ja, thanks — it's good. I need some more.' The waiter had returned with extra slices. 'I wouldn't usually come here. It's too bladdy dear for me these days.'

'I knew her years ago,' he had said that morning very early, before the heat rose and she was still chilled after a swim. 'I spent three very naughty weeks with Naughty Maureen.' He stroked his moustache. 'I picked her up one day at the post office, the main Cape Town branch.' She wondered what difference that made as her hair and the bathing togs and her bathrobe all wept water on to the floor. 'Do look out. You're making an awful mess there. Why don't you get dressed and get yourself organised, you silly cow.' His voice, she thought now, had held a cutting edge since dawn.

'Maureen was a very efficient lady. She'd be sixty now — sixty-one? I don't know. Anyway, take her out to lunch for me. Find out how she is. See if she needs anything.' He was tucking money into the wallet. 'Take all this, darling. Get her a really good lunch, but don't tell her anything. She'd be after me like a dose of salts. Naughty Maureen knew what she liked.' The smile lay brightly on his face, like a flush.

After the ostrich pâté, Naughty Maureen consulted the menu again, lifted the knife and fork in those avid hands with a formidable enthusiasm while awaiting the lobster.

'Just wait till I tell Mother I've had langoustine for lunch,' she said.

'She had lovely eyes,' he had said over breakfast. 'It's the eyes I look at, you know. The eyes are the mirror of the soul.'

'I see.' Her remark hung in the early morning air like a curious irony.

Greedy and glimmering, opaque as those of an ailing tortoise, Maureen's eyes swivelled towards the waiter with the tray.

'All this,' she said, 'for me. Do me good to have a bladdy good lunch.' She was tearing off the claws now. 'I go back to hospital soon. Cataracts. Oh ja, ja.' She nodded to the waiter and raised her empty glass to be filled. 'You're a funny little doll for him to be trotting round with.' There was no break in the dialogue. 'I wouldn't even call you smart.' She fondled the wine glass. It was empty again.

'Would you like some more wine? I'll order another bottle.'

'I'll have some more wine when you tell me where you met him, doll.'

'Don't tell her a thing,' he had said. 'Get her anything she wants, but don't tell her a thing.'

'I met him,' she said, 'in a library,' and was aware that this truth would sit upon the unease of the day like a lie. 'I thought he was a scholarly erudite man on holiday. I thought he was lonely.' She waited for Naughty Maureen's laughter to grow and flower. 'I was sweet then,' she said, 'and innocent.'

'Get some more wine,' said Naughty Maureen, 'and pull the other leg.' She cracked open a forgotten claw. 'What do you do, you bladdy mad little doll?'

'Do you mean for a living? Or just generally?'

'I mean with him.'

'I go swimming during the day and I go for walks, and I meet him in the evening for dinner.'

'So he doesn't spend the day with you.' Maureen's enveloping satisfaction took in other customers also eating ostrich pâté and lobster, and a fat man who had ordered wild boar. 'He always spent the day with me. What does he do?'

'I don't know. I never ask.'

'Why not?'

'He probably wouldn't tell me.'

'I bet he wouldn't.' The laughter was like a rich and abundant mix of scrambled eggs somehow turned into sunny mirth.

'Perhaps he goes to the post office,' she said when the exultation ceased. 'Perhaps he goes to the main Cape Town branch. Didn't he pick you up there, Maureen?' The silence lengthened. 'But he doesn't come back with anything, not even letters. Now? What have you chosen for dessert? He said you were to have anything you liked.'

'Well' — Maureen's heavy hand clutched the list of offerings — 'I'm just tossing up between Cape Gooseberry Meringue Stellenbosch or Kempis Koeksusters or Lemon Tart a la Ochse.' She read with care and relish, then ordered the lemon tart. 'We'd better get that bladdy waiter back, too. You told me we were having Riesling with the pudding, hey doll.'

'Did you get her a really good lunch?' he said, hand on the neck of the bottle again. 'I don't think you need any more falling-down water, do you, darling? Naughty Maureen said you'd had enough today to last for weeks. I hope you didn't eat and drink everything yourself, darling, and leave nothing for poor old Naughty Maureen. She seemed very concerned about you, that's why she rang.'

'Oh, did she?' She placed the glass of champagne on a

little table and gradually began to push her chair away into the shadows.

'And what are you disappearing for, darling? You've got to be able to take constructive criticism. Naughty Maureen thought you had a definite problem with food and drink. She's a very caring person. Now? Do you want me to fill that up?' He gestured towards the abandoned glass.

'No, thank you.'

The gust of laughter was like a gale from the sea where lights on Robben Island shimmered.

'Have you decided to behave yourself, darling? For heaven's sake, watch out. Now you've knocked my diary on to the floor.'

'And what was he doing when you left?' Maureen had asked, oiled by the Riesling.

'He was reading something.'

'A black notebook, hey? I bet he was reading his black notebook. He keeps all the phone numbers of all his dolls in his black notebook.' Naughty Maureen leaned back in her chair, jolly as a teddybear on an outing.

'Does he?' She ordered black coffee.

'Is that all you're having? You should have some of this bladdy pie, doll. He might spend the day with you if you ate more. How long have you known him?'

'A long time.'

'How long.'

'Three years.'

'So he's picked you up and put you down again for three years. Aren't you a lucky doll, hey?'

'No.' It sounded like a pistol shot, startled the people at the next table and they rustled like starlings.

Later, as sirens ravaged the night, birds shrieked in trees outside the hotel and he said, from the windows, 'I hope it's not more bloody riots. I want to get back to London tomorrow. If they close the airport we mightn't get away for days. Now, before I forget, give me the phone number of that place I've put you into. I'll want to ring you.'

'You'll never get away from him, doll,' Naughty Maureen had said. 'He'll have all about you written in his bladdy black notebook and when you're bladdy past it like me he'll send some little doll to see you.'

'Would you like some more wine? He said you were to have anything you wanted.' It sounded like resignation now.

'I'd like some of those postcards in the foyer, those ones with pictures of this place.'

So she had threaded her way through the potted palms to buy what Naughty Maureen wanted.

'Don't take your bag. Don't carry that. You leave it here with me, doll. I'll mind it for you, hey?' Maureen had been strangely helpful.

'She was a very caring person,' he said now. 'Used to give art shows for the poor.' He coughed, as if preparing for something. 'And what did she look like, darling,' he said, 'by the way?'

Maureen had placed one arm across her hollow chest.

'I'll send them to my friends when I move out to Muizenberg. I'm moving out of the city soon. Muizenberg's nine kilometres out.' It sounded like an apology. 'It's not fashionable.' There was another one. 'I'm going to live with Mother. She's eighty-nine. She needs looking after.'

'That's kind of you.' The remark had surprised her.

'She can look after me too.' The arm remained across that chest. 'I had a mastectomy in May and the news isn't too bladdy good, hey.'

The waiter came, as if he had heard the news as well, and poured more wine.

'And they found another lump last week,' said Naughty Maureen. 'I've still got the stitches in from that.'

'Then perhaps' — and she had suddenly been as gentle as a nurse — 'I should take you home. I'll get them to call a taxi. Have you got your postcards? Would you like me to get another bottle of that Riesling? You could take it home and have it tomorrow. Would you like that?'

'I'll ring you when we get to London — would you like that, darling?' he said now. 'Put the number in my notebook, would you?'

'I really must do that, when I get a moment.'

'And you still haven't told me what she looked like. And

104

was there any change?' She handed him the empty wallet. 'You're a little bottomless pit, aren't you?' There was the cutting laughter again. 'Naughty Maureen said you got a bottle of Fumé Blanc to have with lunch, then you bought Riesling to have with some awful dessert or another and then you bought another bottle of Riesling to take away. Where is it, by the way? Not that I like Riesling. However could you touch such stuff?'

'I don't know.'

'Well, where is it?'

'I haven't got it.'

'Downed that as well, I suppose. Naughty Maureen says I'll have to watch you.' There was still no jollity in the laughter. 'Anyway, you've been on such a bender you won't need to go out tonight. Something's cropped up for me so I'll have to leave you. Don't wait up. And you still haven't said what she looks like now. She had beautiful blue eyes.'

'Yes, I noticed her eyes were blue.'

'And I told you she never wore pants, didn't I, darling?'

'Yes, and you told me she was an artist.'

'Learning, aren't you, darling?' He ruffled her hair.

'Yes, I'm learning.'

'Let me look at your eyes, darling. Maureen had the loveliest blue eyes. Yours are a sort of' — and he hesitated now — 'a sort of mud colour, like a crocodile's eyes. They match your funny hair. Naughty Maureen had lovely hair. Blonde. Lovely.'

'I used to have pretty hair,' Naughty Maureen had said in the middle of lunch. From somewhere within the depths of a large red handbag she extracted a mirror, studied her reflection. 'Oh, God.' She dabbed at her mouth with a grape-coloured lipstick.

'He told me you're an artist.' It seemed best to keep the conversation business-like.

'Was an artist. I used to be a graphic artist for Scholefield Magner. You'll have heard of them.' She was very positive.

'I'm not sure.' It sounded like the stirring of a leaf.

'They bladdy cut back eight years ago and I lost my job.'

'What do you do now?'

'When I'm well enough I paint stones.' Naughty Maureen poured herself another glass of wine. 'I paint African designs on stones and I sell them in a gift shop down Pieter Lashansky Street. It's a good street, hey doll.'

'I'm sure it is.'

'Did she tell you about her paintings, darling?' he asked now. 'That's if you can remember anything about the day at all.'

'She still paints. She told me about it.'

'And you won't mind, will you, having a quiet evening here by yourself? I'll fill the wallet up for you again, my little bottomless pit. You can get some dinner or something, whatever you like.'

'Thank you.'

'I know I can rely on you to empty it with great rapidity after today's rehearsal.' Once more the laughter held a contemptuous lack of merriment.

'And what was her house like?' he wanted to know as he changed his tie for a blue one. 'I told you, darling, didn't I, that she had the loveliest blue eyes. She never wore pants, you know.'

'You told me that. And her house was rather pretty. It wasn't far from here.'

'Oh, good.' He stroked his moustache. 'Look all right, do I, darling? Now, what were you saying about the house? Architecture always interests me.'

'I'm sure you'd find it a pretty house,' she said, 'if you happened to see it.' She stretched out one bare, tanned leg, tentative as a dancer about to do an arabesque. 'Wouldn't she have been much older than you are?'

'The age never worries me, darling. It's the eyes. I look for intelligence in the eyes. Now, do you think this blazer looks all right?'

'You look fine.'

'I must say you look a bit white round the edges. Don't say you're going to be sick. You know how I hate sick people. Oh, I'm going. I can't stand this. Eating and drinking all that stuff today — I don't know how you could do it in the heat.' The door slammed behind him, then opened again.

'Darling? Would it be a bit much if I put a silk handkerchief in my pocket?'

'Definitely,' she said. 'Overdone, I think.'

'Right.' The door slammed again.

She watched as the lights of his taxi disappeared into the ornate tracery of streets near the hotel, where little lanes with sweet small houses that were almost historical looked out towards the stain of Robben Island. Then she tied up her hair with red ribbon and went down to the dining-room, ashen as someone who has survived a massacre of the innocents and now joins the barbarians.

'Please leave all that there,' she said when the waiter began to clear the cutlery from the other side of the table. As she calculated how long it would take the cab to reach the cottage with the Dutch gable, how long it would take him to escape and return, she was quietly transferring the notes in the wallet to a secret pocket in the labyrinth of her little velvet bag. 'He won't be here for the main course,' she said, 'but he'll definitely be here for the Stilton.'

# LITTLE VARMINTS

A BROODING VALLEY lay before them as the hired car breasted the last arid hill late in the afternoon. They had passed through other wide, wild gullies on the day's journey, but this one was bigger, deeper. Malign shadows lay with a promise of menace under the gaunt framework of huge and unruly trees, some of them dead.

The valley floor was drawn and quartered by a series of stone fences in a state of profound disrepair, the old grey rocks tumbled from their perches like severed heads lying petrified among rank weeds.

A languorous heat had baked them in the car on that excursion, proved it by leaving inflamed red brands of sunburn across their arms, but a freezing and malignant wind blew in now from a distant glimmer of grey sea. A low and muddy island lay in the middle of a small bay, mocked by sulky waves.

The man, sitting beside the woman who was driving, fumbled under the passenger seat, drew out a pair of binoculars.

'I think,' he said, 'that I can see tombstones out there. I can see crosses. There are graves. I don't think you should just stop like that, suddenly in the middle of the road' — and she waited almost flinching for one of his significant pauses to grow and bloom — 'Mother,' he said, so she knew then that she was rebuked, that he was not pleased with her driving.

'Your father didn't like it either,' she said, watched his puzzled face. 'It doesn't matter,' she said. 'I was talking about something else.'

'I really don't think you should stop in the middle of the road.'

'It doesn't seem to be very well populated. It won't hurt

if we just stop here for a moment. If there's any traffic we'll hear it from miles away.' The car had stalled, the silence impenetrable as the motor died. She watched him as he stared through the binoculars. 'Anyway,' she said, like a schoolgirl caught out in a misdeed, a tiny crime, 'the motor just puttered out.'

'I can definitely see tombstones.' She watched those steady hands on the binoculars. 'It's a cemetery.'

'But, darling' — and there was one of her hidden apologies — 'I wanted you to have a holiday. I didn't want to bring you to a cemetery. I wanted to take you somewhere nice.'

'Your brochure said it was nice.' There was an odd finality about that so she sat with her hands very still and cold on the steering-wheel, watched that mutinous profile and thought about the towering airfares, the escalating costs of the hotels, the clerk in the travel agency who had said carefully, 'Are you quite sure this is where you want to go? I could get you a much better deal in other places. Honolulu? What about Sydney? Sydney's always reliable. Well, what about Melbourne? I know people who swear by Adelaide.'

'But my son says he wants to go here.' Her inexorable little index finger, stained from gardening, poked among the glossy booklets, found the right one. 'He definitely says this is where he wants to go.' And seeing the doubt in those eyes she said, 'He's spent years studying, years and years. I promised to take him to a place of his choice.' She stabbed at the bright pictures again. 'And this is his choice.'

Now she watched him rake the view of ragged towers lost in thorny thickets, a broken blockhouse to the east. The skeleton of a stone prison lay before them, the old walls breached in many places but the barred windows, possessing an unfathomable strength and endurance, remained obdurate within this framework of decay.

'I expected a nice little town,' she said, 'a proper little town by the sea with shops and cafés where I could take you in the evening.' Where there would be other women like me, she thought, who had taken other sons on misguided holidays that were neither wanted nor required, women who would sit trying to gulp down dinners that stuck in their throats because they might begin to cry. 'That is what I expected,' she said, and listened to the squeal of the tyres on the road as she started the car, took off down the hill.

'I don't see why you're so angry.'

'Don't you?'

The wind was blowing in more strongly now from the island, rolling over drifts of dead leaves in the ditches, fanning her small defiance.

'Your driving concerns me,' he said, voice as dry as dust, gravelly as bone meal.

From some stunted eucalypts beside the track came a series of harsh cries.

'Whatever was that?' She almost shouted the question.

'Kookaburras.'

'They don't make that noise on television,' she said, 'or at the pictures.'

'They evidently make it here.' She heard the rustle of paper, cast a glance at him and saw he was reading the hotel brochure.

'If you look at page three,' she said, 'you'll see a lovely picture of a fireplace and big comfortable chairs.' She watched him sigh, sensed that slow expiration of breath as grimly as she might have felt the scourge of birch.

'Watch the road, Mother.'

'I am watching the road.' She negotiated another bend. 'And there was a nice antique clock on the mantelpiece.'

'Watch the road, Mother.' The kookaburras shrieked again. 'I wonder if they'll have any mail for me? I wonder if there's a letter for me?' She knew then that he had been taken away from his friends and his life, that it was not a rest at all but a period during which he merely waited to return to them.

'If I'd stayed at home I'd have got a lot of work done by now,' she said and knew also, inconsolably, that no one would recognise this trite and inaudible scream of anguish.

'Look.' He was pointing to a sign nailed to a stripped tree, and they both listened to the motor die again.

'This car,' she said, 'is suddenly frightening me.'

'*To the lunatic asylum*,' he read. 'I don't think we want to go there, do we?' He was laughing, though. Laughing.

110

'Not quite yet,' she said. 'I don't think we need to go there quite yet.'

'Just inch forward a bit, will you? I want to see that other notice.' Something was nailed to the next tree. 'There you are, Mother. Just what you wanted — *This way to the boys' home.*' His laughter nearly drowned out the screams from the trees.

'I hate the sound of those birds,' she said as she swept round the last bend, the car kicked to unwilling life and sighing like a scrimshanker forced to labour.

'Why do the birds scream?' she asked the porter as he took them upstairs, through the chilled corridors of that old hotel. Like the tread of a man walking the plank, the whisper of his footsteps preceded them up the bare wooden passages and his square shadow, bleak as a sexton's, blocked out the last of the sun from narrow skylights. He did not answer. 'Are there any other people here?' she said. He was unlocking their rooms, jingling the keys on a glittering bunch.

'We don't get many people, not at this time of the year.'

'And who used to live here?' Her own persistence embarrassed her.

'Nobody lived here,' said that big square man who held the keys. 'People were brought here and they stayed.' And when she said nothing, stood mutely holding her small suitcase, he said, 'To serve their time, madam. They came to serve their time.'

'Even little boys?' She took her son's hand then, even though he was so tall and already had a smattering of grey hair. ('But, darling,' she had said when she saw it, 'you're so young,' and she had cried because, again inconsolably, she knew she had begun to see him grow old.)

'Boys in particular,' said the porter. 'Little varmints and sneak thieves most of them, gangs of boys all sticking together like glue, lying and cheating to save each other. A boy just had to be here for five minutes to be part of the herd. I've read all about those boys. Don't you waste your sympathy on those boys.'

They listened to the sound of his retreating footsteps. Finally, from far within the building, they heard a heavy door

111

slam.

'Usually those porters tell you where everything is.' Bag in hand, she wandered into one of the narrow rooms, noted that he followed. 'I think he said you were next door.' But he stayed, perched himself on the only chair, a little wooden one deeply veined and carved with initials. From outside came more harsh cries. 'Those birds,' she said. 'Those awful birds. You won't mind, will you, if I tap on the wall sometimes? Just to let you know I'm here? Just to find out if you're still there?' A bleak dusk was falling, the last of the sun cut suddenly by the height of the encircling bluffs. The entry road, narrow as a rope on a gallows, wound away into mist.

'No,' he said. 'I don't mind if you do that.'

'Why don't you stay for a while?' He showed no sign of moving though, just sat gently on the little wooden chair and regarded her with a clear ingenuous gaze with no sign that he might say at any moment, as he often did, 'Stop fussing. Leave me alone. Get off my back.'

'I've got a bottle of wine in my bag somewhere.' She delved about and drew it forth, wrapped in a black jersey, with a minuscule triumph.

'I like your packing, Mother.' But he stayed. She noticed that.

'And I've got glasses,' she said and found those too, wrapped in scarves. 'And an opener, and everything.'

'Full marks.'

'Your father used to say that.' She switched on a small lamp that swivelled either prettily like the stalk of a jonquil or so that it could blaze on a face.

'When we go downstairs,' she said as she poured the wine, 'I'll change the bookings. I'll ring ahead. That place we're going the day after tomorrow looked nice. It had a beach and things like that, things you'd like. I don't want to stay here.'

He leant back in the chair, balanced it on the two back legs and propped himself against the whitewashed wall.

'I haven't had a drink with you before dinner for years,' he said. 'Not since I used to go home in the holidays.'

112

'Your father really liked that. He enjoyed that — standing up beside the drinks tray pouring you a glass of wine. It was nice for him to have another man to talk to, not just me twittering round the place.' The wine, pungent and almost shocking, nearly choked her then. 'It is,' she said, 'a little young, a bit sharp.'

'I should have come home more.' The chair remained propped against the wall, the hand on that glass curiously immobile, nearly transfixed.

'No, you shouldn't. People have to have their own lives. They have their own things to do. He knew that. Drink that up, and we'll have another one.' What else was there to say.

She sat on the end of the narrow bed, wrapped a scanty eiderdown round her shoulders and with a glass in one hand and the bottle in the other felt irrevocably that these were not suitable props for the occasion, were an unfortunate framework to pin a reasonably pleasant evening to.

'Years ago,' she said, 'when your father was alive, people used to think I was quite amusing. They used to say I was good company. I can't ever think of anything to say now. I can't think how to amuse you.'

'You're all right.' She felt a hand on her shoulder then. 'You don't need to amuse me. You don't need to amuse anybody. You're okay.' So they sat there in the light of the little lamp and nearly finished the bottle of wine, then went down the corridor together to see his room. The porter had left the key in the door so they turned it, like thieves, and entered fearfully as though a shock might be waiting round every corner.

'It looks all right,' he said.

'It's too small, just like a little cell. It isn't like the picture in the brochure.'

He leant out of the open window, seemed about to throw himself upon the mercy of the night.

'For heaven's sake be careful,' she said. 'Don't fall.' From below came the sound of more cries from the trees, harsh but eager screams. 'The birds seem worse here.'

'We're on the second floor. You couldn't get out if you tried. If you jumped you'd break your neck.' She wondered why he said that. From below came more noise from the trees.

'Are you sure they're birds?'

'They must be.' He was closing the window. 'It's so cold here. I always thought it was a hot place. The valley must act as a funnel for a cold wind from the bay.'

'From the cemetery.' She regretted saying that.

'From the cemetery, then.' He shrugged. 'They had to be buried somewhere. It probably kept everyone very occupied rowing out there and digging the holes —'

'Viewing the fatal punishments of others or observing mortality in general. A bad habit of mine,' she said, letting another drop of that fiery wine that was too young and too sharp slide down her throat, 'interrupting. You'd think I'd have learnt by now to keep quiet.'

'You don't have to keep quiet. You can say whatever you like. Shall we have another glass of wine?'

'If you think it might help.'

He took the wine from her — 'I'll do the honours this time,' he said — and she noted for the instant both their hands were on the neck of the bottle they looked like the hands of twins.

'In a funny way,' she said, 'we're very alike, you and I. Our hands are the same. Our bones are the same. But you're better at things than I am. You're better with people. People like you. You've got a nice way with people.'

'You never told me that before.'

'You've got your own things to hear. I've become,' she said, 'terrified of intruding.'

'You're all right.' She felt that hand on her shoulder again. 'You're fine.'

As they listened to more shrieks from the raw-boned trees, the first scud of icy rain struck the window panes like gravel from a rancorous hand. A telephone out in the corridor began to ring, coinciding with this sudden discord like the tolling of a last midnight.

'Do you think we should answer that, darling?'

They went out together into a dim and vaulted hall. From below, down the stairwell, came a faint light.

'I think they're trying to save electricity,' he said.

114

'I don't know what they're trying to do.' The receiver felt very heavy.

'Is that the lady in room 26? With her son in 27?' The voice was gruff, without grace.

'Yes?' She put her hand over the receiver. 'It's someone wanting us. I can't tell if it's a man or a woman.'

'This is Sheryl, from the kitchen.' The name sat oddly upon that harsh voice like a flower on an iron door.

'Yes?' From the stairs the light cast strange shadows, made the hall-stand on which a coat hung look like a claw holding a rodent's body.

'We wondered if you'd mind having dinner upstairs? On trays? In your rooms? It's our off season, you see. The dining-room's closed. We can offer a restricted menu —' Here the voice stopped abruptly and there was a sound of whispered consultations. 'I mean, we can offer you a selected menu — a special selection.'

'But the brochure said —' she began, then gave up.

'It doesn't matter, Mother.' He was putting on an elaborate charade, mouthing extravagantly to her in the half-dark as he stood, almost grotesquely normal, in front of the gibbet's shadow cast by the hall-stand.

'I'll get Selwyn to bring you up the menu.' The wind was howling at the windows, rattling the panes but quietening the birds. More rain splattered in from the bay. 'We've got cold cuts and plenty of bread.'

'Is there a wine list? Could we have a glass of wine with our dinner?'

'No liquor allowed in the rooms.' The voice intoned rather than spoke the words. 'Only iced water on upstairs trays.'

'Have you got a bar then?'

'The bar's closed — for repainting.'

'Fine,' she said with unconscious irony as the rain turned to hail. As she replaced the receiver they both heard, from far below, the slow and shuffling tread of the porter as he began the upward climb.

'I wonder if they've got television. I wonder if I could put in a toll call later. I want to ring ahead, to that other place.' She listened to the footsteps drawing closer. 'I wonder if I

115

should go out and try to start the car.'

'No on all three counts.' That was the porter, addressing them as an invisible presence from a lower landing. 'Couldn't help hearing,' he said. 'Television's on the blink. Only internal phones available. And it isn't wise to go outside, not tonight.'

'And why not?' Rebellious and defiant, her voice sounded like that of a creature cornered.

'Because it's raining.'

'Oh,' she said, as he handed her the menu from the last step on the stairs, and she took it quietly away for the boy whose hair was greying slightly, slunk innocently along under the weight of these possible perjuries.

In the morning the sun awakened them, a stain of light that soaked the sill, faltered and was blotted out in the folds of grey curtains left undrawn. They had wished to see the freedom of the moon's bright passage across the sky.

'You'll have cramp from sleeping in a chair all night.' He padded over to the window, threw up the sash. 'There's a sort of yard down here. I can see marks in the mud where something's walked round and round in circles.'

'Am I better? Do I feel better?' he used to ask years ago, when she sat through fevers in the night.

'You're much better,' she would say. 'If you close your eyes now I'll tell you a story, I'll tell you the story of Barnabas the juggler, and when you wake up you'll be even better.' It had been lies.

'It was probably a dog,' she said now, 'locked in for the night.'

They packed quickly, like people with something to hide, experts at a thousand tiny evasions.

'What about breakfast?' she said. 'Don't you want some breakfast?'

'Hang breakfast.'

Another bar of sun, thick as a cudgel, lay across the head of the stairs.

'Shall we leave a note? No, no.' She was deciding for herself now. 'We'll just go. It's all paid for. They can keep it. Quickly, quickly.'

'I can't hear any sound at all.' She watched him tilt his head

116

to listen. 'There's no sign of life. Is that smell paint?'

'I don't know. I don't care. Come on.'

The sound of their footsteps, the clatter they made on the stairs, seemed to assault the stillness like a series of blows.

'This reminds me of when you were a little boy,' she said. 'When you were ill I used to sit by your bed all night, watching over you, and I used to clatter off to the doctor with you in the morning — just like this.'

'I remember that,' he said.

They stopped briefly to try the car and the sound of that labouring motor punished their ears, faltered into a guilty silence.

'We'll walk,' he said. 'We'll ring the car hire people as soon as we get to a telephone.' He put the binoculars under one arm and a packet of peppermints in his pocket. 'I think that's all our things. Are you all right?'

'I'm all right,' she said, 'if you're all right.'

They took the track that led up to the rim of the valley, past the sign that pointed to the remains of the boys' home.

'The birds are very quiet today,' she said, and felt the handle of her suitcase begin to score a mark on her palm.

'Just keep walking, Mother.'

'When I was a girl guide we used to run a hundred steps then walk a hundred steps if we wanted to get anywhere quickly.'

'Do you think you could do that now?' He had turned his back on the grim lean trees that lined the road like sentries and held out a hand for her to take.

'I can if you can.'

The birds began to call again when they ran round the last bend, the sound as far away as an echo or a cry that was nearly forgotten. As they walked the last hundred steps, just before the main road loomed up, she said, 'When I really listen hard I think I can hear singing.'

'Don't listen, Mother.'

'If I could hear it properly, if I could just stop and listen for a minute, I might be able to tell you what the song is.'

'Keep walking, Mother.'

The main road stretched away over gentle countryside,

undulating sweetly between stone walls and more beneficent trees in groves that sheltered cattle.

'It's nicer up here,' she said, and sat down on her suitcase in the gravel.

'It is.' He sat down beside her.

'When I'm not so puffed, when I've got over the stitch, what will we do?' One hand was pressed to her side.

'We'll hitch-hike when you're ready.' She took a deep breath, counted to ten to make her heart beat more slowly. 'When we're ready,' he said, and she was grateful for that tact.

'Aren't I too old?' she said as they walked past the first quiet and gentle clump of gumtrees. 'For hitch-hiking?'

'You're fine. You're okay,' he said, and they wandered along beside bushes and stone walls that clung to tranquil pastures, where the singing of the birds was as innocent as that of small children with eyes bright as filched sixpences.

'We'll have a peppermint each,' he said, 'when we've walked for exactly fifteen minutes.'

# A DIFFERENT VIEW

'I'LL HAVE TO say goodbye,' he said, waiting by the fruit counter at the supermarket while the girl weighed the bananas. 'Soon I'll have to shop somewhere else.'

'So you've sold your house then?' The hands were very deft, picking out fruit with black spots. He often stopped to talk to her when he did his shopping.

'Mmm,' he said. 'I've had it on the market for more than a year.' It was not actually a lie, he thought. He had merely implied the house was sold.

'Is it a year? Doesn't time fly.' He agreed with her, though he did not believe it himself. He thought time dragged. 'It's taken a while, hasn't it?' She was a bright girl, chatty. 'My cousin had a house for sale and someone snapped it up the first week.'

'How very lucky.' He felt a sudden obscure envy for this relative, this person who sold a property in less than seven days.

'Not really. They brought in a bulldozer and turned the whole place into a car yard. Now? Were you wanting anything else? No?'

He wheeled his trolley away behind a tower of Brussels sprouts, hoping it might provide a brief respite from life's problems, but he was flushed out again almost immediately by someone from the grief counselling course.

'We must get together again sometime,' she said, stalwart with desperation in a red floral frock, so he bolted off towards the butchery section, and the mince.

A car yard, he thought. He would not have minded if his property had been turned into a car yard. As long as somebody bought it, but no one had. He was a victim of lack of mortgage money, astronomical interest rates at the major banks, a marked decline in real estate values throughout the town.

'It's not a bad little place,' the land-agent had told him the previous day. 'Not of its sort, if you follow me. But we've hit a bit of a bummer here, John. The problem is—'

'Peter. My name's Peter.'

'Okay—Peter. Now where were we. The problem is, as I see it, that the sort of man we're looking at here is your first-home buyer.'

'Mmm,' he said, could not think of anything else to say.

'We're looking here, John, I mean Peter, at your little man with a wife and a baby, and they can't service the loans. None of them can service the loans.'

'What will I do?' He stood there, helpless, in his own sunny garden.

*It must be depressing for you*, his son had written, *after the business in the garden. It might be better if you got out, made a break. Sell the place and come up here. You might feel like a different person. You could get a nice place near the cricket ground. You know how you like cricket.* He was as encouraging as a Christmas pixie.

'I'm not so keen on cricket these days.' The boy rang him the day after the letter came. 'I've sort of gone off cricket. But I'll think about what you've said,' and he sat down then and did think about moving as well as cricket, wondered again if the sound of a neck breaking might be as loud as a six? Or a four? Or even just a one-run non-event because his wife had been a small woman. A dainty little thing. And she had tripped over a tree root in the garden, tumbled down a steep bank and lay there with her neck broken on a sunny summer's afternoon while he watched England put a stranglehold on Pakistan at the Oval.

'You could sell a lot of stuff, all the electronic gear, all that sort of thing, when you move,' said his son. 'Buy a whole new lot when you come up here. Might as well be comfortable.'

'I might get a CD thing,' he said, 'for my music. I wouldn't get a telly though. I don't watch it much these days, to tell you the truth. Don't watch it at all, really.'

'Oh,' said his son, and they left it at that.

'What on earth would be the best thing for me to do?' he asked the land-agent yesterday in that bright and pretty domain where menace was attractively hidden. 'What would you suggest?'

'It hasn't moved.' He wondered if they went to courses to learn that mode of speech. 'We haven't had a nibble. We've brought the buyers, John, and nobody's jumped.' He gave up then. 'Why not rest the place for a while, as it were? Try again next summer. The money market might've come right by then.'

He had wanted to go away, wished to live anywhere that might give him a blank face in the crowd, where people would never say, 'And how long is it, Peter, since the accident? And are you still in the house? And what have you done with the garden? You must feel funny about the garden.' He wanted to live anywhere distant, to be known as the man in the grey coat, the man who grows roses, the man who lives in the house on the corner. The remoteness of distance had stirred his heart and he had accomplished it as much as he had been able, so far. He never went to the lower part of the property. Morning glory had taken over there and he allowed this, even though she had died there in the afternoon, and ingloriously. Now he wished to remove himself completely, to never see any of it again. Even the innocent gate, the silver birch beside the letterbox attracted his quiet and unrelenting odium.

*Be sure to feed yourself properly,* his son had written. *We think you're looking a bit too thin.*

I've just slimmed down, he thought. Lost the flab. But the following morning he arose earlier than usual, grilled himself some cheese on toast for breakfast. Protein, he thought. Good for me. The upper element in the oven cast a golden bloom, a sweetness of light that was endearing. In the gentle shadows cast by the oven trays the stale bread lay like a sybaritic offering in the Temple of the Golden Aureola.

While he ate it he turned the oven switch back to *Bake*, watched the stove light up with a horrible glare, a terrifying bleaching of its shadows. Then he turned the bottom element off again and the quality of light in the oven became mellow.

A different sort of light, he thought. A different view. So he wandered away to another part of the house to finish his breakfast, watched waxeyes play in neglected camellias on his forgotten southern boundary. He had never watched the birds before.

'I might buy a bird bath,' he said at the office to the girl who did his typing. He thought she might be called Maxine or Margaret, something beginning with M. The staff changed so often it was difficult to keep up.

'Was there anything you were wanting, Mr Prendergast?' She stood with his letters in her hand, waiting. 'Do you want me to go out and get you a bird bath?'

'I was only talking,' he said. 'I was conversing.'

'Will that be all then?'

He said it was, watched her thread her way through the desks.

That night he moved the kitchen table into the sunroom. It was next door to the old dining-room and had always been a uselessly useful room, handy for the storage of everything nobody wanted. He threw the old umbrellas and the vases with pansies painted on their sides, the raincoats that needed reproofing but might be handy one day, into the rubbish bin. He did not want them either.

'I'll have to get home a bit early today,' he said at the office a day or so later as the old town clock struck four. Usually he was still there at seven or eight, shrinking the hours till midnight when he went to bed and did not sleep. 'I'm having a sort of change around in my house. I'm turning the dining-room into my bedroom. I'd get a different view of the sea from there. I've got furniture to move. See you tomorrow. Don't expect me before half past nine.' He usually was well ensconced at his desk by eight.

In the succeeding weeks he changed his old bedroom into a small sitting-room which he called his parlour. The former sitting-room became an office. His big mahogany desk took on a monumental character when placed in the middle of the room. It was, he thought, an official statement of his new fashion of living and he sat there in the evenings reading better books than he had chosen for a long time. He re-read

122

Iris Murdoch's earlier novels, dallied with dear old Galsworthy and Sargeson, fluttered off at a tangent with Angela Carter.

He had the outlet for the telephone altered after this and rang the garden shop to order half a dozen Italian cypress trees. Amidst winter chill he planted them in a line where his land began to slope to the valley's floor, fencing off the steep part of the garden. Now his gaze was directed upward by the trees to innocent storms the sky provided, to gathering clouds not of his own making. The banks lay abandoned under a shroud of weeds which flowered brilliantly at all seasons and flaunted the subterfuge.

When the spring came he handed in his notice at the office, and thought they seemed sorry.

'But Peter, you've been with us for more than twenty years.' Arthur, the accountant, handed him a small white envelope which contained a large blue cheque. 'We thought you were a fixture.'

'I just feel like a change,' he said. He had a magazine of literary criticism tucked under one arm and planned to head straight for the library to collect a reserved book, V. S. Naipaul's *A House for Mr Biswas*. He had left *Decline and Fall* by Evelyn Waugh for the summer, till he felt stronger. Pinned to the cheque was a gift voucher for one of the better department stores and it was still uncashed when he started work at his new place, right up the other end of town.

'And what made you think of applying for this position?' he was asked during the job interview. 'I mean' — and here the office manager consulted the meticulous cv — 'you've been in computers now for a long time. What made you think of returning to architecture?'

'I felt I wanted something different,' he said.

After his first day there he exchanged the voucher for a Spanish dinnerset in a glimmering shade of pumpkin red and spent the evening packing all the old china from the kitchen.

'Is there any sort of demand,' he said at the local auction mart, 'for household sundries? You know the sort of thing — eiderdowns, blankets, ornaments, tea-sets, mats, just the usual household stuff? These things are just the beginning of what I want to bring in.'

He bought a feather duvet and matching pillows that had been made in China and decided to have only black sheets and pillowcases so all the old bed linen went to the auction as well. The house began to take on a peculiarly sculptural quality, heightened when he had all the old floral carpet taken up. The bare boards of the floor, lightly sealed with Swedish wax, had an exquisite simplicity.

They glowed sweetly in the early morning sun when, at weekends, he sat propped up in downy splendour while he read the newspaper or the stockmarket report. When the most noted economic indicators dipped for the third time in as many months he rang his broker and told him to unload everything.

'But what are you going into, Peter?' The broker was a careful man, utilised just enough air to make the right sound. There was no breeziness of manner, no gustiness of goodwill there.

'Nothing,' he said. 'I'm just going to enjoy myself. I might go to Katmandu next summer.'

'But think of growth investments. And my neighbour went there, Peter, and I can tell you he became a very, very ill man.' There was a silence. 'A very ill man, indeed.'

'Stuff growth investments, and being ill,' said Peter. 'I might even study the renaissance of classical architecture.'

'I didn't know you were an architect, Peter. Is there much money in it?'

'Not really. And I'm a draughtsman. I'm studying to be an architect.'

'Well, never too late, Peter.' It sounded as if it was, already. 'Hope springs eternal.'

When the telephone rang in the evenings he was often curt and never regretted it.

'No,' he said to big bossy Barbara Ainsworth when she rang about the book club. He was busy dragging the antique corner cupboard into the sunroom, now the dining-room, and tripped over his new German umbrella on the way to answer the call. 'I've had my house for sale for ages, as you know.' He nursed a sore toe. 'I won't be joining this year. You've just caught me at a bad moment, actually. I'm busy moving furniture.'

'Oh, so you're doing all the moving yourself.' He could sense rumours of immediate bankruptcy as she provided his own fiction for him. 'Well, good luck, Peter. We may see you anon.' They were like that at the book club. 'Take care — someone said you weren't looking yourself.' He felt pleased then, as if he had remapped his own body's geography.

'Sorry,' he said when the breathless secretary of the Chamber Music Society telephoned about his subscription. 'I'm not available. I've sort of gone away.' He went out and bought a record of the Gypsy Kings, U2's latest disc and a double album of Edith Piaf live at her last concert. In the evenings, to the sobbing of this music, he studied car maintenance manuals from the polytechnic where he had enrolled for classes about specialist motor cars. At the end of the term he went out, with some of the money from his shares, and bought a second-hand Alfa Romeo in a delicious shade of eau-de-nil. It had an aluminium alloy steering wheel that was a triumph in design.

His new supermarket, the Buyrite, was at the other end of town on a westerly promontory overlooking the sea and the parking lot. With its boom of breakers, it seemed wonderfully nautical. He drove there through Barclay Avenue, Poppelwell Drive and Cornwall Street, all routes he had never heard of till he studied the road map for new ways to get about. A new hardware store opened nearby so he went there if he wanted picture hooks for his new paintings or plastic filler when he painted the kitchen Chinese red and his new dining-room an eerie and glowing white. When he sat there eating his dinner alone he felt like a crustaceous being within a pearly shell. And he ceased to cook meat and three vegetables, stopped glumly filling his mouth with alternate manageable helpings of green, white and yellow. He bought French saucepans, black to match the napery, in which he formulated delicious little messes of vegetelli, bacon, mushrooms, basil, white wine, cream and a dash of mustard. A new range hood ensured the kitchen remained a pristine oriental chamber, awe-inspiring in its simplicity, glowing with deep red paint like the interior of a slain heraldic beast.

'It's all so smart,' the wives of the other architects used to say, knee to knee on his Morris chairs in the infinitesimal shell-like dining-room. He gave little dinner parties every second week. 'It's all so very stark and wonderful.'

'When you get the outside painted, what colour do you think?' That was Bernard, the senior partner, thoughtful as a gnome on a better toadstool. He took a sip of the Fumé Blanc. They had all studied wine by correspondence. 'I suggest something really over the top. What about maroon and silver? Your main walls silver and a deep band of maroon round the windows.' So they all tumbled outside, ranging wildly round the house trying to imagine what silver walls would look like in the moonlight and Madeleine, who was married to Bernard, said, 'I'll just run and get the bottle in case we need a top-up.'

'What's down there?' One of them pointed to the tangle of his garden beyond the cypress barrier.

'Nothing. Just a mess.' He was surprised at his even tone. The remark had hardly stirred him. 'Just convolvulus and morning glory. I don't bother about it. I've let it go. I'd rather read. I'd rather study Krier. Have any of you, by the way, seen his drawings for that tower in Florida?' So the moment passed and, shortly afterwards, he passed his final exams as well, used the rest of the money from his shares to buy into the firm as a partner. Twenty-five thousand dollars it cost, but he thought it was worth it to feel he belonged somewhere. He liked the feeling that he had people to talk to, people to have morning tea with or to hear his news. When they stopped for lunch the office girl went out and bought filled croissants for them and they would sit idly, talking about architectural classicism allied with commercial soundness, the merits of Vanbrugh and traditional stone and brick. He liked that.

'You ought to see your old house, Peter. It's very arty, not like the old days.' Once he bumped into the Ainsworths at the pictures. 'And the neighbours aren't that pleased either. They don't like the colour it's painted, some silly silver and red, and the noise, Peter, the noise. They wander round at night, whoever lives there, laughing and drinking in the garden. And the stereo's going all hours of the day and night — French singing, Spanish guitars, you name it.'

'Really,' he said. 'I don't know what I could say about that,' and he headed for the great wide velvet hinterland of the circle and its red plush seats that were almost classical when the theatre was empty.

Two land-agents came knocking at his front door when the Continental film festival was over and he had celebrated New Year by buying seven Italian terracotta pots for his verandah. It seemed a lucky number.

'Yes?' he said, not knowing who they were. 'Can I help you?' He had been reading a supermarket handout with this week's specials and saw that the Iranians and Greeks who had come to town for the oil-drilling had had an effect on the offerings. There were Smyrna dates, olives from Athens, baklava. He thought fondly of how he might manufacture more foreign-ness for his life, might listen to them chattering at the delicatessen counter in sweet soft languages.

'Your house,' said one of the men, 'it's taken someone's eye.' There was that mode of speech again. 'We said we'd come and have a word in your ear. Would you be thinking of selling?'

'I don't know.' He felt at a disadvantage standing there in his paisley dressing gown with a supermarket advertisement in his hands.

'We're talking,' they said, 'big bucks here. Our man's talking turkey. We've got big bickies lined up.'

He wondered, again, if they went to a special school to learn how to speak like that.

'I've done the silliest thing,' he said the following week at the office. 'I've sold my house. Someone just came in off the street and bought it.'

'Did you get a good price?' The senior partner looked up from his drawing board. They were designing a new house for a local businessman who wanted a huge but economical home in which to place a wife who was ambitious, self-opinionated and cunningly stupid and children so alarming they seemed to have been conceived in error. Architraves were not to be of prime timber and all ceiling mouldings must be plastic, not real plaster so the egg-shell residence could shelter them all just until the divorce. The brief had been a saddening one, depressing for them all. 'Did you get them to pay through the nose, Peter?'

'They talked big bucks.' He had learned the dialect himself by now. 'There were big bickies involved so I took the money and ran. Bernard,' he said, 'I just grabbed the dough.'

'Good on you. What say we put all this on hold for a day or so? What say we forget all about this awful house for a while. What say we dream up a new house for you, Peter? What would you like?'

'I don't know,' he said. 'I haven't really thought about it.' He slowly unfastened the top button of his grey cambric shirt and pulled his black leather tie a little looser, tugged it to one side so the knot rested nearly under his left ear.

'Good God, Peter,' the Ainsworths had said when he met them that night at the cinema, 'don't say you're going all arty too. What's this? A leather tie? Next you'll be eating mung beans.'

'That's right, Peter,' said Bernard. 'Loosen up a bit. Take a casual view. Give Madeleine a bell and tell her to put something from the top row of the rack in the old chiller. We'll talk about this tonight.'

They took him to view a nice little section in Artemis Street, which he had never heard of, and later they made a few preliminary sketches on a Peruvian jotter pad. The paper was so fine. Madeleine, meanwhile, gave her thoughts on the state of the nation, current fashions and the price of the better types of cheese, and opened the wine.

'I see you, Peter, in a bijou dwelling.' Bernard's pencil had already provided a miniature but immensely chic portico and a few more hurried lines threw up an Italianate window embrasure. 'We can make it a little showplace for our talents. You can't miss out. Sell it in a couple of years and you'll make a mint. A vaulted reception room' — he was sketching again

— 'with the ceiling lower at one end to designate a library area for your books. What are you reading at the moment, by the way? *One Hundred Years of Solitude* by Gabriel Garcia Marquez? No need for all that, Peter. We'll all be round all the time. *Decline and Fall* by Evelyn Waugh?'

'Oh, don't read that.' Madeleine placed her hand on his knee. 'I'd call you definitely a man on the up and up. I was really happy when that other man left the firm, that one who was so selfish and hateful to people, and they got you instead. I think' — she leaned forward so he saw briefly all the nuances of her silk skirt — 'you're a really wonderful person.'

'Clerestory windows,' Bernard was still drawing. 'Glass bricks let into the walls very high up so you can see the clouds and the sky. It will be like,' he said, 'a goblin hall. It will be magical.'

'It sounds wonderful.' Peter nursed the glass of wine, felt the bougainvillea caress his shins. They were all out on the terrace to watch the sunset. 'And there's something else you can do for me, too,' he said. 'It sounds rather odd, but I was always called Buster at school.' It was like the last lump of mortar in the construction of his myth. 'I'd much rather be called Buster than Peter, if you could remember,' and he sat there smiling, with the wine in his hand and vermilion flowers at his feet, awaiting his new house design, dazed as the newborn.

# THE WIDOW

THE FAT MAN began to perspire in the church, before the funeral service ended. The day was a warm one in high summer but the grease that sprang forth on that domed forehead and capacious upper lip was caused more by the sight of the little widow's white shoulder sliding from her jacket than the weather's heat.

He had placed himself deliberately several pews apart from her, chose a place where all the people lacked stature so he had a clear view to the front. When he saw her gallop in on those long, slim legs, taking the centre aisle with a hasty anguish, he mopped his face again, nodded in glad agreement when the vicar commended the departed to the elements.

Uninvited, he stepped through her front door after the committal, moved his generous stomach before him with the ebullience and calculated ease that the very large bring to their excesses.

'My dear, what can I say?' he said and placed one of his big hands, freshly wiped in the hall, on that shoulder, perched it there firmly like a giant homing pigeon. He looked about him with a rising lust, attention equally divided between pale flesh and the luminous glow of starched dinner napkins placed in formation beside a mountain of sausage rolls. Most of the furniture could be placed in his own home, he thought, and stared at the Derby.

The pall-bearers sat in two trios on facing sofas as if their stint round the casket had set them forever in that mould and while he regarded this he reached for another sausage roll, homed in on her again as a cucumber sandwich dropped from one of those long pale hands that he could already imagine toying with the buttons on his shirt.

The excitement of this thought caused him to withdraw

and he steamed through the ground floor of the house with the purposeful tread of a large valuer occupied by a comprehensive inventory.

After another sausage roll he gave her a few warm glances and, clutching a piece of cold pastry, mounted the stairs with passion, ravished the secrets of upstairs. Her nightdress, an abandoned circlet of green silk, lay on the bathroom floor and beside it he found a pair of Spanish riding boots, wet with dew. When he pressed the garment to his big face he found that the hem was encrusted with mud and lawn clippings to match the soles of the proffered footwear. Did she skip about in the mist, he wondered, like a little fairy? He would stop all that and keep her confined to bed.

A small boy was sitting on a tricycle in the entrance hall when he tore himself away from the upper bedrooms.

'Hello, my little man,' he said with his thin smile that sat uneasily above the big jaw. 'Are you sure you're allowed in here with that contraption?'

The child continued to ride in circles.

'If you were my little boy I wouldn't let you do that.' The fat man bent over the child with an unctuous but assessing look, trying to gauge its age, thinking of boarding school.

'But I'm Mummy's little boy.' The child spoke at last. 'And Mummy says I can ride my bike anywhere.'

'So that's what Mummy says, is it?'

'And Mummy says she's just waiting for all the people to go away and leave us in peace.'

'Oh, really?' said the fat man and waded into the sitting room to say goodbye to her, to please her with his absence. With convenient solicitude he placed a hand on her shoulder again.

'My dear,' he said, 'you're going to be very lonely. Always remember that I'm just a phone call away if life seems empty. Think of taking a little holiday. There's a bed for you at my place anytime, remember that, my dear.'

On the front doorstep he reproached himself for his careless and lusty enthusiasm, while a florist delivered another three bouquets. In a week the carnations and roses would be dead, the water they stood in green and stinking

131

of decay, as the bills began to arrive. While he thought pleasurably of this another florist arrived with more offerings like a tax from the terrified living to keep death away.

'Who are you?' asked the little boy as he negotiated the front steps, one hand on his abdomen to steady it and grinning like a Santa Claus who wishes to hide his draped and tailored delights.

'I'm one of your Daddy's friends.' He bent over the boy with that assessing look. 'And now that you've lost Daddy I'm going to be one of Mummy's friends.'

'Daddy's not lost.' The boy's feet slowed on the pedals. 'If he was lost we'd go and find him. Mummy says Daddy's dead.' The fat man resumed his assessing posture above the small figure. Boarding school would sort all that out, he thought, as the child tricycled vigorously round the corner of the house. A large garden seat, actually designed for two, cupped his form as he judged the size of the property.

'Donegal? Donegal? Where are you, Donegal?' His lovely widow appeared at the front door. The little boy waved a tiny hand round the corner. 'That's all right, darling. As long as you're all right.' She disappeared into the house again, did not catch his hot and willing eye.

Donegal, he thought. An unusual name but it would be a simple matter, through usage, to change it to Donald, then Don. It would be boarding school then, with organised camps in the holidays, and there would just be a little photograph of a tiny face, topped by a school cap. He would allow her to keep it on his mantelpiece.

His car, warmed by the sun, provided him with a Turkish bath's heat as he sat behind the steering-wheel eating chocolates while he thought about her cleavage and how it had glimmered at him with all the charm of moonbeams. Salivating now, like a glutton who cannot eat the entire meal at one sitting but watches tidbits for later consumption, he returned to the house.

'My dear,' he said, 'I just popped back again to say how sorry I am. If there's anything I can do, just anything, you have but to say the word.' He gave his other hand a turn on her shoulder then and trapped a limp wrist.

132

'May I ask who you are?' He had not thought she would be so sharp. 'I don't think I invited you here, did I?'

'Invited me here?' He almost pointed one toe like a playful pierrot. 'My dear, there's no need for that. We don't stand on ceremony, you and me? You must remember me coming here after meetings? I remember all your lovely little bits and pieces.' He suddenly thought that particular reference to her dainty suppers was badly worded. 'I remember all your nibbles.' That seemed only a very small improvement. 'I remember your sandwiches,' he said at last, 'and the clever things you did with caviare.' He even horrified himself then with his own largesse of temperament, placing her tiny hand upon his stomach as his words trumpeted joyfully straight into her face like a gust of hot air from a bakery. He clasped one of her hands between his own and there it remained like the sparse filling in a hamburger bun.

'You must call me Bunty,' he said.

He took the two hundred miles of hills between his town and hers with swooping aplomb, his big car flew along like a giant steel bird preparing for the mating season. In the spring, he thought, she would be ready to be taken, seared to a turn by thunder, lightning and fear of the dark. Difficulties over probate would roast her and she would be baked and grilled by Inland Revenue. Under the heat of fright and misery the widow could marinate nicely for the winter and then all joys would be his.

'It might be better,' he said to his housekeeper that night, 'if you didn't bank on being here past next spring. I'm getting married again then to a very nice little lady, a very lovely little housekeeper,' and he had to excuse himself for a minute or two after that while she sliced into the roly-poly.

That night he went to the housekeeper's room. Her hair smelt quite strongly of onions and jam but he lay happily dreaming of the widow's tumbling curls from which he had extracted a faint scent of rosemary.

Throughout the winter he waited, with voluptuous impatience, for the joint attritions of weather, fright and solitude to do their work upon her. The frost of her gathering distress would have the enveloping delicacy of meringue on

133

Queen Pudding. He licked his lips and watched the newspaper for terrifying incidents in her town, and was well rewarded.

An escaped prisoner strangled a woman only a month after the funeral. There was a rash of flamboyant burglaries involving firearms, mostly sawn-off shotguns. He liked that. There was an unusual winter drought in the area and bathwater was rationed in the ensuing crisis. With pleasure mounting he thought of her discomfort. The body of a little boy was found dangling in a tree beneath a railway bridge and when he consulted a street map he discovered it was not far from her house. The infantile name was not familiar, sadly.

In the depths of winter storms a bus exploded in a freakish accident and six people burned to death in front of horrified Friday shoppers. He pressed a cream caramel to the roof of his mouth while reading this and prayed she may have witnessed the sight, heard the shrieks. Her distress may be immeasurable so he had another caramel and put the kettle on.

The first snow for a century fell and when the power lines came down he imagined her awaiting the long and lonely nights with a torch and candles. With an oily satisfaction he placed his hand on the housekeeper's warm plump thigh.

Sending flowers and gifts were small generosities he discarded immediately. It was best to let her stew till done.

She would be busy, of course. There would be correspondence to cope with and he thought with pleasure about the astronomical price of postage. Friends and acquaintances would assure her, in their best handwriting, that they were thinking of her and would ring sometime. She would hear no more after that. He gauged the life of widows well and had hunted in it before with some gains in funds and flesh, for even an ugly, greedy man might be welcomed into their seclusion.

'Life here for we humble mortals is but the chrysalis before our butterfly wings spread and we are taken to The Beautiful Land of Somewhere,' he remembered one widow reading to him from a crumpled and tear-stained note. He had pressed her to his large, soft chest before launching them both on to the downy comfort of her pink velvet sofa, the cheque for her alleged half-share in one of his little enterprises safely tucked away in his pocket.

Four accidents occurred in as many days on a treacherous bend near the widow's house and he would settle himself for the evening in his big chair to ponder the exact nature of the screams and what damage they might do to a sensitive temperament.

A series of vicious attacks on women kept the police occupied well into the spring. He kept his radio tuned to her local station to hear the latest disasters, her imagined alarm causing a salivating relish as he pictured her isolated house with its fringe of dark trees.

Dresden shepherdesses in a jeweller's window attracted his attention as the scent of summer took hold. Their tiny porcelain hands broke easily in his grip as he removed the figurines from his china cabinet each evening for fondling, crushing the flowers on their bodices and pantaloons.

When the sharemarket dropped dramatically overnight, in conjunction with a nationwide fall in real estate values, he mourned the loss of her funds but rejoiced at her added availability. Joy made him crush the housekeeper against the sink as she arranged flowers in a trumpet vase.

The following day he admitted himself to a private hospital for a vasectomy so he could enjoy her pleasures undimmed and he lay in bed dreaming of their visits to the supermarket. He would push the cart while the lovely creature loaded it with chocolate biscuits, large joints of meat and the biggest size in chickens. She would be docile and demure, plumper but still lovely, and he would insist she had a hysterectomy so he was not inconvenienced.

His gall-bladder trouble cleared up spontaneously after that and he had his narrow teeth capped ready for the nuptial studio portrait, returned to the hospital for extensive infertility tests while they tided up a knotty problem with a cyst on his back. A carbuncle on one forearm required lancing under local anaesthetic and he decided his whole system had curdled with anticipation.

'Inky binky boo,' he shouted playfully through the keyhole of the housekeeper's door as she fumbled with the lock upon his return from the surgical ward.

He received her notice when the blackbirds built their second nest outside the kitchen windows and, before giving her a small bonus on her last day, he trapped her largely on the doormat after scones and cream and again after supper during his favourite television programme about the reproduction habits of the larger quadrupeds.

Summer was well established before he finally drove over the intervening hills to the widow's town, the new suit his tailor had made for the excursion hanging on him with disguising pleats and tucks, and a deeper crotch.

Her garden would by now have become overgrown and the excitement of lawns in disarry, roses unpruned since last season was almost unbearable. Convolvulus may cover her upturned wheelbarrow and through the cracked window panes he would hear the sound of faint weeping from within. It all awaited him and in his urgency he consumed a king-size block of Energy chocolate and four nougat bars without recollection.

With tantalising hope and expectation he stepped inside her front gate. The garden stretched away, manicured and tended, close-cut lawns lapping the branches of magnolias.

She had gone, he thought. The fall in house prices and the sharemarket had snatched her greedily from his outstretched hands. She had been borne away to a small mortgaged flat, without an entrance hall, in a side street. The new occupants of the big house would know her address and he stepped out briskly towards the front portico.

'You certainly took your time.' A sharp voice cut through his happy daydreams and he suddenly noticed a figure in overalls and gumboots wading through the lush branches of a fallen tree near the house. 'I've been waiting for more than half an hour.' The gardener waved a small chainsaw at him and approached with the air of one about to transact contentious business. 'I've rung twice about this thing' — the chainsaw was raised aloft again — 'and I told that girl in the office I wanted to see the manager. How dare you snatch my money for a saw that needs new sparkplugs.'

He thought it was a female voice but the garb posed disquieting questions. The figure tramped towards him and as a leather-gloved hand lifted the safety goggles from those eyes he saw, with a dawning confusion, that it was his own lovely little widow.

She placed one piercing finger against his chest and he was surprised at the pain.

'You need shooting,' she said. 'I want a refund and I want a chainsaw that goes.' She thrust the machine into his arms. 'You can take this and you can bring me back another one and you're not leaving till it starts.'

He stared at that pixie face. It suddenly seemed to possess all the characteristics of a hobgoblin's. Where the goggles had covered her eyes he saw that the skin was white and clean and those two patches glowed out from that grimy visage like a wild panda's spots. The overalls were several sizes too big and were fastened round the waist with garden twine. Round her neck she wore a safety harness and ear muffs to reduce noise. Her tan was a deep and glowing brown and her fingers were thin and sinuous. He took a step back.

'You've got a helmet on,' he said at last, shocked.

'Of course I've got a helmet on.' Even her voice had changed, the sibilance of yesteryear long gone.

'Don't you know me?' He still hugged the saw. 'Don't you remember me? Bunty? Bunty Hall? I told you to call me Bunty.' From head to toe she was covered with a fine dusting of garden dirt, lawn clippings and sawdust, he noticed.

'Bunty blooming Hall.' She was very snappish. 'I don't want to see anyone called Bunty blooming Hall. I want the man from the hire centre.'

'I was on committees with your dear late —' but the little dear did not give him any more time.

'Committees? I hate committees. All that committee stuff went back down to the office months ago. Why didn't you say who you were?' She left him breathless. 'Why didn't you say what you wanted? You go down to the office and ask them about committees. I can't be any help to you.' Already

137

she was walking past him. 'You're just in my way so I'll say goodbye.' As she snatched the chainsaw from him she gave him another painful prod with one of those sharp fingers. 'My God,' she said, 'you're in heart attack country there, aren't you, dearie.' She tramped away from him in those big boots, the chainsaw dangling from one strong thin arm with a frightening nonchalance. 'Oh, goody.' Suddenly she was in a better temper and a slight warmth had come into the voice. 'Here's the man from the hire centre.'

He hurried along beside her, panting slightly.

'I suppose you've been very lonely?' He still possessed the remnants of a hopeful salacity.

'No,' she said, eyes on the man climbing out of a truck at the gate. 'I haven't got time.'

'Other widows I've known say everyone drops them.' She may yet be clasped to his chest like a broken doll.

'Pooh,' she said. 'I just got other friends, better ones.'

She waved at the man beside the gate and held up the chainsaw as if it were a small handbag. 'Over here,' she shouted. 'Over here. This way.'

'Other widows I've known' — he suddenly thought of their plain little faces and their arms twined round his big neck —'say they get prowlers and nasty telephone calls.'

'Pooh,' she said again, seemed to be fond of the word. 'I chased them with the shovel. I blew a whistle in their ears.' Those big eyes never left the man at the gate. 'I've got a bone to pick with you.' She was shouting again.

A sharp pain behind his left knee diverted his attention. The small handlebar of a tricycle had hit him a glancing blow and its rider engaged a self-imposed lower gear to reverse rapidly several times over his feet.

'Donegal,' called his lovely widow from the fence. Her voice contained no rancour or reprimand. 'You really are quite a naughty little boy sometimes. Run inside and get a chocolate biscuit. You can have one in each hand.'

He heard laughter and, spleen expended, she skipped over the pavement and tossed the saw on to the back of a truck.

'I want free fuel,' he heard her say. 'I've used up half my good fuel for a nil result. You'll have to give me some fuel.'

She had turned towards the house again, was shouting across the lawn. 'Donegal? Put the cart on the back of your bike. You can help me put the wood away.'

As he slipped past her he saw that barracuda gaze fasten on the property's latest entrant, a man in yellow oilskins who pulled the starting cord of another saw.

'You're not leaving here,' she was saying, 'till I know it goes.'

# GOOD ORDER AND NAVAL DISCIPLINE

'LAST NIGHT I saw the shadow of a moth,' said Jean.

'Last night I slept badly.' Hilda spooned up the last of the custard. 'Again.' She put the spoon back on the dish. 'That wasn't very good,' she said and, without taking a breath, 'and I slept very badly the night before last, or did I tell you? Tell me if I'm getting repetitive.' They were in the cafeteria because it was Saturday and on Saturdays they always had lunch there. Soup and rolls. Hilda had dessert. They had both become accustomed, over the years, to routine. They had been wives of naval officers and the navy had imposed a discipline on their households, a mastery of rank, protocol, meticulous timing. They had not been naval wives for nothing and now were not naval widows who lacked learned reticences, the symmetries of an orderly life. They lunched in the cafeteria every Saturday — a discipline of a self-flagellating sort because the cooking was so bad — and had even done so during a cyclone last year when some of the roof blew away. Dessert that day had been, prophetically, Upside Down Pudding which Hilda, also prophetically, had declined.

'It seems to be blowing up rough,' she had said then and Jean just said, 'Yes.' And a few minutes later Hilda said, 'It seems to have passed,' and Jean said, 'Yes,' again. They were not women who ever made a fuss.

The cafeteria was sparsely populated today due to an epidemic of influenza. Usually all the people from the villas were there because they played golf on Saturdays, with each other, and did not wish to cook. They wore Argyle sweaters made of cashmere of the most expensive sort and their handmade shoes glistened season after season without repair because they played only nine holes if they were lucky, or five if they had had hip replacements. Their gear never wore out. The actual course suffered the most wear and tear as the players thrashed along with their electric trundlers and their walking frames. It was a retirement village and everything was for the sole use of the residents so the divets and the mud churned up by the passage of wheelchairs and crutches remained private.

The tiny golfcourse was played on by people from the villas, which were expensive, and the studios where Jean lived (cheaper). In the village everything had a socially presentable name. Little separate cottages were villas and were the most expensive. Hilda had one of those. Her husband had been a rear-admiral. Small apartments joined together in a row were called studios and were cheaper. Jean lived in a studio. Her husband had been a captain. No one died — they passed away. They did not become a nuisance or senile. They were bewildered or not having a good day. The cafeteria was just a dining-room which management referred to as the restaurant. The walls were marbled pale blue and there was always a menu even though there was no choice, but you could decline things.

'I saw the shadow of a moth,' said Jean again, 'fluttering around the lamp in the entrance hall. I was sitting in the dark listening to some music — *Dido and Aeneas* — and it was that last sad aria when she sings "Remember me, remember me".' Who will remember me? she thought. Michael never thought about me, even before all that trouble. He never noticed me. 'I didn't like to turn it off,' she said. 'It seemed so rude, interrupting all that anguish to go and look for a moth.'

'My hip still gives me a lot of trouble in the night.' Hilda was looking at the menu again. 'It's the same,' she said, 'week after week. They always have the same thing on a Saturday. I've got a good mind to say something. I don't think I'll have the other one done.' Hilda, anchored to the ground by the infirmity of her aged limbs, possessed an Olympian agility in conversation. 'I often drop off to sleep quite quickly because I'm so tired and then I wake up again with a jump after twenty minutes with the pain of it. Oh, the pain of it, Jean, the pain of it. Have I said that before, dear? About the pain? Don't say I'm getting repetitive.'

'Yes,' said Jean. 'The pain of it.' And it never went away, she thought, that anguish of dolour. 'I watched it for quite a while — the shadow. It looked a big moth, quite frilly, with very wide wings. It looked soft and beautiful and pale. I worried it might scorch itself to death against the lightbulb.'

'Miss Prior burned to death last year, did you know that?' Hilda was looking towards the trolley where the coffee machine always sat on a lace cloth that was renewed every day. It was an expensive place and hidden costs amounted to a sum in three figures weekly for each resident. Perhaps, Jean thought now, some of it went to pay for the new lace cloth every day, in which case they might all have preferred to have yesterday's cloth or none at all. 'Do you want coffee, Jean? It was her electric blanket and she'd just had it checked. And by the way, have you given any thought to the outing?'

'Miss Prior? Who's Miss Prior?' Jean was looking at the crumbs on the tablecloth. The diet rolls were very hard on the outside and possessed the merest of interiors. They shattered open and their crumbs, like shards from a lost world, lay in drifts.

'You must remember Miss Prior. She was that little red-headed woman who brought in the drinks and emptied the ashtrays, dear, at the base. I read it in the paper. It was her electric blanket, and she'd just had it checked. It was all in the paper. Of course, it's the smoke that gets them, long before the flames. It's the smoke that kills them.'

The moth, thought Jean, had been like smoke. It had been as smoky as her recollection of the black eye, as obscure as the sharpness of memory now was. Three years? she thought. Or two? How long had it been, exactly, since the business of the eye? The moth cast itself at the lightbulb and its shadow looked like a pale flounced blot, just as the eye had been a blot on the inoffensive curve of her cheek and her eye socket.

'When I went out into the hall — are you listening to me, Hilda? — when I went out into the hall to see it, to see this moth, it wasn't there. It simply wasn't there.' She had gone out into the little entrance hall which was hardly bigger than a cupboard and did not deserve or earn the name, and there was nothing there except the usual furniture.

The *famille rose* lamp, a present from Michael after a trip to Hong Kong, stood on the tiny table. They were the wives of naval officers, she and Hilda, and they had nice things. It was obligatory to have nice things to gild lives that were often not nice and contained invisible symptoms of neglect and decay. *No, thank you, Jean, he would say. I don't want to go anywhere. I don't want anything. Just leave me alone, will you? And shut up?* Hilda's furniture was monumental. Her husband had been a rear-admiral. His first wife was the daughter of a politician. The lamps and tables at Hilda's still displayed old rank, ancient hierarchies, manifestations of official trips to what was known then as The East. Michael had been a captain. His salary was lower than the rear-admiral's, but substantial nevertheless. Hilda's hall table was a Georgian demi-lune in satinwood. Jean's was of giltwood, Italian, with a minute marble top — a console table attached to the wall with golden screws in a matching bracket. There was no moth on that table. No moth fluttered round the lamp. The moth was nowhere.

Jean had sat down on the floor, on a tiny and tattered Persian rug no bigger than a teatowel, but not as useful, and there was no moth anywhere. In a state of infinite stillness the lamp sat on the table, the table remained screwed to the wall, the rug trailed along the bare boards of the floor and there was nothing else. There was no moth fluttering near the portrait of Michael hanging above the table. Her tartan umbrella with the raffia handle, slightly unravelled (everything was in constant need of mending to a greater or lesser degree), guarded the back of the door and there was nothing else. No scalloped moth looped and swirled round the light. No tawny mottled wing brushed the picture. When she had gone back into her dark sitting-room for the end of that grievous plea, *Oh, remember me, remember me,* the spectre of the moth had fluttered again round the shadow of the lamp.

'You know when people die, Hilda?' she said over lunch,

piling up the crumbs from her roll in a pattern on the cloth. Of course Hilda knew all about dying, she thought. The rear-admiral had died. Her stepson died. Their old Airedale dog died. Hilda had seen Michael die, from a distance. *Dear Jean — the notes put under her door then had been remarkable for their tact and reticence — I was so very sorry to hear about Michael. When they let him come home from the hospital, sometimes they do in the latter stages, do please let me know and I could help you. Perhaps you would let me sit with him if you want to go shopping. My brother, sadly, also died of the same complaint. I remember he used to enjoy orange juice towards the end. It seemed to be all he could take. Do remember we have that lovely tree in our backyard and I have the juicer. You only need to say you need some. I don't know what to say, Jean. Love from Hilda.* 'When people die, Hilda, some people think they become moths. Hilda? Are you listening? Some people say if you see a particularly big moth —'*

'I don't think you should have coffee.' Hilda was rising to her feet, sailing off into the room like a frigate under fire. 'Someone said last week they got a slight shock off that machine. I'm not going to have any today. I've been sleeping so badly I'm giving up coffee. Hurry along, dear. You can do without your coffee for today.' They were in the foyer now where the blue silk hydrangeas matched the rag-rolled walls and magazines and brochures were kept on a table that was a passable Sheraton copy. 'Come with me, Jeannie. Come out to the rose garden.' Beyond its borders of well-clipped box, wild feverfew faded into a shapeless mass of herbage on the eastern boundary where the land became as shadowy as the vision of the moth.

'I've got something terrible to tell you,' said Hilda. 'That's why I brought you out here. I thought it might sound better in the garden.

'I've been trying to tell you all through lunch, that's why I've been babbling on about my hip. I've just been babbling, Jean. Why didn't you tell me to shut up? And the awful thing about it' — she was stumping along the rose border now, ironically labelled *Peace* — 'the really awful thing about it is that if it's her, she might come on the outing and what happens if she wants to sit with us?'

She? thought Jean. She? The outing was easier to deal with. The notice on the board in the foyer said there was a block booking for a concert of operatic arias in the Town Hall later in the week. Circle, $48. Stalls, $35. So there were either 48 or 35 reasons why she wouldn't go. The discrepancies between her own income and Hilda's were sometimes obscurely embarrassing. 'I've got a cold,' she might say sometimes, to get out of things. Or: 'I've been out enough lately, thank you, Hilda. I've just got this great desire to stay home for the next week or two and catch up on things.'

The rose garden lay sweetly on a slight incline, the bushes dappled with a few last blooms under a leaden autumnal sky. Where two paths crossed, a stone statue of Pan blew a silent pipe towards the villas where Hilda lived, the expression on his little flinty face obscured by lichen and moss.

'She?' said Jean. 'Who do you mean, Hilda?'

'It's on the noticeboard.' Hilda stopped in front of the sculpture. 'Do you think he's in a temper?' she said. 'Or is he happy?' The moods of men had governed them, thought Jean, and now they stared at statues for direction or reinforcement of their own contempt or joy.

'What's on the noticeboard?' It was best, Jean thought, to grasp at the heart of the conversation where all the crossed filaments met. 'What are you talking about, Hilda?'

'Oh, come with me. Come with me. I'll show you, Jean,' and when they were back in the foyer she pointed with one wrinkled finger, an arthritic digit that trembled now. 'There,' she said. 'There.'

*Coming in tomorrow,* the notice said. *H. Hartley.*

Helen Hartley, thought Jean. Sweet heaven. Helen Hartley of the lisping whisper, the golden curls, the cause of disquiet in formerly peaceful, if not happy, households, the plunderer of husbands. The idea of Helen Hartley remained in their minds, she thought, just as the scar beside her eye stayed to mark her own later gullibility.

'Hilda,' she said, 'we must stay calm. We must think, Hilda. We must be logical.' She took in the quality of the paper the notice was written on (poor), the ripped edges of the note (unusual), the scribbled handwriting (rare).

'I don't seem to have a hanky,' Hilda was staring into her handbag. 'Everything you want's always down the bottom,' she said. 'And why do they make the insides of bags black, do you think, so you can't see?' She sniffed again. 'It's just my hayfever. It makes my eyes water.' And there were her conversational gymnastics again, looping wildly above and below the subject, the words as supple as string in the wind. 'I thought Helen Hartley might be dead.'

'I haven't ever seen a handwritten notice on the board before.' It was best, Jean thought, to ignore the water in Hilda's eyes. Tears were something they did not discuss. 'It's very untidy, Hilly. It's not the usual sort of thing here.'

The notice advertising her own arrival at the complex had come off a computer and made the facts seem like mathematics. *Mrs Jean Anderson will be moving into Studio Nine next Wednesday. Mrs Anderson is considerably younger than most residents but has obtained a dispensation from the Management of The Village to live near Mrs Corcoran (Villa Five) whom she has known for many years. She is a trained tailoress and will continue to run a small bespoke business from her studio.*

Business since then had not been brisk, but it was steady with discreet orders for relining overcoats and making tailored skirts out of material purchased years ago and kept since then in camphor chests.

The village was a place where falling interest rates were not discussed, where losses on the stockmarket were never mentioned. It was interesting, Jean always thought, that they came in the evenings, as dusk fell, for fittings as though it might be an unpresentable secret that the cuffs of their coats had become worn, that the camel-hair dressing gowns needed re-cording round the lapels.

'You should be living out in the world,' Hilda would say sometimes. 'It's lovely to have you here, my dear, but you should be out in the world. You're a young woman. You're far too young to be here.'

'I'm sick of the world, Hilda.' They might be in the restaurant on a Saturday or out walking in the rose garden.

'I've given up the world, Hilda,' and it was always at that stage in the rehashes of the same conversation, that she thought of the cut eye again. It had not been the worst sort of injury. On a scale of one to ten it might have been a low-key seven or a melodramatic six. But someone who hit her once would inevitably do it again, she had thought, and when Hilda once said, 'Jeannie, what happened to that nice man you met at a concert and he sometimes used to take you out to dinner? You know that one? That nice man? What happened to him?' she had sat, twisting her wedding ring round and round on her finger. 'Oh him, Hilda — I didn't really like him that much. You know what it's like, Hilly — when you've been married to someone for a long time and then they die, well, you don't really get used to other people.'

Hilda limped away through her villa then. It was not long after her hip operation. 'I must show you my new hat, Jean.' So they both sat looking at Hilda's new hat and Jean thought about her eye and Hilda said, 'Oh dear, oh dear,' while sitting very neatly on a newly upholstered armchair. Formality ruled their horrors. 'What's the matter, Hilly?' Jean said that day. 'Don't you like your hat?' even though she was sure Hilda was thinking the man might have dropped her in favour of someone younger with a more, or perhaps less, punchable face. They both sat looking at the hat — a serviceable felt — and never mentioned the man again.

'Your wife's such a good soul,' Helen Hartley said the night of the wardroom party when the rear-admiral, Hilda's husband, took her in to supper.

'You must have an oyster or two, my dear. I insist.' He patted her pale arm with his seaman's hand and they went into the supper room like a lizard with a smooth and secretive snake.

'I haven't been to her little cooking lethonth yet, but perhapth I'll go one day when I've got time.' The condescension, ornamented by Helen Hartley's intermittent lisp, had been as thick as the worst sort of custard. Hilda dodged away behind a potted palm, with Jean in tow. They were friends even then, but she had never told Hilda about the business of the eye even though Hilda knew about

Michael and Helen Hartley and she knew about the rear-admiral and Helen Hartley. It was not possible to think of the eye as hers. It was a black eye. The eye. That was all.

But after Hilda showed her the hat, the day she asked about the man, they both sat looking at that serviceable felt article for a long time and later she could not even remember what colour it was — possibly green or blue, a dark colour anyway, but the exactness of its shading was a mystery of expunged recollection, like the eye. She looked at her own reflection now without interest, but with irony, like that of a lost hunter in a forest of thorns, who has lit a final fire with the last match. The fire has gone out. The forest awaits. That was the look she had, she thought, amidst the cloistered stillness of her studio with the pieces of old silk and embroidery scattered on the floor and another pile of fancy shoebags made from antique fabric packed for the shop she supplied. A stoic watchfulness was all that was left, plus an ability to sew. Bloom and grace and harmless charm had gone with the fading of the eye.

*Pay to Jean Anderson the sum of.* The cheques were invaluable. The money from the shop gave a small, but marked, mobility of action and thought. She could say to Hilda, 'Yes, of course, Hilly, of course I'll come with you to the concert. I'll give you my cheque to hand in for me, shall I?' And she could sign her name with a flourish then.

Sometimes other things nearly slipped out, things like, 'No, I can't go, Hilda. If I go I won't be able to pay the power bill.' It was like the time they were both looking at Hilda's good felt hat and she nearly said he had been a lawyer, with a hidden history of violence. 'And how are you to know these things, Hilly,' she nearly said, 'when a person seems nice? But one day you might mislay some tickets for a concert, just by accident because you were busy sewing and forgot the time, and he might twist your arm, Hilda, and hit you in the eye. And you might be so frightened you'd be sick, right there on the floor. That's what might happen, Hilda.' But she never said that. Never said she had a great urge to be a child again, to be looked after, to go home to her mother who was dead anyway. They were all dead — mothers, husbands, dogs, Hilda's stepson, all dead.

'Hilda,' she had said when the eye healed, 'I've got this yen to live near someone I trust, someone like a mother. Hilda, I've been thinking I might come and live near you, if you wouldn't mind. I could help you sometimes.' Their lives, hers and Hilda's, had been unpopulated except for what the navy supplied. It had given them comfort, status, titles (wives of officers), dinner parties, gilt-edged invitations to meet Helen Hartley and misery incarnate.

'The binoculars. John's binoculars.' Hilda's voice interrupted this calculus of life. 'We can watch the gate, Jean, and we can see if it's really her.' And binoculars, thought Jean. It had given them binoculars which their husbands had taken on permanent loan and never returned, the means by which, in their widowed fastness amid the seclusion of villas and studios, they would view the triumphant intrusion of Helen Hartley. And Helen Hartley, in turn, might note the chips of their tea-sets, the mended handles of china teapots and the scar on Jean's cheek.

'How did this injury occur?' the doctor wanted to know at the clinic she chose for its distance from where she then lived.

'I bumped into a door.' The pain cancelled out any ignominy from the shameless lie.

'You bumped into a door?' She relished, at that moment, his imperturbable face, the bland expression, as he threaded the needle. 'Can you still feel this?' He pinched her cheek, gentle as a child.

'Yes.'

'We'll wait a little longer then.'

Later, when she was at home again, she looked at her battered and mottled reflection in the bathroom mirror and said, 'You are a fool — a fool, do you hear me? A fool,' and listened to her own voice with a rising sense of anomie. The wound healed slowly, puckered as a cruel thought in an inward mind. She did not see the man again.

The following day they took up their positions early, before anyone had brought their newspapers in from the gates. No

149

cat had even walked across the lawns to make footprints in the dew. The day was unsullied, except for the thought of Helen Hartley.

'We should get a good view' — Hilda's voice was muffled by the great dusty swathes of velvet curtains at her bay window — 'if we perch here and just discreetly tilt the blinds like this.' The old hand went out, unerring, efficient. 'We should be able to see perfectly. Now just run outside, will you, Jeannie?' The binoculars were enormous and seemed to cover Hilda's entire face as if every pore in her skin, every capillary, gazed forth to see the approach of the foe. 'You go outside and look in, and I'll sit here like this and you see if you can see me. And stop laughing, Jean, stop laughi—' Her words were cut off as Jean closed the door to the patio. Outside the air was very cold and clear. Winter was well on the way and now Helen Hartley might be arriving as well. Even if she were an old lady — she must be an old lady by now, Jean thought — she would be one of those demanding old girls who always want a wrap from another room, who flirt with old men and who have reptilian blue eyes with smudged mascara, who do not comprehend humourless mirth.

'Are you looking, Jean? I can't stand here forever.' Hilda's voice sounded as if it came from far away, almost from the past.

'Coming,' she called. 'I'm looking now. I'm looking in the window, and I can't see you, Hilda. I can't see anything.'

'Oh goody.' Hilda had come to the door. 'Super.' It was the vernacular of lost schooldays under a forgotten sun. 'The place is a mess with leaves.' Gymnastics again. They had become suddenly childish and ridiculous, Jean thought, had been made into silly girls by fright and pride. 'I'd better get out the yard broom,' said Hilda, 'and give the verandah a sweep. I know it's clean and you know it's clean but,' she said, 'other people mightn't.' They both looked round as though Helen Hartley might be there already with a magnifying glass, looking for dirt and finding their architecture inadequate. 'Are there spiderth?' she might lisp and they would know then that they had sunk through all

150

the layers of polite, and impolite, society and could hope only for the company of arthropods.

'Oh, God,' said Jean.

'What's the matter now?' Hilda was polishing the binoculars with the hem of her apron, something the rear-admiral would never have allowed. 'Come inside and we'll have breakfast. Don't just stand there, Jean, saying, 'Oh, God,' like that. I'm going to make French toast if you give me a minute to get it ready, and we're going to have rum in our coffee. Come on in, Jean. Pull up the big chair. Let me give you a glass of orange juice. I'll just get the glasses out,' and she bent down, grunting slightly with the effort, to open a little door at the base of the sideboard where the crystal was kept. So it was as bad as that, thought Jean. Rum in the coffee. The best Waterford for the orange juice. French toast. 'Is it Tuesday or Wednesday?'

'Wednesday. It's Wednesday all day, Hilda.'

It had been a Wednesday when the builder came to straighten the side fence at her cottage during her last few days there. The place must be left shipshape, she had thought. Things must be left in good order for the buyers whose faces glowed with innocent goodwill. They looked like people who had never been punched, she thought. The Wednesday the builder arrived to do the job was the fifth Wednesday since the eye was blacked. The stitches were out but the scab, black now, lay like a thread along her cheek. The builder found the fence had fallen over because the soil was a quagmire brought about by water from a faulty stormwater drain. That led him to discover three rotten piles on that side of the house. The problem was caused by moisture as if even her own drains wept at her pain. As reinforcements called Ted and Bill worked a hydraulic jack to hoist up that side of the house for repiling, she donned dark glasses and played Chopin badly on her piano, now sold. The pathos of its vanished and trembling notes now belonged to an antique dealer on the main road. Whether she played the piano to reassure herself with noise or to attack the innocent men — it was not their fault the house was sinking — with a cacophony of vile sounds, she did not know. Perhaps she played out of calculated lunacy, to give them the idea that she could neither play nor pay, that she was a gently demented woman with an injured eye and must be taken away in kind and caring arms to a happy land beyond the sea.

The battered notes of butchered Brahms, rattling from the piano, assaulted the neighbourhood after the Chopin was exhausted. She and the instrument, balanced on the hoist and trembling floor, both rocked on the edge of a profound depression, her own as raw and real as a shriek in the dark.

'Aren't you too young' — the trustees of the village had consulted their notes — 'to buy into a place like this? We don't really cater for the under-sixties.'

'I am not well. I am not well at all. I want to live near Hilda, near Mrs Corcoran.' Each word was clearly separate, with no slurring of vowels and consonants, sharp as a punch in the face. The scab had gone by then.

'Here's the orange juice,' said Hilda. 'Just put the glass on the arm of the chair. It doesn't matter. I might have them re-covered anyway. I'm just making up my mind.' She went back to the kitchen and Jean sat in the big chair, watching the sun begin to slant into the tiny entrance hall where the silhouette of Hilda's table looked like a question mark. It was valuable, very dainty, and a suitable piece to have there. Their lives had been lived in miniature, she thought, like an allocation of just enough affection, adequate comfort, some happiness, sufficient respect and male presence. 'Toast coming up,' said Hilda and pushed a plate through the hatch. 'Pepper and salt?' Breakfast had begun. Hilda looked purposeful, even happy. 'I've been doing research,' she said. 'Do you want to come and sit up at the table with me? Well, stay there, my dear. Be comfortable. Don't worry about the crumbs.' Like an invalid child, she was to be allowed to make a mess, thought Jean. She and Hilda had been allocated, at last, a day of generous disorder so they might sit among the slops like clowns on an outing. 'Things are going very well.' Hilda picked up her knife and fork. 'I've been doing research overnight when I couldn't sleep and I've got a lot of information. Things are going well.' Unconquerable, Hilda

152

sat with her plate of toast amidst the battlements of carved chairs and tables with finials like miniature cannons at each corner.

'Things aren't going very well here,' Jean had said last night to the photograph of Michael in the hall, and wondered if other women addressed pictures, memorabilia, old overcoats and other similar signs of lost security and vanished love. 'If I go to a concert with Hilda I have to be a vegetarian for a fortnight, but I take iron pills, Michael, so I hope it's all right. Sometimes I tell lies, Michael. I say I'm too busy to go out but it's because I can't pay. And now,' she had said, 'we think Helen Hartley might be coming here to live, Michael, and we don't know what to do.' The photograph provided no answers. 'You liked her, more than that, but Hilda and I didn't — we didn't like her.'

When she took a step back the face was still shuttered, as secretive as it always had been when she looked along the table at wardroom dinners to see how his attention seldom wavered from Helen Hartley. Later, Hilda's husband suffered from the same melancholy preoccupation. The younger Hilda, still fit enough then to play tennis and to flirt faintly with the older officers, also watched the scene with her small pale eyes that were like the almonds on top of her own Dundee cakes. The rear-admiral, old and wistful, observed the quiver of Helen Hartley's bright curls with unwavering absorption.

'Hartley's being sent on loan.' Jean remembered how Michael came home one evening and said that. 'He's been seconded to the Malaysian Navy and he won't be home till Christmas.'

'Oh yes?' she had said. By then she had become watchful. People had begun to talk. They had begun to say, 'I saw Michael last week with that Mrs Hartley, the young one who's always so bright. I saw them in town, coming out of that new restaurant — the one that's very expensive and where we were going to have the Christmas party and then we didn't. We saw them coming out of there, laughing.'

'Did you?' It was saddening, she always thought, that good-hearted sensible women learn early a camouflaging vagueness, the saving grace of withdrawal. 'Michael's always very kind to people. He's always giving people rides to town, that sort of thing. You know what he's like. Will you just pass me that piece of brown lace? No, not that one — that other smaller piece under the chair.' And her fine steel embroidery needle would pierce the material she was working with, sharp as a stiletto, fierce as a knuckle on a cheekbone. Sometimes now, when she and Hilda caught the bus to town, they would stand looking into the window of the antique shop beside the cinema and she might say, 'Hilly, just pop in there, will you, and see how much they're asking for that little pillow I made out of the old tapestry, that one second from the left on the monk's seat. Yes, dear, that one there,' and when Hilda limped out with the price, they might agree she was not being fleeced yet, not quite.

'I think it's really wonderful, the way you keep yourself amused and you never need to go out or anything. I think it's really wonderful,' Hilda used to say.

'I do so go out, Hilda. I do. I went out with you last week, or was it the week before, to that French film — that one about the sculptress, that beautiful girl who died a tragic death, don't you remember, Hilda?'

'Film? Last week? Don't say I'm getting forgetful.' Hilda's eyes were opaque with cataracts. 'Oh, God.'

'Of course you aren't getting forgetful. Anyone can forget things. I hardly remember what I did yesterday.' She had set to work again, unpicking the sequins from a jersey with a stained front.

'Aren't you wonderful.' Hilda had not even looked up from the newspaper she was reading. 'I see here there's a story on page nine, Woman Makes Attacker Run. That's the headline.' I wish I'd made him run, Jean thought. I wish I'd cut off his hand with the kitchen cleaver. 'Shall I help you put those in the jar, Jean?' The pile of sequins was growing higher. 'It's marvellous what you do with all this stuff. Most people wouldn't have the energy to bother. Just think of all the things you make. Michael,' she said, 'would be proud of you.' Hilda dealt in known faiths, clearly established and unchallenged falsehoods that passed, through long usage, into accepted history.

'My wife's very good at sewing.' She recalled Michael's voice cutting through the chatter at one of Hilda's cocktail parties years ago, and there he had been talking to Helen Hartley in a corner again. 'Spends hours playing round with old buttons and sequins and bits of old silk from this and that.' The voice was nearly dismissive. 'She buys all this stuff at second-hand shops and unpicks it and then she makes it up again into book covers and little pillows and bags and things. God knows what.'

'I'm no good at sewing. I've never made anything in my life.' Helen Hartley's laughter had been like fingernails scraping on glass.

'I feel sure you've got many other talents.' Michael's laughter had been as smooth as treacle from a tart on a summer's day, as rich as one of Hilda's pies. 'Why don't you come and sit with us later? I'm sure Jean won't mind.' Mingled laughter then, pies and fingernails.

*Mrs Anderson has been trained as a tailoress and is prepared to alter suits and coats for a reasonable charge. She also makes luxury gift lines such as embroidered cushions, quilted bags of all kinds and book covers, in many instances using antique fabric. She can be contacted at Studio Nine.* That was what the notice said when she came in the year before last and the words had all the limited generosity of an economical soup made from the tops of leeks, the spines of spinach leaves, the ends of carrots, pumpkin with the skin left on. She thought of her arrival as coming in, like a ship being put in dry dock, an obsolete corvette with rust, on the slips. That notice had been presented in a flowing typed script. But now the name of H. Hartley had been scribbled in blue biro on a piece of notepaper that was stabbed into the noticeboard with a rusty pin.

'Did you notice the pin was rusty?' Hilda flipped more French toast on to a plate. 'Well, Jean, aren't you going to eat anything? Aren't you going to start?' The problem was, thought Jean, that she had no appetite. Dreams had flickered through the night like the wings of that shadowy moth.

'Don't worry about dinner,' Michael said, just as she

remembered. 'I might be here and I might not. And don't keep asking me questions. Don't give me the third degree. A salad'll do, if I'm here which I won't be. I don't care.' And in these nightmares Hilda was in the kitchen doing the cooking while she wept, and Helen Hartley, aged but instantly recognisable, came to the windows of the studio and knocked insistently. Like the brush of the moth's wings, the dreams turned this way and that — a glimpse here, a memory there.

'Would you like to ask the Hartleys to dinner one night, before he goes away?' She had asked only the once, and a long time ago.

It might have been painfully interesting and dangerously charmless to see him compare her with Helen Hartley over their own dining-table.

'I don't think so.' He was very vague that day. 'He's actually leaving sooner than they said. And she'll be busy packing. She'll be busy moving.'

'Moving?' Moving *away*, she had thought in a minuscule moment of mistaken relief.

'Moving into Erickson's place. It's been empty since he retired. When you go over to see Hilda, as you two seem to be such bosom pals, you'll be able to ask Helen over — it's just next door. You could see her from the terrace. She sunbathes a lot. Helen's a sun worshipper.'

The following weekend had been stormy, full of thunder, and she sat embroidering a piece of linen while the windows rattled.

'Are you going out today, Michael? Will you be home for dinner?' Her voice was as careful as her stitches.

'Yes, I'll be home today. And yes, I'll be here for dinner. And no, thank you, I don't want to go for a walk with you later, and no, I don't want to see a French film even if it's wonderfully artistic. And yes, I'll be here next Saturday as well and the Saturday after that and the one after that. Are you satisfied, Jean?' So she knew then that Helen Hartley had promoted herself from captain to rear-admiral and now occupied the second-best house the base allocated to officers with an unparalleled view, through the rear-admiral's binoculars, of her new terrace and herself reclining in a deck chair.

'You're all *tho* clever.' She recalled that pretty lisping voice at the last of Hilda's cooking lessons. Helen Hartley came wandering through a gap in the hedge, in a bikini, to see what they were doing. Already Hilda was looking faded and much thinner. The *sauce hollandaise* curdled that day.

'If you put the saucepan in a bowl of crushed ice that sometimes fixes it.' Hilda, helpless in her chef's apron, wavered over the bench but the clotting in the sauce was not remedied, nor was anything else.

Hilda grew even thinner and paler. She went away, to look after an old aunt. Or that was what she said. The cooking lessons ceased. Hilda's kitchen became a mystery and possibly dusty as well because cooking was no longer done there and the rear-admiral's steward became idle, sometimes close to insolence. People said the rear-admiral dined out a lot, with Helen Hartley, and they had been seen dancing somewhere. Somebody said it was at the Trocadero. They all stopped making a proper *roux* and went back to using the packet mix from the supermarket.

They had learned how to make French onion soup served with croutons of French bread fried in clarified butter and sprinkled with Parmesan. They made farmer's rarebit in a double boiler and had it served on rounds of buttered toast with mushrooms, ham and onion chopped and sprinkled on the bread. They knew how to cook Lyonnaise potatoes, scrambled eggs Magda faintly flavoured with mustard and served mixed with diced toast. 'Like on all the cruise liners,' Hilda said that day, and the class nodded, as if they were wise in the arts of dainty *cuisine*. They made American corn muffins and salmon fishcakes with egg yolks and a little cream to bind the mixture and then Hilda taught them how to make meringues flavoured with ground hazelnuts, to use the whites. They all once had fine tall jars of these in their own kitchens. They boasted of their Crab Royale and their Bananas Brazilian-Style, their poached pineapple and strawberries Romanoff, and all mastered Steak au Poivre à la Crème without difficulty. It ended, though. The whole

157

thing ended when Helen Hartley moved in next door. Hilda disappeared. The cooking classes finished.

'Come with me, my dear,' they used to hear the rear-admiral say at cocktail parties and wardroom dinners. Already he would be placing Helen Hartley's little hand on his arm. 'We must find you an oyster or two, mustn't we?'

The moth had quivered and fluttered round the warmth of the light in the hall and the dreams rippled through the night with an equal agitation of prompted recollection.

'The park's very pretty right now,' she said to Michael once. 'Would you like to come with me to see the daffodils?'

'No thanks, Jean.' His shoulder was a tailored insult, a studied exercise in disrespect. 'I've got a lot of paperwork to catch up on. Yes, I know it's a shame I'll miss the daffodils but I've never been very keen on daffodils.'

'It was a shame about that man you knew,' said Hilda, turning more French toast in the pan. 'I don't know what I'm making all this for. There's only the two of us. Anyway' — she was turning back to the stove again now — 'it was a shame. You're a young woman. You need company.'

'I need some more toast.' It took time to cut it into neat squares, easily manageable pieces like fragments of thought when a whole idea had become too difficult to cope with. He had hit her suddenly, when she had already found the tickets and had them in her hand, and she stood there hardly able to imagine that anyone would punch her in the blameless eye so that something wet slid down her cheek and the bright blood fell on the lapels of her coat.

'I often wondered,' said Hilda, 'if I could have done something to help.'

'You could give me some more coffee.' The cup, Jean noticed, hardly trembled in her hand when she held it out.

'That's not what I mean, Jean. That's not what I mean.' The scent of Hilda's coffee filtered through the kitchen like the promise of a better summer, a sweeter spring.

'I looked in the telephone book last night.' Idle as a girl she sprawled in Hilda's velvet chair. 'No thanks, Hilly, no milk.'

'If you don't want to talk about it,' said Hilda, 'you don't have to. But I'd have helped you if you needed me.'

'There were only three Hartleys.'

Hilda was making more coffee, putting the grounds in the pot with the precision of someone dealing with dust from the dead. 'I do wish you'd confided in me,' she said. 'Sometimes it helps.'

'One of them' — Jean was relentless with avoidance — 'was a C.P.H. Hartley, but I think it was a man. It was an address in the country somewhere, a rural delivery number. I thought he might be a farmer.' Outside Hilda's windows a few early snowdrops had come into flower, the incorruption of the blooms hard to bear. Their dazzling innocence in the greyness of the day was almost shocking. 'She didn't like mud,' she said, 'or hard work. She liked flowers' — she looked out at the snowdrops again — 'but only from florists and done up in cellophane with bows. And there was some Hartley or another, I forget the initial, who seemed to be an electrical engineer with a warehouse and a shop and everything. I felt he could be discounted.' Her voice was dismissive. She heard the dismissal clearly herself, echoing in her ears, just as they had heard it years ago in the voice of the rear-admiral when he said, 'My dear old wife's a wonderful cook — but you know that, of course, don't you, my dear? Gives cooking lessons — all that.' It had been the night of the ball when tulip skirts were in fashion and the prevalent colours that year were lime green and burnt orange. The rear-admiral, with Helen Hartley in tow, passed Jean as she stood in the shadows. 'I can't cook at all,' said Helen Hartley. She wore her hair very long and had it tied to one side with a jewelled clip no one had seen before. 'You don't need to cook, my dear. You're a very talented young woman.'

There was Scotch Woodcock for supper that evening. Hilda supervised the making of it. It was odd, Jean thought now, that details could often be recalled and major issues lay forgotten. Some of the people, those who had not been to the cooking lessons, thought Scotch Woodcock would be poultry, something with a dark and gamey flesh like the dismembered heart of a swan.

'I didn't ethpect jutht thort of thcrambed eggth on toatht.

159

What'th it called Thcotch Woodcock for then?' Helen Hartley's sibilance was piercing that night. 'I exthpected thomething *thtuffed*,' and the rear-admiral said, 'Did you, my dear?' with that crooked old smile.

'I would've made scrambled eggs,' said Hilda, 'but I haven't made scrambled eggs for years. I thought you'd prefer the toast.' She took a deep breath. 'And did you see that B.N. Hartley in some suburb miles from anywhere? I didn't think that would be her.'

So, thought Jean, Hilda had thumbed through the telephone book in the night too, and she would have seen that the small billow of Hartleys had faded into indeterminate shoals of Hartmanns, Hartshornes and even an improbable Hartley-Cartley, the column ending on a prophetic Hartready whose name had all the absurd formality of a hornpipe. In the secret reaches of the night, when she had finished reading the telephone book, she padded out of the bedroom to Michael's picture in the hall.

'It's mutiny, Michael,' she said to those vanished eyes, that square-cut chin. 'Mutiny. Do you hear me? I won't introduce her to anyone. I won't be nice. I won't be good.' The face was as bland as a wall. *No, thank you, Jean, I don't want to look at a book about the treasures of the Louvre. No, not even if it might take my mind off things. No, thank you — I don't want you to read to me. Perhaps later.* His face was like a wall then, too.

Hilda was out in the kitchen again, flipping more toast out of the pan.

'There's enough here for an army,' she said. 'Perhaps the birds might like it. You can take some with you. You can warm it up later. And I'll just hang these up again.' Toast, binoculars, armies. Hilda, Jean thought, sprang from subject to subject like someone on a conversational pogo stick. 'We won't be needing these.' She slapped the binoculars back on their hook in the cupboard without even putting the lens covers over the glass that once held the odalisque image of Helen Hartley sunbathing on a verandah.

'But Hilda, I thought —' The morning seemed to balance on the breeze, on the idea of their plans for the day, on their surveillance of Helen Hartley's possible arrival.

'I know what you thought.' Hilda opened the back door and threw some toast out on to the lawn and the bread whistled through the air like a series of punches, dizzying blows for the unwary or the guilty.

'I wish I could smack her,' Hilda said all those years ago, the night of the ball and the tulip skirts when Helen Hartley went into supper with the men. 'I'd like to smack her. I would.'

'Come with me, Hilly.' So they went to the powder room where they ran icy water on their wrists and then Hilda said, 'I suppose we'd better go out again,' so they did and faced, thus, the disparagement of Hilda's *haute cuisine*.

Helen Hartley's fine high voice was already raised. '. . . I exthpected thomething thtuffed.'

And Hilda, ruffled as a game bird, said, 'It's a traditional thing, my dear, a piece of ridiculous cooking tradition, that's all. It's just scrambled egg and anchovies on toast. It's a sort of cooking joke to call it Scotch Woodcock. It's just tradition.'

'I've got no time for tradition.' Helen Hartley took the rear-admiral's arm then. 'None at all.' They walked away leaving Hilda and Jean standing under a potted palm, only hired and already browning at the edges of the leaves, as the music stopped in every possible way.

'It's time we went,' Hilda said that night and they had gone off together, walking home through the naval base to their respective empty houses. The rear-admiral did not return that night and Michael's hours had, by then, become irregular through duplicity, avoidance or the yoke of work. It was difficult to know the truth of the matter. *Just leave me alone, Jean. Do your sewing and leave me alone.*

That had been the slow cruelty of relinquishment. She must have seemed dull after Helen Hartley, and knew it. The later black eye had been a quick and deliberate piece of arbitrary violence and outrage and, like tickets, both affronts bought her a place in this theatre of withdrawal. In the retirement village people were beginning to stir. Blinds were being put up, curtains drawn back, as if an operetta was about to begin.

'It's time we went,' said Hilda, more cheerful than the night of the ball. 'It's time to go.' She was wiping the pan with a paper towel. The old hand with its swollen knuckles had a compelling inexorability about it, as if the detritus of the years was being cleaned away.

'But the shops don't open till nine.' Did Hilda want to go to town now? Jean stopped flicking over the pages of the newspaper. The news was all bad, anyway. A flood in Pakistan had swept away a thousand people. A gunman in Germany had mowed down six at a supermarket for no apparent reason. The Dalai Lama was on a fast, in New York.

'I don't mean that, Jean. I don't mean we're going to town. I mean we're going. *Going.* You know — going. They buy the places back here, if you decide to go. So we can go. We're going to the office to say what we've decided, that we've decided to go. I don't know where we're going, but we're definitely going there. And you,' she said, sound as a bell, solid as a rock, 'can get something done about your face, something about that eye. You can get something done about that. It would be,' said Hilda the chef, firm as a frigate setting off to sea once more, 'as easy as pie, simple as opening a tin. We're fools,' she said, 'fools, just fools.'

# GOOD NEWS

THE LETTER, WHEN it did come at last, was full of Christmas news.

His daughter wrote that she had made twice the recipe this year for the Christmas pudding so there could be one large and one small. Her husband was late putting the lettuces in, Cos this year, not those old-fashioned cabbagey things that were bitter near the heart, she said. He stood for a long time with the pages pressed against his chest after that. The piece about the lettuces was on the last page and he remained by his kitchen window, holding the sheets of paper, clutching the envelope and looking out over the sea.

He wondered if it would take a long time to drown. Could the clutch of the sea be denied, perhaps leaving time for a change of heart when it was not too late? Or did deep breaths gladly fill the lungs, regardless of the salty pain in the nostrils?

When he glanced at the envelope again she had put the wrong number on it, 22 instead of 23, so Mrs Bailey over the road had put it in his box on her way to the shops. He noticed then that the sea had taken on a glassy glare, glittering and inviting like the eye of a sorcerer.

'I am not loved,' he said aloud in the empty kitchen.

That was Wednesday.

A boiled egg and two slices of thin unbuttered toast made an evening meal. There did not seem much point now in feeding vitamins and minerals to a body he planned to destroy. After he had consumed this food, without relish or realisation, he dragged the television set into the entrance hall beside the telephone, placed his chair there in case she rang, his lovely girl. The programmes showed death and destruction in various parts of the world, so he turned them off and read the newspaper instead. There the same stories were told, but without pictures so the misery did not pierce him so greatly.

While he waited for her call he read and reread one particular headline — Third Prison Suicide Hanging. A convicted murderer had used a towel to form a noose, suspended himself from a ventilator. The instructions in the story were reasonably specific so he ventured into his own bathroom to view his towels, presented himself apologetically before them with the tentative air of one whose confidence and aplomb will never return.

They were all too short, he decided, and he had no ventilators, so he returned to the newspaper and lingered tenderly, enviously, over the Deaths column. There were six lucky ones, two men and four women aged from thirty-nine to seventy-one, his own age.

'I wonder if they were loved,' he said, pondering the gamut of ages from tragedy to merciful release.

That night his own letter to his daughter, written three weeks ago, flickered through his dreams, the paper sliding sideways like scraps caught in the hot updraught from a bonfire.

You couldn't imagine how surprised I was, he had written, when they came in off the street. I thought they were insurance agents or canvassers, something like that.

He thought they were going to produce pamphlets but they were publishers with engraved cards and credentials. It was his garden house, his gazebo glimpsed through the fine spreading foliage of the copper beech, that drew them in.

'My garden house?' he said when they explained their business and he stepped towards them then, glad hand outstretched. 'You like my garden house?' They looked friendly and wore well-cut suits. 'But I've built a garden house everywhere I've ever lived. That's not the only one.' They brightened at that.

Were his gazebos all the same? asked the taller one. Did he always build them exactly the same? That was when he told them about the Gothic one he invented for the old villa in Sedgewick Street and the little square house that had been the first he ever attempted.

'And there was my Chinese one,' he said, eyes fixed on a distant spot in the vanished years. 'That was a beauty.'

It was a real winner, he told them while he made a pot of tea, went into the big chiffonier to get out the best silver teapot and the Derby plate for biscuits. They were nice men, he thought. Nice to talk to someone who was interested.

He loitered in the pantry for a minute or two, vacillating between plain bran biscuits or perhaps the chocolate macaroons, then decided quickly on the Ritz Assorted. It was a great day.

They particularly liked the little house I built for you when you were a little girl, for your dolls' tea parties, he had written carefully afterwards, mindful that he must not let excitement run away with him so that he produced an old man's scribble. I showed them all my plans. You will remember the plans I used to do on graph paper, and they want me to do a chapter about it all in a garden book, with all my drawings and everything. A man is coming to take pictures. Even if they haven't been looked after, Roger and Craig are going to see if the other garden houses will still make a nice picture or two. The men are called Roger and Craig, I forgot to tell you that.

He sat for a long time after writing that much, then picked up the pen and began again.

You know how I have always loved books. You will remember how I always liked to take you into bookshops and libraries when you were just a little thing. All those great stories, such wonderful thoughts and ideas. People do not realise that in books they have recourse to the most remarkable brains in the entire universe.

A thousand times I've stood in the library and wished I could write something, some great idea that will touch the hearts of strangers and I will do it now, quite by accident, with my garden houses in the garden book. I had thought my life was wasted. I had no hope left and now I have some back again. It is a wonderful thing for me, this good news.

Then he waited for his daughter's answer which was all about Christmas cookery and vegetables, said nothing about his book.

'I am not loved', he said again and slid into his tumbled and unmade bed.

'I am not loved.'

The following day, Thursday, he was still thinking about hanging. It was not necessary to have a long towel or a ventilator, he thought. Rope and a beam or branch would do just as well. The distance between the ceiling and floor of his basement was insufficient so he wandered outside to survey the trees. His big plum tree had an excellent branch, high and strong, ideal for a jump and a jerk but it was in full view of the street. The copper beech proved a similar disappointment because it was overlooked by a sandpit played in daily by neighbouring toddlers. It would be hardly fair to give the little souls nightmares into adulthood, his spare figure dangling across their line of vision. In the afternoon he spring-cleaned his pantry and all the kitchen cupboards. When the estate was administered it would be easier if things were immaculate.

That evening he dragged his chair into the hall again in case she rang, but the house remained silent. He sat there, reading and re-reading the letter in case he had missed something, in case he had forgotten to look at the back of a page, but there was nothing. Christmas puddings, lettuces. That was it.

A letter came from the publishers on Friday. They were looking forward to receiving his manuscript by the deadline, late October, and the pictures were fine. The reaction to his proposed chapter on garden houses had been positive and enthusiastic, they wrote, and they looked forward to hearing from him. And when might that be? He detected a slight air of anxiety about them and, gladdened by this, stood holding the message and looked out over the sea, with its inviting glitter.

'Nobody loves me,' he said to the wallpaper as he dialled the doctor's number later that day. 'Nobody loves me,' he said as he waited for the big, bluff nurse to answer.

'I am not loved,' he said to a blackbird singing in a tree as he went into the surgery to lie vaguely about insomnia, and repeated the remark as he came out again with the

166

prescription for only six sleeping tablets.

'Not like you, is it?' the doctor had said and gave that characteristic guffaw of laughter. 'This is just a very temporary disruption to sleep patterns, if you ask me. All you need is a tiny, little bit of help for a day or two.'

The thought that he could possibly ask the doctor for more pills roused him early the next morning. Leave it a week, he thought, then ask for another six and while the bed shielded him from the world he lay within its warm covers and ruminated happily about doubling the number. A dozen may do. Eighteen would be better, but twelve might do. The first six lay spread out on his breakfast tray like small bright promises of better and bigger things while he read the newspaper. Copycat Prison Hanging, he read. Second Prisoner Ends Life.

'They were not loved,' he told the cat from next door as she sat on a fencepost beside his letterbox. He had expected no mail and there was none, but the cat followed him along the front path to have her head stroked under the branch that was just the right height but was too visible from the street. 'Nobody loved them,' he told her as she drank the last of his cream and finished the milk and a piece of fish.

Another heading, missed on first reading the paper, caught his eye. Woman Deeply Unconscious After Fumes Attempt. What a good idea, he thought then rang his daughter's number, carefully memorising it and the direct dialling code so it would click through the computer system without hitch.

A child answered, hesitant and questioning.

'Hello? Hello? Mummy's gone out.'

'Ah,' he said and wondering which child it was, sat down on his chair. 'So Mummy's out, is she? Is Daddy there, then?'

'Daddy's not home yet. Who's that speaking?' It was such a small voice, yet almost accusing. He wondered if it might be the youngest one but was hesitant to ask.

'It's just Grandad,' he said. 'I just wanted to talk to Mummy for a minute.'

'Mummy's out. She's gone out.' There was a long silence while he wondered which one it was. He could not discern whether it was one of the boys or the little girl and he was anxious not to cause alarm. 'Peggy's here,' said the little voice at last. 'Shall I get Peggy?'

Peggy was of no interest to him. He had not heard of Peggy before.

'She minds us.' It was as if the little thing could read his thoughts. 'She minds us when Mummy goes out. She's gone out to her work barbecue, with Uncle Dennis.'

'Ah,' he said. He had not heard of Uncle Dennis. Things were, perhaps, becoming clearer. 'Never mind. You can help me, darling.' It seemed safer to use amorphous endearments rather than pick a name that might be wrong. 'You can tell me whether Mummy got a letter from Grandad. She hasn't answered my letter.'

'A letter.' If reflected on this. 'She read us a letter about a cat.'

'I remember that one.' He was eager now. 'No, darling, that was just Grandad's ordinary letter, the one he writes every week. In a brown envelope, was it? With some clippings from the paper about her old school?'

'I saw her classroom,' said the child, happy now. 'I'm going to school soon.'

'Are you, darling?' he said, careful as a man who strikes out through quicksands. 'Won't that be nice for you, with all the other little girls and boys?' So it was Timothy, the youngest boy. 'That's Timothy, isn't it? Hello, dear old Timothy.'

'Hello, Grandad,' said Timothy. The silence lengthened.

'It's a later letter I'm talking about,' he said, 'the one I haven't got an answer to. Just a note in a little white envelope, a later letter.'

'A letter-letter.' Timothy seemed to ponder this. 'What's a letter-letter?'

'No, darling.' It was such hard going. 'Just a later letter. Another separate letter Grandad wrote after the first one and posted it later.' He waited, hoping for comprehension.

'A little letter,' said Timothy. 'I remember a little letter, with no pictures in.' He thought then that he should always have put newspaper clippings in for the children, innocently winsome shots of kind prize-winning dogs and cart-horses but it was too late now to realise that.

'Oh, I see,' he said, 'so she got Grandad's letter. Did she read it?' The little creature thought she had. 'Well, be a good boy, Timothy,' he said. 'Enjoy life, my boy.' Then he went and looked at the enticing glitter of the sea at sunset.

On Sunday morning he stood beside the sink eating more dry toast. The butter had run out and he did not wish to buy more.

The Sunday paper provided another interesting headline. Exhaust Coma Woman Dies. He poured another cup of tea, watched the dregs drip from the pot and stared into the carshed next door. The view from his kitchen window presented him with a tantalising glimpse. A blue car was housed therein. His own station wagon had been sold just after his seventieth birthday when his eyesight failed badly, but he could supply his own length of hose and there was plenty of string and adhesive tape in his workshop. It might be necessary to tape the hose through the window of the borrowed car in case it fell from position. He might be left merely unconscious, the cat gassed instead. This sobering thought still occupied his mind when lunchtime came, so he made more toast to use his last loaf of bread, found a heel of old cheese and stationed himself beside the window again like a burglar casing a household.

By mid-afternoon he had gone off the whole idea.

It was unkind to involve others in his own private torments, inflicting his purple face on innocent residents of the same suburb. Macabre Pensioner Hot-Wiring Death. He could see the headlines already and gave them up immediately.

Before he went to sleep that night he tipped the six pills out of the bottle as if he wished to surprise them into being more, being larger and poison green instead of antiseptic white. They smelt faintly of chalk and he wanted much more the lingering odour of mould and decay.

He awakened late the following morning, cheering news because it meant the thought that he was unloved came later than usual. The newspaper brought more enviable, coveted tragedies. Husband Of Coma Woman Dies In Blast, he read. Double Tragedy. He boiled himself the last egg, made some toast and said, 'Damn,' when he went to the refrigerator for the butter and remembered there was none. More Prison Hangings. One Saved From Ventilator Death, he read. Six Die In Terrorist Gun Blast. Envoy Disappears. Body In Train. Mummified Octogenarian Found. He thought enviously of these recent flamboyant demises and went out to dig over the vegetable garden. The pristine pantry and now the back garden could await appraising eyes without fear of criticism.

By late morning he had removed all the dying tomato plants but did not burn them, his usual procedure. The spread of tomato blight did not interest him now. In the grip of a greater blight of the spirit he merely threw the old stems on the compost heap, where their invisible infections could contaminate everything while the lawyers and land agents wrangled.

When the ground was clear and clean he raked it over and cast upon the neat scoring a bag of mustard seed. This, he thought, would keep the weeds down while the house was on the market and would create a good impression for would-be buyers.

'And this was his vegetable garden,' he could imagine the agents saying and the buyers would easily see the possibilities of growing courgettes or asparagus on such a warm and sunny site. In the afternoon he pruned the roses quite hard. It was too early but the result would be a neat impression again. The geraniums had outgrown their strength in a late-summer rampage so he chopped them back with the secateurs, received an obscure enjoyment from causing such hurt to the innocent.

They would provide colour and charm as they atrophied through the early winter, might attract buyers to his home's small charms. In the afternoon he sorted through his books and culled enough for three cartons. He erased his own name from those remaining, for he had seen estates sold before, the indelicacy of appellations left within covers always surprising.

The records played that evening on a radio programme of old-time dance music were wheezy with age and he wheezed himself as he climbed up the little kitchen ladder to sort out any damaged china from the cupboards. This kept him occupied till nearly midnight and after he added these packed cartons of cast-offs to the others he suddenly realised that he had forgotten his daughter. She had not entered his mind all evening. Spiders and the pleasant smell of disinfectant from his bucket of hot water had replaced her for hours. He had even sung once or twice.

He stood at the sink again, drinking more tea and looking out into the darkness while he thought about this. In the morning, when he wandered up to the shops to buy his newspaper he inadvertently promised the lady in the dairy some cuttings of his double pink impatiens.

'It's so like a rose,' she said, 'a lovely little rose,' and he nodded his agreement, thinking of his daughter.

During the course of the day, as he worked at clearing out the cupboards towards the back of the house, he covered minutely all other avenues of destruction.

Shooting was impossible because he had no gun. Jumping from a great height possessed a certain attraction because the swift downward plunge might acknowledge, in microcosm, all the characteristics of his own life. But what height would be the correct and fatal one and there was always the difficulty of launching himself forth. Perhaps the kindly arms of strangers might restrain him, young policemen would stand on ledges to calmly address him on hopeful subjects, rescuers might delve into his thoughts and secrets. He could be hospitalised, spoken of without enthusiasm as being unwell, meanwhile sharing a locker with somebody calling himself Napoleon.

He could throw himself under a bus but the timing of this posed problems. At peak hours schoolchildren might scream, or laugh which would be much worse, and in the fallow reaches of the afternoon old ladies could be precipitated into a last heart-attack, leaving cake tins sadly full, bridge parties arranged for next Wednesday at two.

By the time he covered all that mental territory it was midday, so he packed another three cartons of odds and ends from the wash-house — mostly empty preserving jars and an old saucepan or two, a filling hose for the washing machine that would not be required now — and he went to sleep in the sun.

The telephone awakened him in the late afternoon. He sat for a moment, dazed with sleep and hunger for he had no lunch. It was the publishers, requiring information. Could they possibly ask how much he had done already, how many words? And could they have his final draft by the beginning of next month, if it would be possible?

'There's a lot of interest,' said Roger. 'We're using one of your pictures for the poster, and the cover. By this time in a fortnight we'll have a rough ready.' He was not sure what a rough was, but it seemed it was coming in the post and would be a parcel. He stood there, silently holding the telephone receiver, pleased.

'Are you there? Are you there? Have we been cut off?' That was Roger again, anxious to divulge more news.

When he finished lying about the work he had not done he fetched the evening paper. The news seemed suddenly brighter. Two sailors had been found safely after two days' search by aircraft. A politician he particularly disliked had broken a leg in a skiing accident. When he consulted the Deaths column it was sparsely populated, contained only Mrs Pearson, whose demise would bring no gain to him but her absence from the library would be riches.

The evening was a clear and balmy one and as darkness fell he began to write in the large exercise book purchased weeks ago for the task, before he knew that the chapter would have to be composed to please unknown eyes and not those he loved most.

He formed the words carefully, with an old craftsman's skill, and held the pen gently as though it might be a delicate little plant that, with tender nurturing, may bring forth miraculous blooms.

*A garden house,* he wrote, *adds to the graciousness of any residence. Although it may seem to be, in this era of indoor-outdoor living, a mere adjunct to the house for entertaining on summer evenings, it is more than a simple extension of the reception rooms available to a householder.*

*It is,* he wrote, *a sanctuary for the troubled heart, a moment of ease taken on a summer's day, an hour of blessed silence in a noisy and worrisome world.*

He sat thinking for a long time after that before taking up the pen again.

*A gazebo,* he continued, *is a tiny world for a loved small child, a universe for the entertainment of golliwogs and teddy bears, ideal for dolls' tea parties.*

Then he took a scrap of paper from a jotter pad and wrote firmly, in block capitals, SHOPPING LIST and beneath that, BUTTER.

# FIFTEEN RUBIES BY CANDLELIGHT

'SO, YET AGAIN, we miss your friend. We seem to have very bad luck, don't we, with regard to meeting your friend — your mysterious friend, if I might be specific.' Harold was a lawyer and dealt in stated truths, the breakdown of witnesses and the destruction of tissues of lies. 'Just exactly how many times is it that we've missed him? Four is it? Or five?'

'Five.' Greediness, thought Barbara, prompted her to choose the larger figure and perhaps it had been greediness that prompted her to invent the friend. She had been greedy for attention, however mythical, and greedy also for privacy from the small slights of people like Harold. 'Thirty-six? Not married? And not a friend in sight?' Harold always said.

'Harold, stop asking Barbara questions.' That was Jane, Harold's wife. 'We must try and introduce poor Barbara to someone,' Jane used to say. 'What about that land-agent next door, that one who's divorced and his wife said he beat her, but he seems quite artistic and goes to concerts. What about him?' All that had ceased since she invented the friend.

At the head of the table Barbara unwrapped her dinner napkin as if it might be a strange thing never seen before. 'I've never noticed before,' she said. 'These are worn out,' and she held the piece of linen in front of her face. Through two small holes in one corner it was possible to see the light of the candles and Harold's crooked left index finger drumming on the tablecloth. She had set the table tonight with raspberry pink linen and red roses tumbled from an old silver ice-bucket.

'He likes things to be nice,' she had said when Harold and Jane arrived and Jane, tittering faintly, said, 'So romantic. Look Harold, everything's all pink and rosy.'

174

Masked by the linen, Barbara looked at Harold, the executioner seeking truth at the other end of the table. 'You know, Harold,' she said, 'this linen's so thin I can see you through it.' The vague shape of Harold loomed, knife in hand.

'Don't try and change the subject.' Harold was tearing his bread roll in half and piled butter on one fragment. 'I'll just give the old arteries a burst,' he said. Barbara lowered the dinner napkin and looked at him again. It was, after all, only old Harold, ten kilos overweight, too short ever to cross his legs with languid ease and possessor of a bone-headed attention for whatever matter took his fancy. 'I find it very peculiar,' he said, 'that we've been to dinner four or five times in the last year and each time this friend of yours has been called away at the last moment.'

'It might even be six times.' Excess might save her, thought Barbara. Abundance might give veracity to the lie.

'Surely it wouldn't be six?' Jane again. 'Harold, do start your soup and stop asking questions. You're embarrassing Barbara.'

'Yes.' She sighed and watched Harold pick up his spoon. The soup might muffle and muzzle him, she thought. It was cream of carrot, thick and golden, a soup to enwrap the vocal cords, to fill the throat, silence the talkative. 'It's very embarrassing and do believe me I'm very conscious of that. And *he* would be very conscious of it as well. He sent his apologies and said he was very, very sorry.'

'Yet again?'

'Yet again, Harold.'

'*Harold*! Stop it. Barbara looks so sad. Harold, you'll make her cry. He makes people cry, you know.' Jane had turned towards Barbara now, shoulders edging away from Harold the villain. 'I've seen him in court, making people cry. You stop it, Harold, and I mean that.'

'I was looking at my watch today,' said Barbara, dinner napkin crushed in her hand now like a shameful rag, 'and I noticed the oddest thing —'

'I think you're trying to change the subject.' Harold was piling more butter on the roll. 'Another burst for the arteries.'

175

'I couldn't make out the time because the face was so small so I actually got out a magnifying glass to look at it and it was then I saw this wonderful thing.'

'I see,' said Harold. 'Give you the lucky Lotto numbers, did it?'

'*Harold*! Let her finish.'

'Written distinctly on the face of my watch was *five rubies* and then I looked again, to make sure, and I'd made a mistake. It was *fifteen rubies*.'

Harold chomped his bread roll.

'I must say these are rather good,' he said. 'Where did you get them? There seems to be some sort of grain on the top.' He tilted his glasses on to the end of his nose. 'Are they Lebanese? It is some kind of Lebanese bread? Jane and I went to the Lebanon when we were first married, before Digby was born. We weren't impressed.' He sagged in his chair. 'It was a bad year, all round.'

'*Harold*! Let her finish. Nobody wants to know what you thought of the Lebanon before Digby was born.'

'To get back to this little story of yours about the watch, Barbara,' said Harold, 'what happened next?'

'Nothing, Harold. Nothing happened next. Nothing actually happened at all. I just thought it was rather a romantic thing, the watch having fifteen rubies. Usually they just say this many or that many jewels, nothing specific. I think it was the actual word *rubies* I found so fascinating, the idea that there were all those rubies inside the watch somewhere.'

The silence lengthened.

'What brand is it?'

'What brand is what, Harold. She's made the loveliest soup for you, Harold, and all you seem to want to do is talk. I do wish you'd stop arguing and have the soup.'

'I want to know the brand-name of Barbara's watch.' Harold put his spoon down. There was no hope now, thought Barbara, that cream of carrot would stifle his questions.

'I haven't any idea. I've forgotten, if I ever knew. I'm not sure it's written on it, Harold.'

'I really cannot see' — Harold gulped down the last piece

of roll — 'the point of this interminable story about a brandless watch having five, or alternatively, fifteen rubies. I simply don't see the point, Barbara. It is my considered opinion,' he said, 'that you're trying to change the subject.'

'I can't see any rubies.' Jane was finishing her soup. 'Harold, do start. You're miles behind everyone.'

'It's not a matter of seeing rubies, Jane, not a matter of seeing rubies at all.' Harold sighed and stared at the ceiling. 'Is that dirt up there?'

'No, Harold, it's a spider.'

'And to go off at a tangent here,' he said, 'I think I must correct myself with regard to the Lebanon. I think we went there on that tour after Digby was born and just before my Uncle Harold died and after that, of course, I went into the old firm in his place.'

'I never met your Uncle Harold.' Emboldened by this thought, Barbara took a roll herself and ate it with the beginnings of an appetite. Possibly the sickness engendered by Harold's questions might now pass. Perhaps dinner may be enjoyable after all. 'But the fact that I never saw your Uncle Harold doesn't make him less a person and doesn't cast doubt about his existence,' she said.

'Point taken.' Harold, at last, had begun the soup.

'I still can't see any rubies. I'm trying to see the rubies,' said Jane.

'For God's sake, Jane, we're talking about industrial rubies here. We're talking about rubies actually inside the workings of the watch. Industrial rubies, Jane. Probably infinitesimal. Certainly very small.'

'Yes, Harold.'

'Mere specks.'

'Yes, Harold.'

'Grains of sand, Jane, or even smaller than that.'

'Yes, Harold.'

'Not readily discernible by the naked eye.'

'Yes, Harold.'

'And to get back to the fascinating subject of Barbara's friend,' said Harold, 'is it really six times we've missed him by a whisker? I could've sworn it was only five.'

'*Harold*!' Jane leaned over the table and placed a hand on Barbara's arm. 'You mustn't take any notice of him,' she said. 'Harold gets in these moods sometimes. His investigative modus, the boys call it.' Harold and Jane had four sons.

'Don't mention those boys to me.' Harold stabbed another bread roll and took two spoonfuls of soup. The level in his soup bowl was going down slowly, Barbara thought, but it showed signs of being a lengthy dinner and a long evening of scrutiny.

'You must show us the new bathroom, Barbara,' said Jane as if she had divined this thought, 'and the redecorations.'

'You're trying to change the subject.' Harold dug into the soup again. 'You women are all the same. You're always trying to change the subject and you stick together like glue. I was telling Barbara about the boys, about Alexander having a ring put through his nose.'

'It's just a tiny ring, darling.' Jane took a last spoonful. 'You've flavoured this with mace, Barbie. I've only ever tried cinnamon.'

'I do wish you two wouldn't change the subject all the time. It's virtually impossible to have a conversation with you.'

'We haven't changed the subject, Harold.' Jane seemed very cool, thought Barbara. Jane was unruffled. There had, perhaps, been many rehearsals of the melodrama about Alexander and his nose. 'And it isn't actually a ring, Harold. It's more a sort of stud.'

'Jane, it's a ring, definitely a ring. We've been into all this very thoroughly and I think it's been established without doubt that it's definitely a ring and it is, in fact, through Alexander's nostril.'

'Well, it's a studdish sort of ringish thing, darling, but as I've told you lots and lots of times, Alexander can easily take it out when he's sick of it.'

'What about when I'm sick of it?' Harold was finishing his soup now.

'Harold, you don't come into it. Alexander has every right to have a ring through his nostril and when he's sick of it, in a few years' time —'

'Oh, God,' said Harold. He had stopped eating.

'— he can just take it out and throw it away and I'm quite sure a small hole in Alexander's nostril, when viewed in the light of eternity, won't mean the end of the world, Harold. I really don't think it will.'

'Would anyone like some more cream of carrot soup?' Perhaps, thought Barbara, she could become one of those people who never repay hospitality, never return dinner invitations, never endure investigation by friend or foe over her own table again.

'Oh, cream of carrot, was it?' Jane seemed brightened by the clash with Harold over Alexander's nostril. 'I thought it was pumpkin. Sorry.'

'*Jane*!' Harold's turn now.

'Well, they're much the same colour, Harold, and much the same consistency. And in this light, Harold' — Jane waved a languid hand and the candles guttered — 'the error may be understandable.' It sounded like a plausible defence for a minor crime. 'And furthermore, with regard to the Lebanon, I feel certain we went there after Digby was born, not before. We were there over Christmas, if I remember correctly, and Digby was born the previous September.'

'Let's leave the whole thing, shall we, Jane?' Harold bent his head over his bowl of soup like someone at devotions. 'We're supposed to be having a pleasant evening.' He spooned up the cream of carrot as if it might be a series of liquid pills. 'Very nice.' He had finished. 'There's this frightful woman at the office who makes pumpkin soup,' he said, 'and she purées the skin and all. Jenny and Rodney have been to dinner there — you know Jen and Rod, don't you, Barbara? — and they say it comes out khaki and stiff as a board. Rodney says it'd stand up and bark at you.'

'*Harold*!'

Barbara was gathering up the dishes now, flurrying out to the kitchen which suddenly looked like a refuge, a pristine little temple dedicated to pleasantries. She stood leaning against the sink for a moment, looking out the window into the garden, but it was like looking into nothing. The stars had gone. There was no moon tonight.

'Barbara?' Harold's voice was inexorable. 'Barbara? Where

are you? You still haven't told us about your friend. Where exactly is he tonight?'

'I'm really very sorry he isn't here.' She was taking the big blue dinner plates from the cupboard now, making a melancholy game of it. One for Harold, one for Jane and one for me and one for nobody. 'The table always looks kind of lonely with only three.' The clatter of the china gave the words a plausibility, she thought.

'Don't worry about it, Barbara. Don't let him upset you. Harold, you're not to upset Barbara. Why don't you have another of these rolls? Barbara got them especially for you.'

'I don't think Barbara got them for me, did she?' Harold, though, looked mollified. His hand went out, took a roll. 'Pass me the butter,' he said. So they had muffled him again, thought Barbara and opened the oven to get out the casserole and the potatoes. A salad as large as a felled tree in bloom waited in an African bowl. Comprehensive and magnificent in its variety, it was a new recipe supposed to be rich in the B complex of vitamins to promote calmness and well-being.

'Good God,' said Harold when she put it on the table.

'*Harold!*'

The main course had begun.

'Can I pass anyone a potato?' Harold was wielding the big silver spoon. 'One for Barbara? One for Jane. Another little baby one for Jane. And let me pour the wine.'

They seemed happier now, Barbara thought, and sat back in her chair slightly more at ease. But the untenanted side of the table, where the friend was supposed to sit, looked emptier than ever.

'Shall I?' Harold had taken up the ladle and prepared to attack the casserole. 'Always a good dinner at Barbara's,' he said and she watched the spoon explore every angle of the big dish, winkle out every morsel in each corner. 'And to return to the subject of your friend,' said Harold, 'it seems a very great pity he always appears to miss the culinary delights.'

'Yes.' Barbara made the word as long as a sigh, turned it into a gracious acceptance of absence. Even she had begun to believe that the invention was not actually there. Perhaps,

180

she thought, it was best to sail boldly close to a lie, to lay it out for public examination, to flaunt one's sad and saving fibs in front of breakers like Harold.

'Did he,' said Harold, 'give you your watch?'

'No, no. It's quite old. No one's worn it for years. I found it in one of the drawers.' The house had been her mother's, much of the furniture also. In nooks and crannies, cupboards and shelves, lurked the detritus of the years. 'I just happened to see in a magazine that these old watches are in fashion again so I got it out.'

'Let me see.' The candlelight made Jane look rosy and almost eager. 'Hold out your arm, Barbara, so I can see the watch,' so she held out her thin, tanned arm, freckled lightly on the back of the hand, as a woman may hold out her arm at a dance when someone says, 'Please? Will you dance with me?'

'It's a shame you can't see the rubies.' The little silver watch with its square domed face glittered up at Jane, bright as Harold's sharp pale eyes. 'Imagine, Harold,' said Jane, 'fifteen rubies. It sounds quite romantic, doesn't it?'

Harold was helping himself to salad.

'Delicious,' he said. 'He doesn't know what he's missing, that friend of yours.' Harold buttered his last fragment of bread roll, the knife spreading into every corner, every space explored. 'There are,' he said, 'just one or two tiny details I'd like to get straight, just for the record. For instance, Item One, we've got this mysterious friend, this doctor, who seems to be sometimes called Gerard and other times Jeremy, according to the lady's mood. Or is it the other way round?'

'*Harold!*'

'His name, if you must know,' said Barbara, 'is actually Gerard.' And she began to eat the beef which was surprisingly good, like the inner kernel of a beast, perhaps its heart.

'What delicious meat, Barbara. Where did you get it?' Jane, in her white dress, looked almost like a nun.

'At the supermarket, just like the bread.'

'Amazing. Isn't it amazing, Harold?'

'I don't think it's amazing at all.' Harold helped himself

to more casserole. 'Modern marketing trends and techniques mean that the consumer gets first-rate produce in double-quick time.' Relentless Harold skewered a French bean in the salad. 'Got you,' he said, 'and, furthermore, I think you're both trying to change the subject so to get back —'

'He was actually christened Gerard by some very high-ranking bishop or another, I've forgotten the name.' Barbara took another mouthful of the strengthening beef, like invalid's beef tea only solid. 'They're a Roman Catholic family.' Jane's bowed head looked very nun-like, she thought, bent in supplication over a large rich dinner. 'Gerard is a Roman Catholic name but it's one of those names that always gets shortened or altered a bit so sometimes he's called Jeremy and sometimes he's even called John. It just depends on the people and how they know him and so on and so forth.'

'And what do you call him?'

'I call him darling.' That silenced Harold for the rest of the main course. 'I would think, just in my own mind, that the bishop would call him Gerard, though, having christened him,' she said as she began to clear away the dinner plates. The myth, during the last two hours, had been wonderfully fleshed out. It now had a religion, a definite name which altered according to circumstances and knew a bishop.

'Item Two,' said Harold when she brought in the big platter of cheese and biscuits, dried fruit, green grapes mounded high as a fortress. 'We have never so much as glimpsed this friend. What was it exactly that you said he did in the medical world?'

'*Harold!*'

'Grapes anyone?' she said. 'Do help yourself to cheese. The one on the right, that biggish square piece, is a very nice sharp Cheddar. I know Harold likes a good Cheddar. As for Gerard — I've already told you, Harold, he specialises in heart surgery on children and babies in particular. That's why he's never here, you see.' She sprawled in her own chair, like a woman relaxed and easy in her own home, a loved woman explaining a sad but necessary fact. 'It's a known medical fact, Harold, that most births occur at night. It's a relic of the Stone Age when birth had to be safe and secret and even now the human body obeys these age-old rulings. So,' she said, 'the fact is that the poor man often has to interrupt his own arrangements to try and save the life of a child and, sadly again Harold, it's often late at night. We're quarrelling with Nature here, Harold, and I'm not sure there's a lot we can do about it. Now, do let me give you some grapes. I feel sure they're very nice. And let me give you some crackers as well, Harold, and what about living dangerously for once, Harold, and try a bit of Brie?' She piled the food on his little plate where it lay in a gagging array. 'I do hope that satisfies you, Harold?' Emboldened now, she made it a question. The little watch on her wrist had the time perfectly enshrined. Eleven o'clock. The evening was nearly over. 'Wine?' She filled the glasses.

'I thought you said once he was a lawyer.' Harold took a grape and ate it as if it was an eye.

*Harold!*'

'No, I didn't. I've always said he's a doctor.' That was the one true thread in the whole thing, in the whole invented grace of her withdrawal. 'We must try to introduce poor old Barbara to someone,' they used to say. 'What about the man next door? What about your awful brother Bob? What about the butcher on the corner?' And so it had gone on till the myth of the doctor saved her. She had never slipped up on his occupation, though once she said he had red hair and another time blond. 'Well, Harold, reddish-blond, blondish-red, what does it matter?' she had said that night. 'Beauty's in the eye of the beholder, anyway.'

Ugly old Harold had snorted a little, like an elderly porker. 'I've never heard Barbara say he's a lawyer.'

'Just testing.' Harold was eating the Brie.

'*Harold!*' There was a long silence. 'Have you been to see the new plant centre, Barbara?' The nun, Barbara thought, had changed into a nurse and was trying to poultice the injuries of the evening with talk of flowers and the gentle art of tilling land. 'Harold and I went over to have a look yesterday, didn't we, Harold, and they've got fifty-six varieties of daisy, some we've never seen before.'

Harold cut some more Brie.

'I'll just eat Gerard's share,' he said, 'since he's been delayed by hole-in-heart surgery. And if I may ask one more question, if he's a Roman Catholic, why did you say you went to the mosque?'

'I never said he went to the mosque.'

'Just testing.'

'*Harold*! Harold, why don't we talk about something nice? Why don't we tell Barbara about the plant centre? For heaven's sake, Harold. You've nearly made her cry.' Harold took another cracker. 'Harold cut out the coupon for potting mix in the big size at half price, didn't you, Harold?' Jane looked very flushed, Barbara thought. Almost ill. 'Did you get the booklet in your letterbox, Barbara, with all the specials?' She shook her head. The evening had made her speechless. 'We've got a spare one, haven't we, Harold? We can drop it in for Barbara. She likes gardening. I think, in all, they had fifty-four varieties of daisy.'

'I thought you said fifty-six earlier.' Harold had been eating grapes and had a pile of seeds, like tiny gallstones, on his plate.

'Harold' — Jane put her head in her hands — 'Harold, I feel I must say this to you. Harold, I'm sick of you.'

Harold ate some more grapes.

'Equally, my dear Jane,' he said, 'I'm sick of you, but there you are, Jane — that's life for you.'

'Perhaps we should talk about something else,' said Barbara. 'Harold, do have another grape. Jane, help yourself to more coffee. And don't forget, either of you, the wine. You've hardly touched the wine. Do have some more wine.' Perhaps, she thought, wine might help. It might have been better to leave Harold and Jane in their own home to quarrel amidst their own cutlery and dinnerplates, to waste their own Cabernet Merlot. Like a defeated child, baulked at every turn, she wondered what to do. Like a child again, she seized at the idea of the alphabet. 'A is for apple,' she said, pouring the wine into their glasses, the generosity nearly hysterical. 'I can open another bottle,' she said. 'Oh, do have some more. Tell me, Harold, what's your favourite kind of apple?'

'The Braeburn,' said Harold. 'If you must know, the Braeburn is my favourite apple in all the world.' He sighed and looked at the other side of the table, the empty side. If Gerard really existed, thought Barbara, then Harold would have had someone to talk to about batting averages, the price of the better whites this season, how Cabernet Merlot was better than Cabernet Sauvignon and why. It would have been better for Harold if the myth existed, better for them all. They could have talked about holidays together, jointly owned cars, specials on barbecues.

'The Braeburn is my very favourite apple of all time.' Harold, though, looked nearly happy. 'Nothing can touch the flesh of the better Braeburns. After that I'm exceptionally partial to a Cox's Orange — all that nice white crispness and the gold and pink stripy skin, quite lovely visually.' He sounded like an apple salesman. 'It is my considered opinion that after the Braeburn the Cox's Orange, at its best, can hardly be surpassed. Are you sure I can't give you any of Barbara's very wonderful Cheddar, darling? Let me top up your glass.'

'Thank you, sweetheart,' said Jane.

A for apple, miraculous in its childish simplicity, had saved them, thought Barbara. B for bananas gave them time to have another cup of coffee and at C for cats she brought out the Cointreau.

'I'm sorry,' she said as she put the bottle on the table, 'you might prefer Benedictine.' But that would be incorrect, she thought. They had done B. B for bananas. 'Or Drambuie.' That would be D, though, and they had not yet reached D.

'No, no.' Harold was nearly ebullient now. 'Cointreau's our favourite, isn't it, darling?'

'I'm worried,' she said, 'that the coffee's cold. Shall I make some more?' C for coffee. C for cold.

'No, no.' More of Harold's sudden ebullience. 'Let everything get cold. Sit and relax for a minute, Barbara. Don't worry about it. I wouldn't worry about it at all, if I were you. This has just reminded me of Dr McPherson. We met him — do you remember, Janey? — on the way to the Lebanon. Said he preferred all his food cold. He told us he'd had so many years of missing dinner and having everything cold he'd come to prefer it.'

'*He's* probably like that.' Jane nodded towards the empty place at the table, the cutlery still pristine, plate waiting. 'It's a noble profession and they all get their own little ways.'

'They do indeed.' Barbara sat now with her chin on her clasped hands, elbows on the table, the watch with its fifteen invisible rubies encircling her wrist like a large wedding band, an enormous wedding ring placed on her whole arm so that the world might know she had been claimed from the millions of unwanted women wandering the globe.

'Aha.' That was Harold. It was a short sharp noise like the barking of a small watchdog. He was looking at the half-empty dishes, the beef congealing slightly in the big iron casserole dish. 'Cold food,' he said. 'Quite so,' and she divined immediately that they thought the doctor would be coming to see her later, would eat his dinner by candlelight while she spooned out chilly potatoes like marbles and beef coagulated in its own juice. In her blue chiffon negligée she would be sitting there at three in the morning feeding him cold meat and on her banded wrist the watch with fifteen rubies would capture the passage of rapture.

'We're very happy for you, Barbara.' Jane patted her hand. 'Aren't we, Harold?'

'Couldn't be happier.'

The clock was striking M for midnight and Harold was rustling through his pockets.

'Oh, Lord,' he said. 'Is that the time already? Where are those keys? Where did I put the car keys, darling?'

But they were not there yet, Barbara thought, not at the safe harbour of L for Lord, lassitude, labour and loneliness or K for keys and karma.

'We must get on our way.' Harold had found the keys now. 'I've got a very early start in the morning. Must be in court by ten at the latest.' He drank the last of his Cointreau, tilting the tiny glass so it caught the light from the candles and there it was, sparkling, like an E for eye. 'Enchanting,' he said. 'An enchanting evening, Barbara, as always.' So that was E, she thought. E had been done.

Harold was looking at the table, assessing what was left, counting the crackers.

'He's got plenty here,' he said. 'We've left tons for him. Perhaps,' he said, 'Friday's not a good night for him to come out to dinner. I've heard that Friday's their very busy night at the hospitals with all the accidents and so on.'

So that was F. F for Friday.

G for goodbye took them out on to the terrace in the front of the house.

'It's a great old place.' Harold thumped a wall. 'I think you were wise to hang on to it. These old places — they're fetching money these days. The whole area's coming up. Your mother saw it go down and now you're seeing it come up.'

But they were not as far as L for legacy or R for real estate or renovations, she thought. Or P for pretender and plain.

'And we never did see the bathroom,' said Harold. 'Never mind. Next time.' They were climbing into the car now.

'Such a lovely evening.' Jane had wound her window down. 'We both think you're looking wonderful, don't we, Harold? Gerard must obviously agree with you. We've sometimes thought you've looked a bit peaky but you're looking lovely tonight, Barbara, quite lovely.'

Harold had begun to back the car down the drive, then stopped.

'Harold, there's no need to brake so suddenly like that. I nearly hit my head.' Jane's voice, clear and sharp, echoed the altercations of earlier in the evening. 'Really, Harold, you're just hopeless. I might as well drive myself, the way you go on.'

'I haven't said goodbye to Barbara properly.' Harold was stepping out of the car, walking past the D for daisies, striding on the V for verandah. The way in which he put his arm around her shoulders was nearly embracing, verging on concupiscent.

'Harold?' That was Jane again. 'Harold, what's going on? What are you doing?'

'Barbara and I are just having a tiny chat about your birthday,' called Harold, 'and you're not to listen. It's a secret. Now, wind the window up, Jane, and look the other way.

187

One never knows the full extent of your talents. You may be able to lip read.'

Jane began to turn away, looking at other gardens in the street, gazing up the road as Harold's arm tightened.

'You tell that neglectful bastard Gerard or Jeremy or whatever he calls himself,' he hissed in her E for ear, 'that if he doesn't get himself organised and turn up when he's supposed to, you tell him I'll be here myself. You give him that message straight from the horse's mouth, straight from H for Harold, and see what happens.'

Much later, towards dawn in that dim and shuttered house, she began to dream of rising from her narrow bed and walking with a stranger on a gently rising road in high summer with the grasses whispering dry. 'Please,' said the stranger, 'can you tell me the meaning of love?' and she awakened battling with the pain and mystery of her I for inability to answer.

ACKNOWLEDGEMENTS

THE ANTIQUE DEALER
Published in *Listener & TV Times*, 1990

PLEASURES OF THE PAST
Published in *NZ Listener*, 1988

EDWARD AND LALLY/TED AND PAM
Published in *Me and Marilyn Monroe*, Daphne
Brasell, 1993

THE FACE OF THE LAND
Published in *NZ Listener*, 1989
and *Vital Writing I*, Godwit Press, 1990

NAUGHTY MAUREEN
Published in *Subversive Acts*, Penguin, 1991 and
*Vital Writing 3*, Godwit Press, 1992

LITTLE VARMINTS
Published in *Listener & TV Times*, 1990

A DIFFERENT VIEW
Published in *The Literary Half-Yearly*, The Institute
of Commonwealth and American Studies and
English Language, India, 1991

THE WIDOW
Published in *More Magazine*, 1987

GOOD NEWS
Published in *More Magazine*, 1988

The author gratefully acknowledges the assistance
of the Literature Committee of the Queen Elizabeth
II Arts Council of New Zealand in awarding her a
Creative Writing Grant in 1993. The author also
gratefully acknowledges the University of Auckland
for awarding her the 1993 Writing Fellowship.

# OTHER NEW ZEALAND
# TITLES AVAILABLE IN
# VINTAGE EDITIONS

*Available only in New Zealand
†Available only in Australia and New Zealand